FREE FALL

SPRING HILL BLUES

BOOK ONE

By
E. M. MOORE

Manufactured in the United States of America
First Edition August 2019

Cover by 2nd Life Designs

Special thanks to my beta readers for helping me with Free Fall! You all are so very much appreciated!

Falling For Darkness

Surrender To Darkness

Ravana Clan Legacy Series

A New Genesis

Tracking Fate

Cursed Gift

Veiled History

Fractured Vision

Chosen Destiny

Order of the Akasha Series

Stripped (Prequel)

Summoned By Magic

Tempted By Magic

Ravished By Magic

Indulged By Magic

Enraged By Magic

Her Alien Scouts Series

Kain Encounters

Kain Seduction

Rise of the Morphlings Series

Of Blood and Twisted Roots

Safe Haven Academy Series

A Sky So Dark

A Dawn So Quiet

Chronicles of Cas Series

Reawakened

Hidden

Power

Severed

Rogue

The Adams' Witch Series

Bound In Blood

Cursed In Love

Witchy Librarian Cozy Mystery Series

Wicked Witchcraft

One Wicked Sister

Wicked Cool

Wicked Wiccans

*M*y brother had the Spring Hill blues.

I don't know that I ever did. I was content living my life here, even if Spring Hill is a small town by anyone's standards and we don't have the greatest variety of things to do. I was the best in my class. I had great friends. My family was amazing.

I didn't see that I was missing something.

Now, I do. Now, I'm definitely missing something, and the hole is greater than I ever imagined. Made worse because I know I'm never getting back that void no matter what.

So, yeah, my brother had the Spring Hill blues, and when he died, he passed them on to me.

I blink up at the school. The flags wave high out front above the main entrance door. The wind whips at them while I stare. Underneath, kids I've known all my life are walking through those doors, hurrying to get to their first class before the bell rings. I had no intention of being back at Spring Hill High for my junior year. In fact, my only plan was that I wasn't going to be here. Maybe I would drive up the West Coast, the sea air tangling my hair. Maybe I'd hitchhike to Arizona and see the cool rock formations. Maybe I'd check out the East Coast for once. I didn't care where I ended up as long as I wasn't here—in Spring Hill. The place Brady couldn't wait to leave.

I guess those blues are why I'm in trouble now.

I sense Jules next to me. I don't even need to look up to know it's her. First, because I'm barely on speaking terms with anyone else right now. And second, her sad vibes are as familiar as my own.

Jules is Brady's girlfriend. *Was* Brady's girlfriend.

"Hey," she says softly.

"Hey," I say back, mustering up all the excitement I can, which isn't a whole hell of a lot. I sound like a fifty-something year old on his birthday while he's going through a mid-life crisis.

It's not a lot, but it's all I've got.

"You ready for this?" she asks.

I can handle the walk into school, but what I can't handle is living the rest of my life without my big brother. That's the scary part. That's the part that seems so wrong that nothing will ever be right again.

Jules nudges me. "Come on, Briar. You know he wouldn't want this."

I'm not going to be the petulant one and say something like, *Yeah, well, he doesn't really have a say anymore, does he?* Even though those same words are on the tip of my tongue. I don't know why it seems like I'm mad at him sometimes. I think I'm just mad at the world.

"I know," I tell her. The thing is, I just can't get my feet to move. I'm telling them to start forward, to take one step followed by the next and the next, but they aren't cooperating. Jules nudges me again, giving me the momentum I need to finally take a step. Then, we start our slow, steady walk toward the main doors. There aren't very many people in the parking lot anymore, so I've successfully avoided pretty much everybody at this point. Yes, school hasn't even technically started, but this feels like a win to me.

But that's where my day stops winning.

As soon as I walk through those doors, it feels like I get punched in the face. Jules runs into me from behind after I stop abruptly. I'm sure she'll have the same reaction as me, but there's no way for me to stop her from looking up, from seeing the banner already announcing Spring Hill football games. This *is* Spring Hill after all. This town is football through and through.

Jules grabs my arm, and for a moment, we hold each other upright, our gazes locked straight ahead. One step, the next, and the next. Eventually, we get to my locker, and I lean against it as if I've just run a marathon. My forehead rests on the cold steel. I try to slow my heartbeat, but I can feel my pulse right through my palm as it quivers on my neighbor's locker.

"They've been up for a week," Jules says. Her voice is still quiet. She's so quiet now, sometimes it's as if she doesn't even know how to talk anymore.

"Hey, Jules," someone says, calling out to her.

I'm still turned the other way, so I don't know if she greeted the person with a wave or not, but I know she didn't answer them. Believe it or not, Jules used to be a lot of fun. She wasn't loud for the sake of being loud, but she was happy and didn't mind sharing that with the world.

"I got to get to my locker," she says finally after I don't move.

I nod against the steel. "See you at lunch," I manage to choke out.

With that, she's gone. The air in here still feels stifling though. Maybe even moreso now that I'm by myself. There are shouts and laughter and just a thick tension layered in the air. People are excited. There isn't much to be excited about in Spring Hill, but this is one of them. New school year. New football season. That about sums Spring Hill up.

"Miss Page?"

I carefully remove my forehead from the locker and look up at the school counselor. She's young. She graduated out of Spring Hill exactly seven years ago. Just enough time to go get her degrees and then get hired back here. I envied her once for that. For applying herself, going to school, and then coming back to our perfect little town. Now, I think she's an idiot. She had a way out. Hell, she *was* out of here. She had her chance, but she blew it.

I try on a smile, but those things are as foreign to me now as pastel colors.

Ms. Lyons appraises me. She looks me up and down, taking in my appearance, which even I admit has drastically changed from last year to this year. There's no hint of disapproval in her eyes or dissatisfaction in her face or next words, but I still feel the weight of her gaze. "You remember you're to come see me during your study hall period, right?"

"Yes, Ms. Lyons, I'll be there."

She gives me a small smile, but then turns on her

short heels and walks away. A few of the male students turn around to check her ass out as she turns down the next hall toward her office. It makes me roll my eyes, but at least it spurs me into motion. I finally unlock my locker and put the books I won't need until later in the day there just in time for the bell to ring. *Oh goody. I'm late for homeroom.* The old me would die before she was tardy to anything, but this new me couldn't care less. There are too many other thoughts swimming around in my brain to make room for worry over being late to an arbitrary class that means nothing in the grand scheme of things.

The first few periods drag by at the speed of a snail in a race for last place. Everywhere I go, people stare at me. It might be the drastic black-as-night hair I dyed just recently or the fact that I think everyone can smell my sorrow, but I wish they would stop. I want to blend into the background. I want to slip by unnoticed.

This is why I did what I did.

When I walk into the lunchroom, it's loud and overcrowded. The deafening hum of hundreds of conversations taking place right this very second only serves to remind me that I'm more alone than I've ever been. I scan the crowd for Jules, but I don't see her. I carefully avoid the table my brother would be sitting at and go all the way to the back corner, setting my tray down on the far end of a table, away from another group that's taking solace here. I accidentally look up at them and when I do, their eyes widen, and they immediately turn to look at one another and hide their lips with their hands while they talk.

Real subtle. I wonder if they're defining me to one another as the girl whose brother died? Or the girl who couldn't stand it here, so she had to run away?

Maybe I should ask them…

It doesn't matter. I sit, take out my cell phone, and type out a text to Jules, telling her I'm in the back corner of the room so she knows where to go when she gets in here. Who knows with Juliet though? She could've stayed after class to get direction on homework or any number of things. My brother's death had somewhat of the opposite effect on her than it did me. Instead of wanting to "throw her life away", she flipped a switch to good girl gone great in everything she does. Trust me, I'm a bit of a connoisseur on grief now, and I've heard—in many different forms recently—that we all heal differently.

Just not like me, apparently.

I push around the chicken on my plate after eating a few mouthfuls of the carrots that came with it. I set my fork down and stare at my plate. The buzz of electricity that's coming from my back is almost impossible

7

to ignore even though I'm trying like hell to block it out. The football table is too loud though, too alive. Just last year, my brother would've been in the thick of things. He would've been right in his glory, eating and talking with his teammates, strategizing, and dreaming.

"It's okay, I'll get her," a familiar voice says, breaking into my thoughts.

My back tightens, and I sit up straighter.

"Oh, come on," another voice says. I'd know it as well as the back of my own hand.

I recognize it like I recognize my own. I squeeze my eyes shut to block it out, but it only keeps getting closer.

Moving to my feet, I pull my bookbag toward me and step away from the table. I turn in the opposite direction, but then I hear my name called by that same voice and it makes me want to vomit.

"It's okay, Cade," I hear Jules say. She's trying to intercept, and I kind of love her in that moment. The last thing I want is to come face-to-face with my brother's best friends.

"What the hell?" Cade says. Strong fingers grip my arm as I try to make my escape. The fingers tighten and pull back until I'm forced to look up at Cade, to see his face. His brows are pulled together as his stare peruses me. He cocks his head. "I didn't even know it was you at first. What the hell are you wearing, Briar?" His stare moves up, and his eyes widen at my now raven black hair. "What did you do?"

"Shut up, Cade," Jules says, giving me an apolo getic look.

Cade barks out a laugh as he does another once-over of my clothes, hair, and makeup like he's a judge of a modeling show. To be fair, if he wasn't the best tight end Spring Hill High has ever seen, he could probably judge a modeling contest. He sure seems to get the prettiest girls in school without even trying.

I don't know if it's the way he's looking at me, the humor dancing in his eyes, or because he seems so familiar, but my hackles rise. "Screw you, Farmer," I say, hugging my backpack tightly to my chest, his last name rolls off my lips like it would have if I were my brother. He never called him Cade, always preferring to use his last name.

Cade's gaze narrows. After a beat, he says, "Reid says you should come sit with us."

Reid, Reid, Reid... I'm not even going to look back at their table. I know what I'll find. Reid Parker, quarterback of the Spring Hill High Varsity football team, reigning over his table with his girlfriend by his side.

"No," I say simply.

His expression tightens. I'm sure he thinks they're

doing me a huge favor, but I don't want to be coddled, and I certainly don't want to be treated differently just because my brother died and they have some sort of misplaced integrity to treat the little sister of their late best friend with sympathy. Fuck that shit.

"Get your ass to the table, Briar," Cade says through clenched teeth.

The nerve of him. The nerve of them all. "I'm sorry, I don't think you heard me the first time. I said fuck you." I smile. "Actually, I said, no, but I meant fuck you."

He shakes his head, his lips pulling up in an incredulous smirk. "You think you're all grown up now, huh? Because you went to the big city by yourself for a whole week?"

I swallow bile rising up my throat. "No, I *know* I'm all grown up now, and I don't need to sit with you or Reid or Lex, okay?"

He frowns down at me, but it's all just for show. I'm dead to them. The thing connecting us is gone, so I'm gone too. "Grown up, but can't even wash your hair for your first day of school or put on decent clothes?"

I flinch, but it's to be expected.

"Just leave her alone, Cade," Jules says, trying to intervene on my behalf.

Ignoring her, Cade grabs my arm. "Come on, Briar,

get your smelly ass to our table. Juliet's already sitting there."

I snap my head back at Jules. She lifts her shoulders as if she's asking, *What did you want me to do?*

I thought we were sticking together. That's what I imagined would happen. My brother's friends have never known boundaries, but it's gotten worse since Brady died. Now they try to stick their nose into every aspect of my life when I just want to be free of them. Instead, Cade drags me to the middle of the lunchroom right before the football table. There are various players sitting there along with their girlfriends. Surrounding the main table are little satellite tables. If you're good, you're expected at the main table, which is why all my brother's friends are there and why he sat there once upon a time too.

My throat closes as the world swims in front of me. This is exactly what I didn't want to happen.

"Cade," Jules says behind us, but she's too quiet now. No one is going to take her seriously with how mousy she is. That's why I dyed my hair and picked out new clothes. I don't care that I stick out at Spring Hill like a sore thumb. I don't even belong here, so why try to fit in?

"What the fuck?"

Reid's voice sends a shiver down my spine. It

makes me want to cower, to bow my head and submit, but I lift my chin anyway. Sasha snickers next to him as she looks me over with distaste.

Reid rises from his seat. He draws the attention of everyone. It's been like that since we were little kids. He just has that aura, a phenomenon about him that makes people want to sit up and take notice. He's staring down at my clothes with contempt. I don't need to look at the oversized sweatshirt and baggy sweatpants I put on that morning. The old me wouldn't have been caught wearing this outside ever let alone for my first day of school, but I know now how ridiculous all this high school posturing is. Who cares? None of it matters.

"Go home and change," Reid says, dismissing me with a flick of his hands.

"E-excuse me?" I sputter.

Reid turns his head, catching on me again. Then, he moves closer. His chestnut brown hair shines underneath the fluorescent lights in the cafeteria and with each step, my heart thunders louder and louder. "You heard me," he says.

I feel the weight of everyone's stares on me. Not just the football tables, but everyone in the cafeteria. Talking has stopped. At most, there are low murmurs as everyone watches what's going on.

I grind my teeth together. "I'm not going home to change," I tell him, making sure my voice has just the right amount of bite that's hopefully telling him to fuck off without saying the actual words.

The tips of his shoes hit mine. My eye level only hits his upper chest, so I have to tweak my neck back to look into his eyes. He's glaring down at me like I'm an inconvenience to him. It's okay. I've been used to that look lately. His Adam's apple bobs up and down once. "Go home, wash your hair out, and get new fucking clothes on. Now."

I just smirk and shake my head at him. I swear he thinks he's God or some shit.

The thought makes me laugh. God is a lot more frightening than Reid fucking Parker.

The green of his eyes pop against the deepening crimson blush of anger stretching out over his cheeks. He lowers his voice until it's barely above a whisper. All the hostility is there, though, stealing away any calming vibes I had for the day. "You're disgracing your brother's memory."

A gasp ricochets out of me. My stomach clenches painfully at his words. I don't even think. I raise my hand and slap him. It happens so quickly I don't even realize I've done it, but the collective surprise that ripples through the cafeteria brings me back to the present.

"Bitch!" Sasha yells. She jumps to her feet and comes at me, but Lex gets in her way, holding her easily back while she shouts hurtful things at me that my mind just erases as soon as it recognizes them.

All the while, Reid just stares at me, his jaw ticking. He hasn't moved an inch. His green eyes molten as he stares at me like he's burning up from the inside out.

"Miss Page," a voice says. "My office. Now."

The last thing I see when I turn away from Reid is the growing red patch on his cheek. I know I didn't even hurt him. He's a big, tough football guy, and I'm just little old me. What I did do was awaken a beast. Reid doesn't let anyone get away with shit like that, even if I am the little sister of his dead best friend.

What he doesn't realize is that I'd already declared war on them.

2

I sit waiting for my turn in the principal's office, my head resting against the wall behind me. I think I even fall asleep for a little while. As I'm sitting there, though, I get ragier and ragier.

Reid, Lex, and Cade have it all. During my brother's funeral, they sat next to their parents with stoic faces. Lex even had his hand wrapped around his sister's forearm like he never wanted to let her go. Me? I was stuck in a black hole of dark, dark thoughts. I had no one by my side. Brady, who'd always been there for me, was currently being lowered into the dirt, leaving me alone up here to fend for myself without him.

The hatred started then, I think. Then it just grew and grew. The more they asked me to do things with them just ended up pissing me off. I'm glad they were able to go to the county fair and not think about Brady, but I couldn't. I'm so happy they could continue to play football and have their epic parties afterward and not think about my brother every second of every day, but that's not me. Hell, I don't even want that to be me.

Brady had an out. He was going to get the hell out of Spring Hill just like he always wanted. Instead, he died of an aneurysm during football practice. They say it was brought on by a tackle, so no, I don't want to think about football. I don't want to hear about football. And I sure as fuck don't want to be buddy buddy with my brother's football playing asshole friends who think they run everything in this fucking town.

The principal's door opens and Reid steps out. He doesn't even look at me when the principal says, "Thank you so much for talking to me about this unfortunate incident, Mr. Parker. I hope you'll still be one hundred percent at practice today."

My gut twists. Don't they know none of that stuff fucking matters?

"It's no problem, Mr. Dade. Barely felt a thing."

My face burns at that, and I lean further back in my chair. I must draw their attention because Mr. Dade says, "I'm sure Miss Page will want to apologize for the physical altercation."

I lift my gaze to meet his. "I'm sure Miss Page doesn't."

Like hell I would. I wonder if Mr. Parker told Dade what he said to me. Fuck him. Disgracing my brother's memory. He doesn't know a thing about my brother, not like me.

"Miss. Page," Dade says, turning my name into two separate anomalies. He looks to Reid and shakes his head like they're on the same level, like he's apologizing to Reid for my behavior as if they're equals of some sort and I'm just a troubled student they both have to deal with. "I'll handle this. You run off to class, so you can keep those grades up for those scholarships."

The knife in my gut twists again. Brady was going to get a scholarship. He called it his Spring Hill Blues Scholarship for getting the hell out of Spring Hill. I always admired him for that. He didn't just want to leave Spring Hill for college, he wanted to get the fuck out for real and never come back. He wouldn't have returned to teach P.E. or coach Mighty Mites. No, he was done with this place.

"Of course," Reid says. Again, he doesn't even give me a second glance as he turns and leaves the sitting area. Outside, I hear Dade's secretary typing away at her desktop, more than likely adding notes to my usually stellar file. Hell, maybe they're even writing me up. That would take the cake, wouldn't it? My first referral?

"Inside, Miss Page," Dade says, gesturing toward his sparse office.

I stand from my seat and slip past the middle-aged man. Did I mention he went to Spring Hill too? Class of Sixty something, I think. It's just sad. I'm not going to be one of these people who can't get the fuck out of here.

Dade shuts the door behind us and then moves toward his office chair. When he sits, he doesn't waste any time getting straight to the point. "We're worried about you, Miss Page. Reid Parker, especially. You know that nice young man just told me not to punish you. Now, I told him I couldn't do that because rules are rules, but—"

I make a sound of amusement. "Rules are rules? Like when Cade brought in a Super Soaker to Home-coming last year and nothing happened to him? Does it explicitly say somewhere in the Code of Conduct that water guns are allowed? I'll make sure to bring mine in. I mean, if so. If that's what we're saying here."

Mr. Dade levels a glare at me. I don't care. I just want him to know I'm aware of the hypocrisy of everything.

"Do you deny you slapped Mr. Parker?"

"No," I tell him, leaning back in my chair. "I'm pretty sure you saw the whole thing, so it would be stupid of me to deny it. Besides, he deserved it. I'd do it again."

His face tightens, deepening his skin's creases which become more like craters. "We don't allow physical altercations at Spring Hill, Briar. You know that."

"Unless they're out on the football field?"

His nostrils flare.

This is kind of fun. I don't know why I was so meek before. Pushing the envelope has its own set of positives.

"I'm afraid I won't be able to abide by Mr. Parker's wishes."

"That's a first," I quip.

"Miss Page," Dade says, his voice laced with anger.

The door pushes in behind me. For a moment, I'm startled, but then I hear my mother's voice. "Thank you, Reid. I don't know what I would do..." Her voice breaks, and with it, a little piece of my armor chips away. Don't worry. It's replaced by fury in the next second. We don't know what we would do without Reid fucking Parker? Is she serious? We already know what we would do without Brady. Surely Reid Parker could get hit by a bus and it wouldn't change our lives at all.

Mr. Dade stands. "Mrs. Page, thank you for coming."

The door behind me shuts, and my mother's heels click forward. She and Mr. Dade shake hands. I'm getting daggers, but I don't look up. Instead, my mom sits in the chair next to mine, her back as straight as an arrow. I'm too tired to put on airs. "Thanks for calling me, Roger," Mom says. She shakes her head. "Mr. Dade. Sorry about that."

He waves her use of his first name away. Everyone in Spring Hill knows everyone else. The names we use for one another are dictated by the social interaction. One second, Sheriff Thomas is Sheriff Thomas, the next, he's Daryl who likes to play darts down at the pool hall and gets sloppy after too many drinks. "I know you have a lot on your plate. Did Mr. Parker explain the situation to you?"

"Yes, he certainly did." Dagger eyes again. I'm already digging my fingernails into my skin to try to keep my mouth shut. People don't like opinions in Spring Hill, especially those that go against what everyone else thinks. "I'm sure Briar has apologized profusely."

"Actually," Mr. Dade says. "She's refused to apologize at all to Reid."

"Briar!" my mother exclaims, true shock forcing through her lips. The sound makes me wince a little.

"Even so," Mr. Dade continues. "Reid has asked that she not be punished for what happened, but I'm afraid I can't abide by that. She'll have to serve after-school detention for two weeks."

My mother's fingers grip onto the armrests. "Of course. I completely understand."

I can feel her eyes lasering into me, but I avoid her look like the plague. Tonight will not be a fun night in the Page household. Not that any night has been all that great since Brady's death.

After that, they continue to talk about me like I'm not even there. My mother asks if I've seen the school counselor yet even though I don't have study hall until the last period of the day. She should know this. I've told her only about a hundred times since she set the appointment up for me after I was dragged back home. They're all worried I'll run away again.

They should be.

"I think that's perfect," my mother says, her tone clipped. "She can talk about what she's done with Ms. Lyons and then she can think about what she's done while sitting in detention. Right, Briar?"

I nod.

The accusatory eyes have gone, but what's replaced them is sometimes worse. They're her sad eyes. The eyes that wonder what's gotten into me lately.

Honestly? I'm just fed up with everything.

After that, Principal Dade tells me I can go to class while my mother hangs back to talk to him. It doesn't matter to me. I'm sure my mother will have plenty to say to me tonight. I'm only getting a few hours leeway on the scolding that's sure to come in private.

I grab my bookbag from the chair I'd been waiting on out in the sitting room and head back into the hallway. The football banners and streamers are everywhere, making my gut clench. My teeth gnash together. I seriously can't get away from any of it.

Because it's in the middle of a period, there's no one in the halls. I glare up at one of the signs that says SPRING HILL TOUGH in block letters. Part of the cord it's strung up with his hanging down next to the wall. I set my bag down and jump at it. I land without the cord, so I jump again. This time, my fingers just graze it. I make an annoyed sound in the back of my throat and jump again. My fingers find the cord, but at the same time, strong hands pull back on my hips. I let out a yelp and then I'm tripping over my baggy sweats and hit the ground hard on my ass.

I stare up at the fiery green eyes of Reid Parker. "Just what the hell do you think you're doing, Briar?"

I push myself to my feet. "Tearing the fucking sign down. What does it look like?"

He shakes his head at me. "Is that what Dade and your mom dismissed you to do? Rip the football sign down?"

I blink at him. I don't even know why I'm even standing here answering his questions. I don't owe him shit. I stretch my arm around him to get my bookbag, but he steps in the way. Reaching out, he grabs a few strands of my hair and sneers at them.

I yank my head away. "Don't touch me."

He glowers. "When did you turn into such a little bitch?"

I smile at him. Of course, he would think that. I don't fall at his feet, so that must mean I'm a bitch. "I guess it's always been begging to get out."

"Well reign it in. We've all had enough."

"Oh God." I smile. I legit smile. "This is hilarious. You know that, right? I mean, you can feel it, too, can't you? The ridiculousness of it. I don't know how many times I need to make this loud and clear but let me do it again. Don't touch me. Don't come near me. I don't care about you or Lex or Cade or anyone else for that matter. If my bitchiness offends you so much, look the other fucking way."

He growls low in his throat. He sets his hands on my shoulders and pushes me until my back's against the wall. "Grow the fuck up, Briar. Get your shit together. Dress for school. Take a fucking shower. And for God's sake, dye your hair back. Your mother's a fucking mess, and she doesn't need you acting out like this just for attention."

I raise my hands to shove them into his chest, but he easily plucks them out of the air.

"I'm not messing around. I'll make your life a living hell if you don't get your shit together. You think you don't want anything to do with the football team now? You wait. You'll be on the sidelines during every fucking game and practice. I won't let you out of my sight." He tosses my hands aside. "And that's a promise. Do you understand?"

The bell rings above us as I glare at him. His words sink into me. With the steady heat of his eyes, I know he means every single word he says. I've seen him use his will over people my whole entire life. I've laughed with him and my brother, but that's all been in fun. It was just a little teasing. It was a way for us to get exactly what we wanted. This time, he's gone too far with someone who gives no fucks.

He wants me to bring the old Briar back, but I can't. She's gone for good, and you know what, I don't even miss her.

I loathe the person she was. I hate that she lived for approval. That she did extra credit to stay at the top of her class. She lived in a bubble is all she did. That bubble called Spring Hill. She didn't understand anything in the outside world.

The hallway starts to fill with students. People slap Reid on the back, and every time it happens, it's like someone slides a blade a little further into my heart. Why my brother? Why not someone like Reid?

"I'm not afraid of you, Parker."

For a second, he's taken aback, but then the creases in his face deepen as his lips thin. "Why are you so determined to ruin your family?"

I swallow before snatching my bag up from the other side of him. "In case you haven't noticed, that's already happened."

I barrel right through Cade and Lex who are coming up behind Reid like usual. Both of them are wearing matching surprised faces as I knock their upper arms with my own. It's only pure determination that gets me through them because they're huge football players, and I'm just me. It's hate that's driving me now.

I head straight for the main doors and out onto the sidewalk that leads to the parking lot. I refuse to look to my right where the football bleachers rise up in the distance, but I cross the lot, heat rising from the asphalt, to get to the other side. I take a seat just under one of the huge lamplights and fish my cell phone out of my bag. I go into the last conversation I had with Ezra and stare at the last words he sent me. **You look beautiful, baby.**

Tears start to run down my face. Sometimes I just feel so heavy I need to release things. Emotions, baggage, decisions, whatever it is. It just needs to come out. I send Ezra a heart and clutch my cell phone close.

Sure, some would call him my online boyfriend, but he's much more than that. He's the person I tell everything to. He doesn't care that I didn't wash my hair this morning and didn't bother with dry shampoo or makeup. He actually likes my dark hair, and he didn't balk when I sent him the selfie where you could see the collar of my baggy sweatshirt.

Everyone else had shit to say about it, but he didn't. He thinks I'm beautiful.

And right now, when I feel like the lowest shit on Earth, can't I just have one person who thinks I'm beautiful?

3

I'm lying on my bed staring up at the ceiling when lights flash through my window. I blink, thinking the intrusion was just something my eyes did to try to trick me, or because it's late and I've been staring at the ceiling for hours like it can give me the answers to all my problems.

The lights flash again. Two in quick succession. My stomach lurches. I pull myself up on my forearms and peek out the window directly to my left. There it is. The familiar silver Honda Civic that I haven't seen since I tried getting the hell away from Spring Hill.

I peel the covers off me and plant my feet on the floor, still staring out the window. He's parked just far enough away from the house so that the lights only shine in my window, and so he can't be seen from the other parts of the house, even though it doesn't matter, my parents are already sleeping. Gone are the days where they would stay up after we had gone to bed. They're too tired now. Too lost.

I stand and lean toward the window, taking the screen out like I used to. I set it carefully aside, not wanting to clue my parents in on what I'm about to do. If I thought the tongue lashing I got earlier was bad when they realized I hadn't gone to see Ms. Lyons and skipped out on school for the rest of the day after I slapped my brother's best friend in front of the whole school, they certainly wouldn't care for the way I want to cap off the whole day.

Once the screen is off, I sit on the window ledge and jump, allowing myself to fall the few feet to the ground. The grass is crisp, a little wet from the dew as I walk across the yard toward the side of the road. There aren't any houses directly nearby, no one to notice what I'm doing outside, crossing the lawn at midnight.

I tug on the car door and it opens easily before sliding into the passenger seat. The car light illuminates the entire interior of the car, so for a few moments, I just get in and stare ahead until the light goes off.

"Hey," he says.

"Hey."

We're silent for a few beats longer. I don't always know why this happens. We only do this for one thing. Well, it didn't always start out this way, but it quickly turned into it.

"I didn't think you'd ever show back up."

"Me either," he says. I feel him move to face me. He sighs. "You're not wearing pants."

"I figured why bother? Aren't you just going to take them off?" He's silent. He never likes me to talk about it so in his face like this. "I have underwear on."

"What are we going to do with you, Briar?"

My stomach twists, and I finally look up into Lex's deep brown eyes. He was so quiet at school today. I wasn't sure if he'd ever talk to me again. I take him in, his large shoulders, his expansive chest. He's too big for this car. Twisted in his seat like he is now, he's taking up the entire space between the seat and the steering wheel. It's good that he's this big. It means he does his job on the football field well. No one gets past Lex to sack Reid. It's been like that for forever. In football and in real life.

I'm not going to answer his other question, so instead, I ask one of my own. "Did you miss me?"

His eyes darken. "Not in the way you think."

A stab of guilt hits me. I know exactly in the way he thinks. We've lost ourselves in each other too many times to count. It's exactly what he wants. Maybe he thinks I've developed some sort of crush on him, but I haven't. I love the way it is between us now. A means to forget for however long it takes to make the memories subside. "Well, I missed you." I reach my hand out to traverse the distance between us. I slide my palm over his knee and start to move the fabric of his athletic shorts back when his hand lands on top of mine.

"I don't think you missed me. If you did, you would've come back sooner. Hell, you wouldn't have left."

"Is that why you haven't come until now? You're trying to punish me?"

Lex lets my hand go. "You do enough of that to yourself."

I blink at him, take a deep breath, and ask, "Do you like my hair?"

He shakes his head. Not about my hair, but about everything in general, like he can't find words to express enough how much he dislikes everything now.

Lex started showing up at our house because he missed Brady so much. We used to talk about everything, sitting here in this cramped car. We'd talk about different memories, and we'd cry with each other. We haven't talked about anything that in-depth in months. Not since we gave in that one night when crying turned to kissing. Kissing turned to touching, and then there was no turning back. He fingered me until I climaxed around him, my body clamping around him like even it didn't want to let him go.

I didn't know I could feel that way after Brady died. Then, I craved it and craved it. I'd watch out the window until Lex would show up flashing his lights, promising me intense moments of relief.

I brush my hair aside. "I take that as a no."

"Why can't we talk about anything anymore?" he asks, voice soft. He's so different than what you would think if you only saw him. He's a gentle giant. Except for out on the field. When he's playing football, he becomes his own monster.

"What fun is talking?" I ask, a smile on my face. Now that he's here, I want nothing more than to lose myself in the bliss of not having to think. I love that this is our little secret. Reid and Cade don't know. Jules doesn't know either. Nor my parents or the school counselor. This time is just for Lex and me, to forget, to heal, to live.

I run my hand further up his thigh, but he stops me again. He's straining in his shorts. I can see his erection from here, even in the low light. It's not surprising he won't let me touch him. He never has, but I always try.

"I just wanted to talk to you," Lex says. "With

everything that happened today, I thought you could use someone."

"Oh, you mean Reid telling me I'm disgracing my brother?"

He flinches. "He's just worried about you."

"Is that how you act toward someone you're worried about?"

"You shut us out."

My anger spikes. "Listen, Lex, are you going to psychoanalyze me, or are you going to bury your head between my legs? Or maybe even your cock this time?"

Lex's eyes flare.

"I see you straining." I try to move my hands up once more, but he pushes down harder to stop me from moving. "Don't you want to know what it feels like?"

I'm under no illusion that he hasn't had other girls, but he hasn't had me and he wants to. It's so evident.

He swallows. "What we did together was so wrong."

"We live in wrong, Lex."

He squeezes my hand. I can see the conflict on his face. I'm not above egging him on. Otherwise, what did he come here for? We both know why he's here. We best just get to it. The longer I'm out here, the better chances I have of getting found out.

I use my left hand to cup my breast over my form-fitting tank top. His eyes immediately zero in on my movement. I moan and bite my lip, thrusting my hips into the air. Then, I pull on the scooped neck until my bare breast is revealed.

"Jesus, Briar," Lex says, his voice heavy with desire. He squeezes my hand again. I close my eyes, hoping he'll move my palm over his cock. I want to feel him, feel his need for me.

I pluck at my nipple, rubbing it between my two fingers until it's peaked and heat settles between my legs. I pull back on my hand, and he lets it go. I move it to my core and brush it over my nub. "Oh, God," I groan.

I'm lost now. I'm not going to stop until I come. I don't care if he does it or I do, it's going to happen. Blissful moments of peace, that's what I think of them as.

I open my eyes to see him feasting on me. Lex has always been handsome, just like the rest of my brother's friends, but when he's like this, he's downright sexy. It was easy to fall into this arrangement with him. Too damn easy. "You know what would be better now? Your tongue on my pussy."

"Fucking Christ, Briar," he curses. "Where did you get a mouth like that?"

"You like it," I tell him.

I rub my nub again and another shock of pleasure warms me. The truth is, he's made me this bold. Ever since this started, he's made me feel sexy and wanted. For so long I was just the annoying little sister, but one moment with Lex changed all that. He's brought out a side in me I don't want to hold back any longer.

I squeeze my nipple until pain blooms, but all it does is make me want more.

"Please, Lex," I groan.

His large body moves forward. He takes up so much space in the car it's impossible not to look at him. His stare is still conflicted while at the same time he eats me up with his eyes. "This is so wrong."

"Taste me with your tongue, Lexington Jones. Let me feel you."

He pulls my knees apart and leans over the console. It's not by any means comfortable, especially when he physically moves me, so my head is pressed against the passenger door before kneeling over me, his hot breath caressing the inside of my thighs. He nuzzles my apex right over my panties.

"Oh, fuck me," I breathe. The tension ratchets up inside me. He's going to give me exactly what I want. "Maybe tonight you can finally slide your cock inside me."

He groans.

I raise my hips into the air, searching for him. He rewards me with a kiss just to the side of my panty line. "Rip them off. Push them to the side. I don't care."

His hands slide over my ass, pulling me to his mouth. He pulls my panties to the side and I look up, watching his face as he stares right at my drenched core that's waiting for him. "This is the last time," he growls, before diving forward and licking my folds.

When he does that, I don't even notice how uncomfortable his car is. I get lost in his expert strokes. The way he plays my body like he's been doing it all his life. I relax because I know he'll take me where I need to go, suspended in a rush of pleasure where the only thing I can think about is what he's doing to me.

I start moaning his name over and over. He brings his hand up to cup my breast, and I cry out. We don't kiss anymore. Not like we did the first time. We just do what needs to be done. I'm not his girl-friend, and he's certainly not my boyfriend. For a moment, I think of Ezra, but at the same exact time, the tip of his tongue flicks over my clit, and my body jolts.

I love when Lex gets like this. He loses himself too. He's not the reserved center who'd rather watch his friends get into all the trouble. I know I'm helping him just as much as he's helping me. He comes alive between my legs. "Oh fuck. You taste so sweet. You like that, Briar? You like my tongue on you?"

"Yes," I stutter out. "More."

My whole body starts to tighten, preparing for release. I want to hold onto this moment. Don't get me wrong, I fucking love the rush of my release, but I don't want it to end. I want to stay forever in this state, this precipice of bliss where it's impossible to think about anything else.

"Lex!" It's both a warning and a cry of triumph.

My body flings itself over the edge. Lex moans into me, softening his strokes while prolonging the moment until I'm putty in his arms and his grip slowly starts to relax.

After I catch my breath, I stay with my head at an odd angle against the passenger side door as Lex extricates himself from me. I stare up with my eyes firmly closed, my front teeth digging into my lower lip as I try to grasp on tightly to this moment. But it never fails to fade away on me.

When it does, I maneuver my panties back into place and sit back up. I peek over at Lex to find him already staring out the front windshield of the car like he can't wait to get out of here now. My head starts to thump. I stuff my breast back into my tank top and reach for the door handle. I'm not even going to attempt to take things further with Lex. He doesn't look like he's in the mood at all to ward off my advances. I even tried straddling him once, rubbing my bare pussy over his cock, but he won't give in. If I ever did get him to give in, I think I would count it as a personal victory.

I swallow the lump starting in my throat. Everything has already started to come rushing back to me. My hand closes over the door handle, but Lex's voice stops me. "Do me a favor, Briar?"

I stay silent. Everyone knows not to ask me for favors right now. I am completely self-aware I'm being selfish as fuck. The thing is, I can't bring myself to care.

What the fuck is wrong with me? My brother dies, and I lose my fucking mind. I let one of his best friends eat me out. I slap the other. I don't even keep up with his girlfriend because I'm too inside my own head.

The first tear falls.

This usually happens, and Lex pretends he doesn't notice, but I'm sure he does. I'm sure he thinks I'm so fucked up, which is why he's refrained from sticking his dick inside me. Isn't that a saying every guy hears growing up? Don't fuck the crazy ones?

Well, I'm crazy. I'm fucking losing it, and I can't make myself stop.

"What's that?" I ask, my voice choked.

"Forgive me?"

I close my eyes and start to swallow the pain those words conjure. He's done nothing that needs forgiving. It's all me. Poor sixteen-year-old girl who lost her brother and is now ruining her own fucking life. I mean, I must be a sight. I know why my parents can't stand to be in the same room with me. I bet part of them would've liked if I'd stayed hidden in the city.

But for Lex, there's nothing to forgive. At least not in the sense he's asking.

I just don't know why, out of every single guy on that team, that it had to be my brother.

Instead of releasing him from his guilt over burying his tongue inside me, I just get out. I slam the car door and walk back toward my bedroom window, tears tracking down my face. There isn't a square inch of skin that isn't wet and salty. I'm not sobbing. I'm not even overtly crying. It's just the tears that won't stop. I'm not sure if they ever will.

4

The next morning, Lex and I pass each other in the hallway like we don't even know one another. I'm acutely aware of him. The hair stands on my arms, but I'm immediately thrown back into what happened last night and the way I cried myself to sleep afterward. It's not just that Brady's dead, it's that I don't think I even like myself anymore.

Jules has been acting weird all day. She can barely look me in the eyes. So much so that I wonder if she actually happened upon what Lex and I were doing in the car last night, but I know that's just my guilt talking. There's no way anyone saw us. Now, I'm just chalking up her odd behavior to missing Brady. It sucks being back in this school without him, so I feel her pain.

"You know what's strange?" she asks as we walk to our next class. "I feel like Brady was everywhere. In the hall talking to a group of people, texting me on my phone, waiting for me at the end of the day to ask me how my day went just before he went to practice. And now he's...just not anywhere."

I swallow, hard. I may as well have a chicken bone in there for how difficult it was to choke that emotion down. She's right. Because Brady was one of the football greats, he was literally everywhere. People talking to him, talking about him. For a lot of my life, I was happy to stay in his shadow, looking on at what my brother had been able to do for himself. It was only until I got to high school that people noticed me because I was his sister. Then I got attention and looks, and Brady got to act like the protective older brother, and his friends followed suit. His absence is a huge hole. "I know what you mean."

As siblings go, Brady and I got along really well. Sure, I may have been the annoying sister from time-to-time, especially growing up, but in the year before he died, I think he liked me being around. I was there with Jules when he couldn't be. He used to tell me to watch out for her. God, he loved her so much.

"Sometimes it feels like nothing will be normal again," Jules muses.

I'm so with her there. I don't even want it to be normal again. What's normal when Brady can't be here? It's an impossibility.

Up ahead, right outside my next class, Reid and Sasha are pawing at one another. I don't remember Reid being like that before Brady died. Maybe he's using her like Lex and I are using each other. Though, that can't be entirely accurate, Reid has been dating Sasha since middle school. It's like they were meant to be. She's the head cheerleader, he's the quarterback. What other options are there? It's so cliché it makes me roll my eyes.

Reid's kissing her neck when Sasha drops her head to the side, her eyelids fluttering open. I look away, but not before she catches me looking at them. "Ugh, get a life, Briar," she says.

You'd think I'd get a grace period on the bullying with my brother dying and all, but Sasha didn't care about that. I'm pretty sure she only kept her mouth shut before because of Brady. Now that he's not here, there's no one to shut her up. In truth, Sasha's pretty territorial. She's cool with Jules, or used to be, because she was dating Brady. If Lex or Cade get a girlfriend, she's cool with them too. What she doesn't like is for other unattached girls to be hanging around. It makes her drama-fueled head explode.

I would've ignored her, but the mention of my name makes Reid come up for air. He steps back, so there's only an inch of space between him and his girlfriend and gives me another once over. He shakes his head, and I just shrug my shoulders. I did take a shower this morning. Sure, I'm still wearing a long-sleeved shirt and baggy jeans, but my hair is freshly washed even though it's still black.

"Maybe you should find a guy to fuck that look off your face," Sasha says, her nose scrunching up.

"Why? That hasn't worked for you yet."

Her gaze narrows, and I can't help but smile. She thinks she's so smart, but she's an idiot. She's using Reid to get her ass out of Spring Hill. She thinks he'll take her to college with him and then beyond if he ever makes it into the NFL. She sure as hell isn't going to take her hooks out of him. It's her only chance, and honestly, I can see she was thinking ahead. So maybe she does have some sort of brain in her.

"Watch your mouth," Reid says, eyeing me.

Jules tries to tug me into our class, so we avoid a confrontation, but what's the fun in that? I just eye him until he sighs.

He steps away from Sasha and moves forward. His green eyes appraise me, and I know that whatever ridiculous standard he's set for me in his head on how I should be acting hasn't been met. "You didn't go to your meeting yesterday."

I shake my head. No, I didn't. I sat there and texted Ezra on that little piece of grass just outside the parking lot.

"You should go."

"I've got another chance today," I tell him.

"You're going to run out of chances."

"Why do you care?"

"Come on," Jules says, tugging on my hand again.

Reid gives her an apologetic look. Why is it always Jules that people feel sorry for? "No, I need to hear this," I tell her, not ever taking my eyes away from Reid's. "I need to know why somehow I don't meet the approval of the quarterback of our football team. I mean, that's something we should all strive to meet, isn't it?" The sarcasm is just oozing off me. I'm practically swimming with it.

"You want to know why I care," Reid says. He moves forward. He comes at me so fast I have to step back. Before I know it, my back is against the metal locker and Reid Parker is in my face. His chiseled jaw jumps. Beyond his shoulder, I see Sasha standing there, hands on her hips, her eyes are practically bugging out of her head as she stares me down. "Your brother's not

43

here, so if I'm the one who has to make you toe the line, I will."

My face heats. "You're not a stand-in for Brady." I can barely get the words out. How dare he talk about him right here right now. I want to spit in his face. Like anyone could step into my brother's shoes. "I don't need you."

"You obviously need something."

"Trust me, I've got things handled, so whatever fucking ridiculous...thing you have over making sure I'm fine, you can let it go. I don't want it."

"Until your mom stops calling me, crying in my ear, you're going to get it."

I suck in a breath. I narrow my eyes at him, trying to figure out whether he's lying or not. Why is mom calling Reid of all people? If she is even calling him.

"Leave her alone, Reid," Jules says.

His head snaps to her. He gives her a slight frown. "I'm sorry, Juliet, but this has nothing to do with you."

Sasha's hands close around Reid's bicep. It's only then that I realize how close we'd gotten to one another. The stench of her hand lotion permeates my nostrils, and I pull away only there's no place for me to go. Reid takes in our proximity and lets Sasha move him back. "Be careful, baby," she says. "You'll get a disease."

He ignores her. "Tomorrow I want to see regular clothes. I mean it."

"These are regular clothes."

"Something presentable."

Sasha snickers. "Who cares? Let her look like a homeless person."

"Fuck off, Sasha," Jules snaps.

Both Reid and Sasha stop to stare at Jules. I can tell Jules is shaking, but she crosses her arms over her chest and lifts her chin in the air. That's the only thing that gets me to move. Both Reid and Sasha are too shocked to say anything, so I take her forearm and we walk into class right before the bell rings. The teacher glares at us until we take our seats in the back, but I don't care. Jules may finally be getting her voice back.

In lunch, Jules doesn't sit with the football table. She and I take over the end of the table I found yesterday and spend the whole hour chatting quietly or just in silence. She's one of the only people I can stand to be around after Brady died. I don't feel like I have to fill the silence when we're together. There's no pressure to talk or be quiet or to try to figure out the right thing to say. I wish it was the same with my parents.

"Let's hit up the boutique shops after school, okay?" Jules asks.

My brows pull together. She's not even looking at

me. She's dangling her fork into her mashed potatoes. "You want to go shopping?" Then it dawns on me. "You want me to buy clothes I'll wear, don't you?"

Her head snaps up. "No. No, of course not. I don't give a shit about that. I was going to look for something, but we can do something else. Maybe get some ice cream or a bite to eat. I'll drive you home afterward."

I bite the inside of my cheek. Jules hasn't been to my house since Brady died. I figured she didn't want to because it would hurt too much. I know for a fact she lost her virginity to him in his bedroom. Maybe she's finally ready. Maybe this is just the way she's broaching the subject. "Sure. Fine. Whatever you want."

"So, you'll be around at the end of school? You're not going to skip again?"

"I don't have any plans to skip at present," I tell her with a short smile.

She rolls her eyes in a moment of normalcy. But then it's as if we both realized that we forgot for a second, so we go back to the all-encompassing sadness instead.

Behind me, I can hear the football table going crazy like normal. Because I was Brady's sister and because I was friends with Jules, I got to sit there last year. We laughed, talked, and joked. I actually had fun, but as soon as Brady died, I didn't want anything to do with it. In fact, when I finally came back to school to finish the year, I didn't even eat lunch in the cafeteria at all. I ate in the library. We—my parents and me—figured I had so much studying to do anyway. No one wanted me to fall behind since I'd already skipped a grade anyway.

Yeah, that's right. The one who doesn't want to even think about school anymore skipped a grade. In middle school, I was a year behind Brady and his friends, but I skipped eighth and went right to the high school with him in the same grade. He was proud of me. We walked into Freshman year together with his arm slung over my shoulders. It's one of my favorite memories. It felt like the Pages were about to take over Spring Hill High. He was the big shot, soon-to-be captain of the football team, and I was destined to be Valedictorian.

Without thinking, my gaze wanders the cafeteria to find Theo Laughlin. He's off in the corner at the smart kid table. His glasses are pushed up his nose as he reads his Chem book. He was the only true competition I had to get Valedictorian. When I look at him though, I can't muster up any of the warrior in me to want to challenge him for that spot. I used to stare at him before, and it would make me want to work harder, do better, especially if he was doing schoolwork during lunch. *Who does that?*

Freshman year, I came out ahead, but last year, he beat me, and not by just a little either. He slaughtered me. My grades from before Brady's death were so good that I wasn't in much danger of failing, but my whole average went down by the time school ended.

The bell rings overhead, and Jules and I go our separate ways for the last classes of the day. Then, we meet out in the parking lot next to her car after I talk with the counselor and serve my detention. She just happens to be parked right next to Lex's silver Honda Civic. I stare into the passenger seat, imagining how I would've looked from an outsider if they'd spied us in there yesterday.

With a quick shake of my head, I get in her car and she drives us down to the small downtown that Spring Hill boasts. It's just a few boutique shops, a small dessert place alongside a hairdresser, a pizza shop, and a diner with terrible food. I have no idea how they stay open, but I see a bunch of elderly in Spring Hill still eat there, so my only guess is that the place used to be really good and they just can't seem to let it go.

We go into a few of the clothing shops. I finger a few of the tops. Some of them are really pretty despite the small selection, and I have no problem helping to pick out outfits for Jules, but not for myself. When we get done, we walk down to the dessert shop and get small ice cream cones before getting back into her car.

There's no mistaking it now. The tension in the air has skyrocketed since Jules pointed the car toward my house. She's driving extra slow and super carefully as if to put off the inevitable. "Jules," I say, unable to keep quiet about it any longer. "You don't have to do this. Just drop me off down the road. I'll walk the rest of the way."

She blinks. "What?"

"Drop me off. I'll walk."

She shakes her head like she has no idea what I'm talking about. "Oh, no, I'm fine." This time, she makes an effort to press down on the gas a little harder to appear normal, but the tension never leaves the inside of the car. She even makes my stomach queasy like I've downed an extra shot of adrenaline.

When we come around the corner and we're within seeing distance of my house, her foot on the gas falters a little. I look up to see what she's staring at and notice a bunch of cars in the driveway. "W-what's going on?"

Jules shakes her head. "Nothing."

I look from her to the house and back again. Her

free leg starts jumping up and down. "What the hell is this, Jules?"

She doesn't answer until we pull into the driveway. I see Lex's silver Honda Civic, and even Reid's Escape sitting there. My stomach flips over itself. I'd actually been feeling a little better this afternoon after the talk with the counselor and then the little break with Jules after school, but I feel like my life is about to turn upside down...for the second time.

The front door opens, and my parents step out, staring into Jules's car. "What's going on?" I say again, my voice breaking. Sometimes it feels like there's so much inside me that needs to be felt that I don't know how to feel it unless it's in tear form.

"Your parents wanted to talk to you," she says quietly.

I blink up at her, the puzzle pieces coming together. Jules is here for the first time since Brady died. The guys are here. My parents, and God knows who else. "They talked you into this, didn't they?"

"We all care about you, Briar."

Holy fuck. I know what this is. I'm about to walk into a goddamn intervention.

Fuck me.

5

*W*e're all in my living room. Mom and Dad are sitting on the arm rests on either side of the couch. Between them are Lex and Jules. Cade and Reid are sitting in the armchairs while I'm seated in a chair from the dining room table surrounded by all of them.

I can't keep from staring at Jules. She knows, too, because she hasn't looked up once since my parents coaxed me into the house. My first thought was that there aren't a lot of people here. Easier to deal with. Then again, are there really so little people who "care" about me? And I'm not even counting Brady's friends in this. I stare at my mother. "Why are they here?"

"Who?"

"Them," I say, pointing at Lex first then the other

two. I don't even want to think about how Lex's tongue devoured me last night, and he must have known about this the entire time. That's just something I can't fathom right now. At least he can't really meet my eyes either.

"Come on, Shortie," Cade says.

I shake my head. "No, I'm not going to 'come on'." I stare at my mother to implore her with my eyes. This is embarrassing enough, but to have to go through it in front of them. They're not even my friends, and they don't care about me. According to Reid, they only care because my mother's been calling to cry to them. If she needs them, fine, but I don't.

"They're here representing Brady," my father says.

I grind my teeth together. For the love of all that is holy, they are not fucking substitutions for my brother. You can't just replace one with the other three. My foot starts to bob up and down, but I keep my mouth screwed shut. If they like having my brother's friends around to help remind them of Brady, fine, but it shouldn't be shoved in my face. They certainly shouldn't be here during this. But since they're already here, I guess I just have to grin and bear it. That's what everyone wants from me anyway. "Poor choice," I say, leaning back in my chair with my arms crossed.

"We're trying to reach you, Briar," my mom says.

She's looking at me now like she's been looking at me since Brady died. Like she doesn't even know me, like everything out of my mouth surprises her now.

"By embarrassing me. Good call."

"No," my father intervenes. "By showing you the people who care about you."

I stare at Reid then. Why is *he* doing this? Why are they all doing this? Brady died. That should have been the surgical removal of them from our lives. "Don't you have football or something?" I ask, staring straight into Reid's green eyes.

"Yes. We do," he says. His voice is curt, filled with the vitriol I've come to expect from him. Like he blames me for them being here.

"I didn't ask you to be here," I say flippantly.

A low growl starts to pour from his mouth, but Cade cuts him off. "Well, we're here anyway. I would just like to start off by saying that the baggy look is not doing you any favors, Shortie. Also, the dark hair just makes you look that much paler than your already pale ass."

"Thanks for the beauty tips," I deadpan.

"Thank you for sharing that," my father says, nodding at Cade like what he said was mind-blowingly revealing.

I glare at him. What, did he read some sort of

manual on how to give an intervention? "Oh yes, thank you for sharing that, Cade. I'm glad you find me repulsive, but I'm even happier that I don't give a fuck what you think about me."

"Briar!" my mother snaps.

Cade just laughs it off though. Nothing gets to that guy. He's too carefree. I give him a smug grin and he returns it.

"Who else wants to share something?" my father asks. His hair has gotten a lot grayer in the months since Brady died. Maybe it's the loss of his only son. Maybe it's because I've been losing my damn mind. Or a combination of both. I don't know.

My mother places her hands in front of her mouth, teepee style, then brings them down to her lap. "Briar, I love you. You know that. I've tried to get you the help you needed to feel better. I feel like I've done all I can and all I know how to do. You can't let your life go to waste because Brady's dead. You can't."

If I knew how to get my shit together, I already would have. Why doesn't anyone get that?

I don't know how to answer her, so I don't. "Anyone else?"

Reid shuffles his feet. "Yeah, I've got something to say." When I turn to look at him, some of the anger has seeped away from his face. He clears his throat. "Do

54

you know how proud Brady was of you?" His face twists and it looks like he's wrangling some sort of emotion under control. "For skipping a grade? For being kind of cool for a sister? I guarantee you he would not like this person you are now." He gestures toward me with a dismissive wave.

My heart cracks, but I slap some super glue on there and harden up. "Cool. Who else?"

"Jesus. Are you even listening?" Reid asks.

I ignore him. I glare at Jules until she shifts uncomfortably. When she lifts her gaze to mine, her eyes round. She tucks her hair behind her ears, and says, "I know you're super pissed at me right now. For not telling you about this and for telling you I wanted to hang out just so I could bring you here, but you know I care about you." She takes a deep breath. A small smile flits over her face. It's not long lived, and it's almost whimsical in a sense. "Your brother loved you. He *was* proud of you. I'm not going to say he wouldn't like you now because he would love you no matter what, Briar. But I do know he would be intensely concerned for you." A single tear runs down her face. "He used to tell me you studied too much. He was concerned about that, so I know for a fact he would be worrying about you right now. If he—" She chokes on her words and starts over. "If he'd been alive when you ran away..."

She shakes her head. "Oh, God. He would've been devastated."

I'm trying to strengthen my resolve, but it's quickly dissipating. It happens every time I think about Brady. I know he'd be worried about me. Hell, I'm worried about myself. I'm making decisions now that are going to change my future, but I can't fucking stop. How do I tell them this though? How do I tell them I can't figure out why I'm behaving like this? They won't get it. "I know," I tell her.

She's crying now, tears streaming down her face unchecked. Lex places his arm around her shoulder, and I just stare blankly at the spot they connect. My dad claps her on the back a couple of times while pinching his nose. That's about as comforting as he gets.

"Right, so..." Mom looks around. "Lex, do you have anything to say to Briar?"

He clams up. His hand falls from Jules's shoulder, and he looks at me. Guilt is written all over his face. All I can think in that moment is that I'd much rather be spending this time with him in his Civic than talking about all this. He runs a hand down his cheek. "I have something to say, but I'm going to say it to her privately. On top of that, I just want her to know that I want her to get better."

"I am sitting right here," I tell him. "You can actually address me."

Lex's jaw ticks as he looks me in the eye. "I want you to get better, Briar. I want you better for a whole slew of reasons that I can't even begin to list, but maybe the number one reason is because you don't deserve to spend your whole life in Spring Hill, waitressing at that shit diner downtown because you dropped out of high school. But you also don't deserve to hide away in the big city and still be nothing either. The Briar Page I knew before wouldn't take any of that. It wasn't good enough for you then, and it's not good enough for you now."

By the time Lex finishes talking, he's out of breath, and his voice is raised several octaves. I just blink at him. Then, I take a slow perusal around the room to stare at everyone. I don't know how to end this, but I know I want all of this to end right now. I don't want to ever think about this again, and I sure as hell never want to go through this again.

"Good," my mom says, still wiping tears from her face. "Now, Briar, is there anything you have to say? What can we do to help you?"

I shrug. "I'm fine."

Her lips start to thin. "We'll do anything to help you. Just tell us what it is."

"I actually think I just need space. Also, I need to pee."

Reid's hands turn to fists at his sides. "You had space when you were in fucking Calcutta for the week," he roars. "When none of us knew where you fucking were."

Even my mom jumps at that. I don't. I'm used to it from him.

"Space isn't working," my dad says, taking the more tactical approach and ignoring Reid's outburst.

I shrug again. "Then I don't know what to tell you that I need." *I don't know what I need* is the real answer, but I refuse not to have an answer. How can I not know what will make me better? Or better yet, what do I tell them when the only thing that can make me better is impossible? I need Brady. Right here, right now. That's what I need.

"I told you this would be a waste of time, Pam," Reid says. He rises from the chair, his face pinched and angry. I'm sure he would've rather been at football practice, but I'm not the one who invited him here.

Mom glares at me as if I've done something wrong. I watch as Cade and Reid leave. They don't bother to say goodbye to me, and I wouldn't have bothered answering if they had. Lex and Jules are still on the couch, my father on the armrest, but all I

58

really want to do is tell Ezra what a fucking mess today was.

Mom returns after the front door opens and closes. She waves her hand in the air. "I guess you guys can leave too. I appreciate you trying everything you can."

Jules stands. She gives me an apologetic look, then comes over to throw her arms around me. "Don't hate me."

I squeeze her back. "Never. Just please don't do that again."

She doesn't answer either way and soon my mother is walking her toward the door.

Lexington Jones rises next. He dwarfs my father who gets to his feet now too. But instead of leaving, Lex says, "Can I have that private conversation with Briar now?"

My stomach drops, and I look to my father for his answer, hoping he'll say no.

"Sure," he says. He waves his hand toward me as an invitation. He's totally exasperated, but it's about a tenth of the feelings I feel in relation to myself, so I don't even have the heart to feel sorry for him. He goes out through the kitchen to the garage. It's his sanctuary away from us. Well, me. He and Brady used to watch football games out there on the TV hanging on the wall.

I turn to head toward my room, grabbing my bookbag from the dining room table first. "Where are you going?" Lex asks.

"To my room. If you want to talk to me, I guess you'll have to follow me there."

"Briar, come on," Lex complains, but he follows me to my room anyway.

When we get there, I close the door behind us and dump my bookbag by the foot of the bed. "You knew about this last night, huh?"

When he doesn't answer, I turn toward him. He's leaning against my dresser. When he meets my eyes, he nods. "I shouldn't have let it get that far."

A smile plays over my lips. "I wonder what my parents would think if I said the only thing that makes me feel better is when Lex and I are together...alone?"

He shakes his head. "Don't say that. You don't even mean it."

"I beg to differ. You know I mean it. How many times have you made me cry out your name now? In fact, I'm thinking you owe me big time for what just happened." I stalk toward him, putting my hand on his chest and roam upward. I still for a moment when I feel his heart beating underneath chiseled muscles. His heart beats once, twice, then I move my hands around his pectorals. His skin is warm, even through his t-shirt.

"I've let everyone down, including you."

"You haven't let me down once, actually," I tell him, my voice a little breathy. Lex is alive. He's warm-blooded and breathing.

His hand closes around my wrist to stop my slow perusal of his massive chest. His brown eyes stare right through mine. It's like he can see right through to my very core. A sliver of anxiety works its way up my spine at his next words. "I've let you down every day, and for that, I apologize." He brings my hand up and kisses my knuckles before letting me go. "I'm not going to do it anymore."

"Lex," I say, emotion thickening my throat. "I don't think you understand what you do for me."

"I know you always leave the car crying, and that's all I need to know."

"I cry all the time now," I tell him, dismissing his concern. I try to reach my hand up to touch his chest again. It feels so good to be this close to another human being.

He catches my hand before I make contact. "Call me crazy, but I don't want someone I do that with to leave upset."

I swallow. "So, I'm not good enough?"

"No, you're not good enough," he says, his voice clearly pained. He places his hands on either side of my face, his thumb trailing across my bottom lip. "You're even better than that. You just have to start seeing it again."

I move forward. His lips are calling me. The heat of the moment, the desire his touch raises inside me. My lips don't even brush his before he's angling away from me.

"I'm not going to hurt you anymore. That's the last thing I want."

My hand sneaks down, and I cup his semi-hard cock. He moans at the contact, and so do I. "I know you want this."

My words break him free of whatever spell he was under. He pushes my hand away and moves to the other side of the room. "I can't do this anymore, Briar. I know you don't see it yet, but I *am* hurting you. I won't be showing up outside your house anymore. Okay?"

"Lex," I say, amusement coloring my words, but then I can see how serious he is about this. He already has one hand on the doorknob. I nod. "This is what you wanted to say to me out in my intervention, huh? You wanted to tell me this is over and blame it on being for my own good, but shouldn't I get a choice in this?"

"Not when you're not thinking clearly."

My jaw hardens at that remark. I cross my arms in

front of my chest. "Fine. Get out. I'm sure I can find someone else who wouldn't mind helping me."

His eyes turn hard. "Briar."

"No, it's cool. I get it."

"Briar," he growls. "Sex isn't helping you heal."

"But it's helping me forget!" I scream, losing myself in the fear of having to feel everything again.

His eyes widen, and I step back a few steps, shocked at the emotion that rocketed out of my body just now. I take in a few deep breaths to get myself back under control.

He starts to move forward, his hand outstretched, but I hold my hand up to stop him. "Just leave, Lex. I'm fine." I smile, but it's wobbly on my face. It's obviously fake.

He looks like leaving is the last thing he wants to do, but there's really nothing he can do for me.

"Bye, Lex," I tell him. I turn my back and pull my bookbag onto the bed, acting as if I'm about to do homework.

He doesn't know what to do at first. I can see him in the mirror over my dresser. He rubs the back of his neck, looks at me then the door. "I'm just a phone call away."

"Yeah," I say, keeping my head down and pulling out a notebook I have in there.

"Bye, Briar," he says. With that, my bedroom door opens and closes.

When he's gone, I turn and stare at the closed door. The first track of tears fall down my face. I'm sad when we do stuff, and I'm sad when we don't.

I'm just a mess of haywired emotions.

6

I'm startled out of bed by the sound of my alarm. I blink, gasping for air like the sound of the incessant beep is choking the crap out of me.

What the fuck? I didn't set my alarm.

"Good morning, Shortie," a too bright voice says.

I cock my head to the right and see Cade Farmer sitting in my desk chair where I left my bookbag still half open from yesterday. "What are you doing here?" I snap, pulling my covers up to hide my exposed skin.

He laughs. "You don't have anything I haven't seen before, Briar. Get your ass up."

I look at him like he's crazy. "Did my parents let you in here?" That doesn't sound like something they'd do. They especially wouldn't do it if they knew his reputation.

He smiles, displaying his perfect set of white teeth. "Of course. They actually like me."

I groan and flop back on the bed. Cade has always been an early riser. When they all used to spend the night here once upon a time, Cade would already be up by the time the rest of us got our asses out of bed.

"I thought it might go like this," he tsks.

Suddenly, I hear the trickling of water and a pitter patter as liquid hits my sheet. Soon afterward, I feel a splash on my arm. "Cade!" I throw the sheet off me, but Cade just ends up throwing an entire cup of water in my face. I blink. Droplets of water settling on my lashes. "What the fuck?"

He smiles like he's won Student Athlete of the Year. "I figured you'd be more likely to take a shower if you were already wet."

"Goddamnit," I growl as I look at the mess he's made.

"Come on," he says, whipping the sheet all the way down the bed. The front of my tank top is soaked, clinging to my breasts. "Well, hey there, Briar." His eyebrows raise suggestively. "Nice to see you this morning."

When I look down, I notice my nipples are standing at attention. "You're such a pig."

He just laughs. His reputation around school is well known. He's never had a steady girlfriend because he likes to sample a lot of different girls, and I mean a lot. "Get your ass in the shower. I'm picking your clothes out today. And don't think about running to your parents. They okayed this, and it won't work anyway because they've left for work already. It's just you and me, baby."

Cowards. They probably didn't want to hear my wrath when all this started. "I really fucking hate you," I grumble as I get out of bed.

"Not the first time I've heard that and certainly won't be the last."

When I stand, I'm in a wet tank top and underwear. The same outfit I greeted Lex in the other night. A string tugs on my heart again at the conversation we had last night. I certainly fucked that one up. For a while, it felt like the only person I could talk to was Lex, but then things escalated, and all I wanted was him. His body, I mean. His skilled fingers. His freaking tongue.

Jesus. I'm giving myself hot flashes this morning. I need to reroute my thoughts pronto.

A piece of clothing gets thrown in my face. When I

pull it away, I notice it's my mom's robe. "Put this on when you come out. Your mom made it mandatory. I mean, I wouldn't care if you walked around naked, but..."

I groan in frustration, grasping the robe in my hands as I stalk off toward the bathroom, grumbling to myself the entire way. The nerve of him. I slam the door behind me and stare at myself in the bathroom mirror, leaning over the sink. Part of my now dark hair is matted to my head from where he dumped water on me. My heart still hasn't calmed down for the intrusion of my alarm clock either.

A loud knock comes on the door. "I don't hear that water running."

"Are you going to barge in and make sure I'm actually under the water too?"

"If need be, but I'll need special permission from Mama Page."

I throw the bathrobe across the sink and start to strip. I turn the shower on before peeing because I haven't heard Cade's footsteps walk back toward my room, so I wouldn't be surprised if he is still on the other side of the door, listening to everything going on in here. I hate wash my hair, muttering the entire time about a gross misuse of my personal space, but by the time I use my special body wash, I'm calmed down a bit. The heat from the shower helps soothe my tense muscles. I even take the time to shave my legs and underarms before relaxing in the spray a while.

When I'm done, I turn the water off and go through my usual routine. Well, the routine I used to have. After towel-drying my pitch black hair that's started to fade a little already, I throw the robe on and stalk back to my room. Cade isn't outside the bathroom still, but he is sitting in my desk chair texting. "Who's that?" I ask. "One night stand?"

"Nope," he says, smiling. "Lucky Number Seven."

I roll my eyes. They call Reid that sometimes because he's had the number seven on his jersey for forever and he seems to be the luckiest mother fucker on this earth at times. "And what's good old Reid doing this morning?"

"Probably tapping Sasha's ass."

I groan at that, and my heart squeezes. "Hard to text and tap someone's ass at the same time."

"How'd you know about that, Shortie? I'm pretty sure I...Yep. Done it once or twice. May have been drunk out of my mind, but whatever."

Cade certainly uses his football prestige to bag girls. It's kind of ridiculous how they all come out of the woodwork for him. I glance over at my bed and see an outfit laid out for me. It's a cute little sundress that

69

my mom bought me for school in the beginning of last year. I used to pair it with these cute little booties. "I'm not wearing that, Cade."

"I know it doesn't go with your hair," he snipes. "But yes, you're wearing that today. Also, I'm calling my cousin about how to get that black shit out of your hair too. Now, hurry up. I can't be late for school. Game night, you know." The thing about Cade is, he gleams when he talks about football. He loves the sport. Sure, he might be a flirtatious pig who'll get sex whenever he can, but his one true love is for the game. He likes the teamwork and the rivalry. He thrives on competition.

"I don't want to wear that today," I tell him, staying steadfast in my resolve. I really don't want to go through this with him.

"Listen, Shortie," Cade says as he rises to his feet. "You only have one option. If I have to stand right here while you change, you're putting on that dress."

"You're not watching me dress."

"How's this then? If you're determined to put on your ugly ass sweats and shirt, I am watching you dress. Every last revolting second," he says, sneering down at the black clothes at the foot of my bed. "If you don't want that to happen, you'll put that dress I laid out for you on."

70

"Why do you care?" I ask. I mean it to come out snippy, but all my anger dies on my tongue. I actually really want to know.

He cocks his head to the side. "You keep asking that, and I feel like we keep answering you, but you're somehow not getting it. Come on, Briar. Humor me. Put the dress on. I'll get Peter Phillips to kiss you on the lips."

I drop my head back and groan. I used to have a huge crush on Peter Phillips, another football player. "I don't like Peter Phillips anymore."

"Good because I'm pretty sure he likes chicks with dark brown hair, so you've already gone and fucked that shit up."

"Just get out of here, Cade."

He walks to my door, then turns back with his hand on the jamb. "Put the dress on, Briar. Don't make me call in the cavalry to force it on you."

He raises an eyebrow when I raise mine at him. For some reason, I think they'll actually do that. If I walk out with the same outfit I've been wearing for the last few days, I'm sure Reid and Lex would both be knocking the door down within a few minutes. "I'm not promising anything."

"Don't mess with me on this, kid. I mean it." With

that, he exits my room and closes the door softly behind him.

I stare down at the dress he's laid out for me. I loved this dress last year. It looked so cute on me. Then, I stare down at the clothes I wore yesterday. The truth is, I'm tired. I don't have enough energy to fight with Cade this morning. I grab my silky nude bra from the dresser and the matching panties, pulling them on before I pull the dress over my head. I face my full-length mirror in the corner. The dress is a little shorter on me this year than it was the previous year. I must've grown some. Since my hair looks like a bird's nest, I grab my hairbrush, which is stained from black dye, and pull it through my damp shoulder-length hair.

A knock sounds on the door. "Do I have to call reinforcements?"

"No, jackass. I'm dressed."

The door opens slowly. He looks around the edge and then smiles when he sees me standing there. For a moment, he doesn't say anything. He just stands to his full height, his stare perusing me from my head down to my polish-chipped toenails. After a moment, he nods once. "Alright, let's get some breakfast."

I see the cute boots I wore with this outfit last year peeking out of the closet, but if he's not going to make me wear them, I'm just going to put on a pair of flip flops. At least I'll have a little semblance of control over my outfit today. I follow him into the hallway while simultaneously fluffing my hair, trying to get it to dry quicker. "I don't eat breakfast."

"Since when?"

"Since..." I say, trailing off. "Just since I stopped eating it."

"We can't skip breakfast, Shortie. It's the most important meal of the day." He checks his watch and frowns. "We don't have a lot of time. How about a bagel?"

He doesn't wait for my answer. He just goes right to the bread box where we store the bagels and then to the toaster. He knows exactly where everything in this house is. The three of them have been here so many times before they probably know it as well as me. Seeing him move around the kitchen brings a pain to my chest. So much so that when he puts the bagel down in front of me, I start eating it without thinking. I'm numb now, going through the motions, just wanting this day that hasn't even really started yet to end.

Cade disappears down the hall for a minute before walking back in with my bookbag. He holds it up just as I stuff the last piece of bagel down my throat. "Kind of light, don't you think?"

I shrug. "I forgot some books in my locker."

"Correction. You forgot *all* of your books in your locker."

He hands it over to me, and then puts his hand on my shoulder. "Come on, Briar. You're too smart for this." I'm silently seething when he says, "I can't get over how different you look." He looks into my eyes, and for a moment, he isn't Cade Farmer, my brother's best friend, he's Cade Farmer, the Spring Hill High playboy.

Perhaps I could convince Cade to take Lex's place... I don't know why I didn't think of him in the first place. He has no problem sticking his cock into people for fun.

I smile up at him, and Cade's dark brown eyes seem to sparkle as we look at one another.

We're interrupted by a chirping in his pocket. He checks the clock over the stove. "We got to go, Briar. I'm driving you to school today."

On the way out the door, I slip my flip flops on and grab the house keys from the peg on the wall next to the front door. I lock up behind us as Cade jumps into his busted-up SUV. Hiking my bookbag on my shoulder, I walk toward it. Once I'm in and Cade starts to reverse out of the driveway, I pull out my phone and send a message to Ezra. **You're not going to**

believe how I'm dressed today. Then, I snap a selfie with some generous cleavage, which also shows the flowery pattern of the sundress, attach it to the message, and send it off.

It's weird that Ezra has become like my Dear Diary. I tell him everything, and he always seems to know what to say. It's too bad he got held up when we were supposed to meet in Calcutta. I stayed in a shit hotel for five days waiting for him. One thing after another happened, and he couldn't get away from home. When my parents finally found me and dragged me back home, I still hadn't met him, and I think that hurt me more than the fact that I'd let everyone down and pissed off a bunch of people in the seven days prior to them finding me when I didn't want to be found.

We haven't tried to meet up again, but we will. I know he felt horrible about what happened. If he'd been there when my parents found me, he would've saved me. We could've run away again and kept running away. I just want to get lost sometimes, where no one knows me or anything about me.

"That selfie better be for Jules."

I quickly put my phone away, so he doesn't violate my privacy any further. I could totally see him having no problem going through my phone.

When I don't say anything, he says, "Don't be too upset with her. One of us had to do it."

I know exactly what he's talking about. He's talking about lying to me and then taking me to the intervention my parents planned. "Trust me," I say, smiling over at him like I'm the sweetest girl in the world. "I hate you so much more than I hate her right now."

"Really?" he asks with feigned excitement. "You mean that?"

"Wholeheartedly."

He knocks me in the shoulder. "That's my girl."

Despite myself, I find I'm smiling as Cade drives me to school. That's the first time that's happened in a long time.

7

*W*alking into school with Cade is so much more enjoyable than walking in by myself or just with Jules. He's like a freaking celebrity. Everyone gives him high-fives, they ask him how much Spring Hill is going to win by tonight, and to top it off, everyone seems to notice me too. It might be because Cade wound his arm through mine as soon as we stepped out of his car. He's got a tight hold on me. To outsiders, it might look like Cade has a new conquest, only I know it's because he doesn't want me to run away again.

This attention, I don't mind. I just don't want people to see me as the dead guy's sister. That's when I want to hide. But this, this reminds me of how it used to be.

Ever since Freshman year, I'd walk in with the football gods. It's super pretentious to think, but I like being noticed in this way. Or maybe I just like that Cade's being noticed and I happen to be with him. The way he walks through the school, he acts like people should worship him. His chin is held high. The shirt and tie he's wearing commands attention. By the end of the day, the tie will be off, and the first few buttons of his shirt will be undone, but that's just Cade.

Before I even realize it, we're past my locker and heading toward a part of the school I begin to recognize. I try to hold back, but the fierce grip Cade has on me isn't letting up. Up ahead, I spot where we're going. It's where all the jocks, mainly the football team, hangout in the morning. It's right by Reid's locker, practically under the set of stairs that lead to the second story Science wing. "Cade, I have to get my books," I tell him, trying to get out of this.

He laughs. The sound projects through the hall and those who weren't looking at him before are looking now. "Shortie, we know you're not taking books to class. Come on. Do you think I was born yesterday?"

I'm too nervous to speak let alone come up with a witty comeback.

"Ready for inspection, Seven," Cade says as we walk up to the group.

My face flames. There are so many students around. Not just other athletes, but the other people who want to be around the athletes, whether it's girls who have crushes on them or the guys who want to be them.

Cade forcefully spins me around in front of Reid. Everyone's eyes are on me. I'm on full display for everyone to make assumptions about. I can practically hear the whispers now.

Hey, isn't that—?

Did she come here with him?

Wonder what that's about?

The area behind my eyes heat, but I lock my jaw down and will myself not to cry even though my body is trembling.

Reid peels Sasha off his side, who's currently sneering at me. Despite the fact that Cade just turned me around in front of him, Reid walks around me, inspecting. Everywhere his gaze touches, my skin pricks. It heats so much I wouldn't be shocked if I have blooms of red all over my body by the time he's done making his trip around me right there in front of everyone. When he gets in front of me, he tilts my chin up, forcing me to look him in the eyes. Sasha makes a strangled noise behind him, but he doesn't pay her any attention. "How do you feel?" he asks.

Reid, in his shirt and tie, with his overpowering green eyes, and his gelled brown hair is a sight to behold. My stomach quivers. A lot of it's nerves, but some of it is something else. Something I was never meant to feel for one of my brother's best friends. As soon as I recognize the feeling, anger surges inside me. Here he is parading around me like the asshole he is, and I'm what...*liking* him? It can't be. I just think he's hot. That's all it is.

His grip on my chin tightens. "Well, Briar?"

I bite the inside of my cheek. I went from feeling almost okay this morning, grateful that Cade had shown up and made me put on this dress. I thought I looked pretty even, but here I am being harassed in front of a bunch of people. "Actually, I'm feeling a little like your bitch at the moment. Can't say that I enjoy it."

Sasha squawks. Literally. There's no other word to describe the derisive noise that pours from her mouth. "Like he'd want you to be his bitch when he has me."

I shrug, never losing contact with Reid's eyes, so I notice when the green in his eyes turn more of an emerald shade. A muscle jumps in his jaw. "Wrong answer."

"I'm not sure I can give you a right answer." I push

his hand away from my chin, his short nails slicing me in the process.

My dismissal doesn't bother him. He looks at Cade. "What about makeup?"

Cade shrugs nonchalantly. He's got the ever-present small smile on his lips. "I thought she looked good without it."

Reid makes a face that says he doesn't agree, but he also doesn't verbalize it. In the background, I notice movement, so my gaze flicks to behind Reid. It's Lex. His upper arm muscles are practically bulging out of his crisp, black shirt. He has the cuffs rolled up to mid forearm. The three of them together? Damn. I don't know as if I've ever noticed it before. I was on the inside. They were like brothers to me, but not anymore. The thing linking us together is gone.

"But you'd fuck anything," Sasha says. "So, I don't think your opinion counts."

Cade laughs along with everyone else, but I swear he tenses at her comment. When everyone looks away from him, the smile leaves his face. No, Cade Farmer did not like that comment one bit. "You would know," I strike back.

For a second, nothing happens. I know I went low, not that Sasha doesn't deserve it. She's a horrendous bitch. There's always been a rumor that Cade fucked her. I honestly don't think it's true. No way the guys would do that to one another, but the fact that I just brought that up in front of all their adoring fans, I know I'm about to get a whole pile of shit.

Sasha marches forward. Her face is beet red. "You little bitch. You think because you're wearing a dress today that you're all of a sudden hot shit. You're not. You're nothing. You always were. Just because Brady was somebody doesn't mean you are or ever will be."

I always thought I was more of a passive person. But the new me is more of a strike first, ask questions later person.

I lunge at the bitch. How dare she even say my brother's name? But, apparently, my new habits aren't as strategic as I think because Reid steps in between us at the same time Cade reaches out to grab my arm while it's flying through the air toward her face. He spins me toward him until my back is pressed against him. "Alright, feisty Shortie," he says, practically cooing in my ear. "That's enough of that."

Reid's eyes are hard as he holds back a foul-mouthed Sasha like she was going to be the one to kick my ass. It's nothing for him to hold her back, just a single arm across her midsection. I glare back at him. I can't believe he's going to let her say that to me. "You're so stereotypical, you know that?" I ask. He's like the fucking jock you see on TV who only cares about himself and picks on the lowly people that dare walk his halls. He's a character sketch, that's all he is.

I struggle out of Cade's grip, snatch my bookbag up from the floor that must have dropped sometime in the whole process, and start walking the other way. The bell rings overhead. There are going to be a lot of late students to homeroom this morning because most of them were watching the free show that was going on in the jock hallway.

My chest constricts as I head to the girls' bathroom near the library. I barrel through it, but I never hear the door shut behind me. Instead, someone else has followed me inside. I twist my head to see who it is. Black hair and a small smile greet me. "You can't say shit like that," Cade admonishes.

"You're in the girls' room."

"Like I haven't been in here before, Briar. Come on. I'm the school slut, right?"

"He shouldn't have let her say that to you either."

Cade's lips thin. "She was out of line," he agrees.

"You're *all* out-of-line. Parading me around, inspecting my dress, my makeup, *me*. Fuck you, Cade. Get out of here."

Cade shakes his head as he turns toward the door. After he leaves, I smack the ceramic sink in front of me until the tears dry up behind my eyes and pain blooms on my palm and fist. Then, I get out the eye makeup I keep in my bag and layer it on. I go heavy with the eyeliner and dark shadow. By the time I'm done, I'm looking pretty goth, but it's still not quite right. I find a pair of nail clippers that I happen to have in my bag and snip my dress below the collar. I make five curved gashes that make the dress look more punk skater than sundress, then throw the clippers back in my bag. I stand back in the mirror. They want to pick out my outfits, fine. I can always do this. I turn to the side, smiling in the mirror. Honestly, I think this looks pretty damn good for a job I cobbled together.

I pull my phone out and take another selfie, sending it to Ezra. **This looks better.** Immediately, he responds with heart eyes emojis.

Feeling much more confident, I pick my bookbag up and head toward my first class. I'll probably get another detention for not making it to homeroom, but oh well, they can just add that to the ones I got when I slapped Reid. He fucking deserved it.

The day passes, and I don't see Jules or the other guys until lunch. "Whoa. Nice," Jules says when I walk up to the table we've now claimed and set my tray down. "I like it."

I smile for her. "Thanks." She opens her mouth to

84

say something, but I interrupt. "I don't want to talk about what happened last night. Can we just forget it happened?" The truth is, if I stayed angry at Jules, I would literally have no one. Also, none of it is really her fault.

We eat in silence for a little while, then she says, "I heard what happened this morning."

"Oh yeah?" I say with a roll of my eyes.

"Reid's not very happy."

"He needs to put a muzzle on his girlfriend instead of being pissed at me."

She tilts her head to the side. "That's what I mean. I heard him give her a hard time for saying something to you about Brady."

I flick my gaze to her. "You're serious? He said something to her?"

"I think his exact words were, 'I should have let her kick your ass.' So, yeah, they're fighting."

"Breaking news," I deadpan. Reid and Sasha are the quintessential couple who you always wonder why they're together. They're either always fighting or kissing. I don't see any in between with them. No times where they're just having fun as a couple, unless people count ganging up on others as fun, but I wouldn't.

"Ha. Right?"

A sadness takes Jules over then. She and my brother were couple goals. It's not as if they didn't fight, but they had more good times than bad times, and even when they fought, it was never nasty. It was never a cut-the-other-person-down-to-the-quick harsh words battle. They were seriously perfect for each other. It makes me wonder how much Jules has lost without him here. A future, possibly? A future filled with love, marriage, children, perhaps. When I think about things like this, I realize how selfish I'm being for only thinking about myself, but I'm at a point where I can't seem to stop myself either.

Instead of saying all that to her, I ask her how her classes are going, and then, she asks me the same. Is it weird that I kind of miss learning? I don't miss the homework or the studying, who would? But I miss learning new things every day. I glance over at Theo's table and find him again with his nose in a book. I hate that guy. I'd like to see how he'd handle losing a family member and see if he was still gung-ho on being perfect at everything.

Or maybe everyone is just better than me? They seem to have everything well-handled while I'm sitting nearby drowning.

"Oh shit," Jules says.

I snap out of my own thoughts and look at her. She's staring over my shoulder with wide eyes.

"Shit," she says again. "Move!" Jules jumps up from the table. I jump up too, but when I turn, it's too late. I'm flooded with hot, brown liquid. I gasp as it runs down my skin and over my dress. The metal serving tub falls to the floor, and Sasha stands there with her hands on her hips, one of her bitchy minions beside her.

"Figured you were used to dressing like shit, so I wanted to make you feel more comfortable."

She takes one of the brown spatters that hit her in the arm on the tip of her finger and then sucks the gravy served at lunch today into her mouth.

Stepping forward, she smirks, but I'm too shocked to move. "Stay the fuck away from Reid."

By the time she moves away, the cafeteria attendants are already on us as the whole cafeteria either laughs or stands there with wide eyes, gawking at me. "Miss Pontine," one of them gasps, chastising Sasha.

There's a tug on my hand. When I look over, it's Jules who's got me. "Don't worry about her," she says, then she yells, "She's just a fucking bitch."

"Careful, Jules." She smiles, barely raising her voice. "You'll be next."

Right before Jules pulls me away, my eyes find the table my brother used to sit at. Reid is glaring at the whole scene, his arms crossed over his chest. Lex is shaking his head, and for once, Cade isn't smiling. Their eyes hole into me, and it's as if they're saying I deserve all of this. I'm not following their status quo, and they don't like it. Anyone who doesn't fall in line, gets shit.

Jules tugs me into the girls' locker room and shoves me in the shower, dress and all. I'm shaking as the water runs from brown to clear. "Hey," she says, her voice soft. "I got you some clothes." I peer behind me. She's placed a stack of gym clothes on the concrete divider. "You'll have to go commando though."

I don't know whether to hug her or cry. I was right earlier. I could never be so mad at Jules that I would never speak to her again. And not just because I need her since she's the last person who'll tolerate me, it's because I like her too.

I turn the showerhead off and dress in the gym clothes Jules gave me. With every piece of clothing I put on, I tell myself that it's armor. The shirt is to protect my heart. The pants to hide my position.

This isn't high school, it's a freaking war zone.

n my way to detention, I notice a certain person lounging against the wall next to the classroom I have to go into. I stop to stare at him. I'm still so pissed about earlier. Sure, Jules told me he gave his girlfriend shit for saying that about Brady and me, but did he really? She could still be trying to protect me. I go to turn the other way. Screw detention, it's not worth having to talk to him. But he's already seen me.

"Briar." His voice comes out like a demand, and he's only spoken one word—a name. How can that be? How can someone be that sure of himself?

My jaw clamps together, and I turn back toward him. He's sauntering toward me casually like he has all the time in the world, except he doesn't. He has a freaking game tonight, and I know for a fact he should be in the locker room right now.

His shirt is still buttoned up. His tie still in place. Nothing about him says he's about to apologize to me for what happened earlier and the shit he's pulling, so I hike my bookbag up on my shoulder and wait for him to say whatever he's got to say. It must be important if he came to talk to me before football. Though, I guess the game can't start without him. He is the quarterback, after all.

"You're coming with me."

I blink up at him. "Um, what?"

"With me. Now." He grabs my arm and starts walking me down the hallway toward the locker rooms.

I pull my arm out of his grip. "Stop grabbing me. Christ. I have detention, Reid. I can't just go with you." I realize those are awful strong words for someone who was just about to bail out of detention, but I hate that he keeps ruling over my life. Telling me what to do. What to wear.

"Actually, you can. I told them you'd serve your detention with me."

"With you? But you have a football game."

"That's exactly where you're spending it."

I stop in my tracks, my heart dropping to the hall floor. "No, Reid. I can't do it."

I wasn't there when my brother passed out during practice and was taken away in an ambulance, but I have plenty of imagination to know what it looked like. When I think about football now, I think about poor Brady who was dying from an aneurysm that no one knew about until it was too late.

"Don't worry. You won't get in trouble."

He goes to reach for me again, but I slip out of his grip. "I can't do it, Reid," I seethe. I don't want to say the words, but I feel like he's going to make me.

He steps up in my face again. I'm becoming used to this position with him. "You *will* fucking do it because every time one of us isn't right by you, bad shit fucking happens."

"Bad shit happens when you *are* right by me, asshole. And you deliver it."

He blinks. "You're going to the fucking game, and that's that. You're going to sit your ass on the Goddamn sidelines and cheer us on because that's what Brady would want you to do."

My heart skips a beat. It skips a beat for so long I feel its absence and wonder if there's a hole in my chest where my heart should be pumping right now. Brady loved football so much. Not to get too sentimental, but if it's at all possible, he'll be watching this fucking game from heaven or whatever there is on the other side. He'll be rooting for his friends. He'll—

"Come on," Reid snaps, giving me a sharp tug on my hand.

The only thing making me move with him right now is the thought of my brother. I don't know if I can handle this. I told myself I wouldn't go to another game for the rest of my life. I'd feel Brady's death too much. I'd feel his love of the game overwhelming me and remember everything that he's missing out on because he's not here.

Walking numbly behind Reid, I barely notice when he pulls me right into the boys' locker room. The guys all cheer when we walk in, which is what brings me out of my cathartic stupor. "Shit. Reid." I immediately shield my eyes at the amount of skin and muscle showing.

"You guys don't mind if Brady's sister hangs out here with us, do you?" he asks, though it's not a question at all. His statement is approached in a way where no one would dare contradict him.

He sets me down in a row of lockers no one uses. I sit there with my bookbag between my legs, listening to the jock talk going on. There's talk about the game, but there's also talk about hot girls, who's easy, and of course about the celebratory party they're going to have tonight to commemorate their win. I always wondered why they bothered. They always win.

When Coach Jackson walks in, things get serious. He probably doesn't even know I'm in the back. He talks strategy. He talks about their opponents. I find myself enthralled in the way the game is discussed. He doesn't just give a go out there and play your hearts out speech, there's real playmaking and decision talk going on.

I know, being the sister of a guy on the team, I should've known. I knew how much hard work Brady put into football, but I guess I always just thought it came down to pure skill in the end. If you have it, you have it. If you don't, you don't. Hearing Coach talk, I know there's a lot more that goes into it.

I run my hands through my hair. I must've been sitting here for an hour plus already, but it doesn't feel like it. The time goes by in an instant. My heart is happy, I realize, sitting back and listening to them. It's almost as if I can hear Brady's voice right alongside the others. No wonder why he fit in so well here.

Their win chant breaks me out of my reverie, and then Lexington Jones the Third peeks around the row of lockers. He's dressed in his football jersey now, all padded up. He's holding his helmet in one hand and reaching out to me with his other. "Come on," he says. "It's show time."

It's unsurprising Lex is the one who comes to get me. It's just so like Reid to bring me here, but make Lex actually do the grunt work of making sure I follow them onto the field. We pass Coach, and I swear the guy doesn't even blink. He pats Lex on the back and tells him to keep his head in the game, and then we're walking toward the field and the stands which are already bursting with people.

Football is a major thing here. It always has been. My decision not to go to tonight's game was the opposite of most other people's in Spring Hill. Football is the only trophy we can carry from one year to the next.

"And where exactly does Reid want me to sit, Lex? On the bench with the other players? On his lap?"

Lex's muscles bunch. "I'll find a place." He looks over at me. "Once I set you there, can you please stay where you are? It's football, Briar."

The way he says it, I know he means business. He isn't forceful like Reid would be, but I know how important these games are to all three of them. They won't be able to concentrate if they think they have to look out for me too. "No promises," I tell him, but then I smile, so he knows I'm just kidding.

The crowd starts off as a volcano, grumbling and

grunting, little spurts here and there of fire, but when Reid gets on the field, it fucking erupts.

The energy in the air settles into my stomach, making my nerve endings fire. Last year, I would've been front and center in the bleachers with my school colors on with those cheap plastic pom-poms. Today, I'm wearing someone else's gym clothes, pale skin, and might have spots of gravy in my hair that I didn't wash out completely. Who knows?

Lex takes me behind the player bench and sits me down in the grass, my back against the fence that sections off the crowd from the team. I'm pretty much between two worlds. I don't belong with the football team, and I don't belong with the crowd either. This is just a reflection of my real life.

Without another word, Lex joins the team in calisthenics before the game. While they're doing that, the other team comes out onto the field. There are a spattering of people in the small "away" stands across the field from us. I know without looking behind my shoulder that ours is filled. People will start lining the fence soon, but hopefully no one stands directly over me. Creepy.

Down the field a little, I hear Sasha start her cheerleaders up with a rousing cheer to get the crowd going. The smells from the concession stand, the busy nothingness and excitement fills me just like it used to. I suppose I shouldn't complain though because I am getting out of detention for this.

Which, when you think about it, is a crock of shit. Who can go demand that someone serve detention with them instead of with a teacher? I roll my eyes just thinking about it. Like, how is this Reid's real life?

He's going to have a big fall one day. I don't know when it will be, but at some point, he has to realize he won't be treated like this his whole life. He won't get special athlete attention and the come hither looks from girls, or the people wanting to be around him. At some point, he has to be just like the rest of us. That goes for both Cade and Lex, too.

The referee blows the whistle, and the captains from both teams move to the middle for the coin toss. We win. Reid jogs back to the sideline with a huge smile on his face. I bite my lip, noticing just how good looking he is in his football jersey and pads. The shape the tight pants give his ass.

But then I remember he can also be cruel, so I focus on the game as a whole instead of one person.

It takes a lot for me not to clap and cheer along with the rest of the crowd. I almost fall into old habits, so instead, I chew on my thumb knuckle and watch each play go by, trying not to think about my brother lying in the middle of the field, unconscious and life-less. The vision keeps poking up now and then. Every time someone is slow to get off the field, it's hard not to notice. During halftime, I pull out my cell phone. I automatically text my mother that I'm at the football game. I don't know why I do it. I haven't been so forth-coming with information for her lately, but I just feel like I need her right now. I remember her talking to Dad the other day at dinner, wondering if they should make an appearance here. For all I know, she's some-where up in the stands, and maybe I just want to feel that connection with her. Is she upset too? Does she feel like her heart is twisted in her chest, not knowing what to feel?

I don't get a response back from her, so I look through my past messages with Ezra. We haven't talked much lately. Both of us are lazy in responding to the other. For myself, I feel like I have too much stuff to worry about. I'm either being bullied by my brother's best friends or feeling sorry for myself. I don't know his exact excuses, but I know he's back to school too. He's probably doing homework or out with his friends. What's going on between us now isn't like what it was when we were messaging all summer.

The whistle blows again, taking my attention once more. I put the phone away and stare back out at the field. Lex is walking to the bench in search of a water bottle when he glances up to make sure I'm still there. I lift my chin at him, and he looks away automatically, keeping his head in the game and all that.

Spring Hill is winning, but the other team must've gotten a surge of energy because the second half is a lot closer than the first. There are harder hits, bigger plays. There's some damn good football going on right in front of me. The other team's quarterback throws a ball toward the receiver on our side of the field. It's just out of reach. The ball and the player fall and roll, the former rolling right at me. I stop the ball with my foot and the player runs up to me to get it. When he sees me, he smiles. "Wish I could've caught that and looked like a badass in front of you." He winks and then jogs away.

I'm almost taken aback by what he said. I read the name on the back of his jersey as he runs in the opposite direction. Winthrop. No one has been nice to me lately. And I mean no one. Except for this morning when I was wearing the dress, no one has looked at me with interest either. I can't keep myself from smiling while watching him cross the field either. It may have something to do with his tight pants. Though his ass is far skinnier than Reid's, it's still nice. Plus, he was nice to me, so that makes it even better.

When I look around again, I notice Reid has turned his head to glare at me. His sopping wet hair is matted to his forehead. He has two black lines underneath each eye, his helmet sitting by his side on the bench. When he sees me looking at him, he looks away, watching the other team out on the field. I swear I can't do anything without getting dirty looks from Reid. The guy talked to me, it's not as if I could help it. Plus, I liked it.

I guess it's just the things that make me feel good that piss Reid off right now.

The clock ticks down the minutes in the second half. There's really no danger of the other team coming close to winning. We nail them to the wall, and then Reid even puts the punctuation mark at the end of the game when he throws a Hail Mary perfectly to one of our wide receivers. My breath catches when our guy easily catches it and walks into the end zone.

My stomach lurches. Any other year and that would've been Brady. He and Reid were a terrific duo. They could read one another like no one else. It should be Brady scoring that touchdown. It should be Brady still breathing, still living, still playing.

The world in front of me goes out of focus. It's weird when grief hits you sometimes. It could be out of nowhere, and you don't know what triggered it, but I know exactly what triggered it this time. It's seeing the real-life absence of him. I blink rapidly, trying to get the tears to go away. When I do, I see Reid out on the field. Everyone else has run up to the player who caught the ball. Not him. He watched long enough to know that they'd made the play, but now he's turning, looking back toward the sideline as he makes his way over. His eyes immediately find mine, and I don't know, I think I see the same grief in mine mirrored in his.

Maybe he's thinking the exact same thing.

Maybe he's not heartless after all...

9

*A*t the very end of the game, after Coach talks to the team out on the field, the three of them —Brady's best friends—huddle together, helmet against helmet against helmet. I'm not privy to what they're saying, but the rest of the guys on the team leave them alone. The crowd's dissipating too. The students know where to find the guys now—at the after party. The adults don't care. They leave the field and the high school behind.

I won't be doing that tonight, no matter how badly I want to.

As soon as Reid and the guys break up their huddle, they start toward the locker room, Reid with a full-on scowl on his face like they didn't just win a great game. I hear Sasha calling his name, but he either doesn't hear her or ignores her. It's Lex who comes over and gets me. He reaches his hand out. His skin is glistening with sweat, and when he pulls me up, my hand slides up his slicked arm. I remember thinking that boys who sweat are gross, and maybe it's because I've done things with Lex, but it makes my mind go somewhere else this time. It makes it go to exertion and force and a certain physical activity.

He holds on to me for too long, his brown eyes staring into my own, and I know he's thinking about the same thing.

Finally, he lets go of me, but asks me to follow him toward the locker room. I hear Sasha say, "What the hell?" behind us, but I don't pay her any attention. Lex is so big, he stands over me, especially in his football gear. Everything about him is accentuated. His shoulders, his hips, his calf muscles popping just under the hemline of the tight football pants. He makes me feel so small. I've been feeling that a lot lately. Like everything else in this world is bigger than me. I think that's natural after someone goes through a death, but even though I feel small next to Lex, it's only in stature. He doesn't make my shoulders curve in or my insides start to constrict. In fact, it's the exact opposite.

He makes me come alive. These feelings are batting back the empty hole Brady's death left. The in-your-face moment I just felt of Brady not being here is slowly receding. I don't know whether to jump up, grab Lex, and thank him, or run away.

"It's only going to get worse," Lex says as we approach the locker room door.

I shake my head. That was not anywhere near where my mind was at. "I'm sorry, what?"

"Reid. And Cade. And Sasha for that matter. They're—we're—not going to leave you alone. And because of that, Sasha's going to hate you."

"Oh really? I hadn't figured that out yet," I dead-pan. I think the gravy clearly spelled that out for me.

"If she touches you again, you come to me."

"And you're going to do what?" I ask. "Reid isn't going to let you touch his girl. Besides, he'll probably help her drop acid on me next time."

Even though Lex just played a full two halves of football, he doesn't seem the least bit tired. He says, "You did kind of ask for it. You ruined the dress. You put all that makeup on."

I stop just outside the locker room door and look up at him. "Can I just ask why you three think you have anything to say about what I wear? It's utterly ridiculous."

"So is dressing as someone you're not."

With that, he drags me into the locker room. I have

to shield my eyes immediately because there's cock and bare ass everywhere. I'm talking hard, sinewy ass muscles that make me want to peek through my fingers, but Lex pulls me to the corner of the room as fast as he can as the players laugh at my reaction. My cheeks heat. Fire radiates over my skin. When Lex tries to let me go, I hold onto him. I peek up through my lashes and he must understand the look in my eyes before I do because he just shakes his head and walks away from me.

I don't know what girl wouldn't have been turned on by the free show I just got. Next time, I shouldn't shield my eyes. They wanted me here, they got me. That should mean I can ogle all I damn want. From the sounds of it, the guys wouldn't mind.

I listen while Coach gives them the end-of-game speech, which basically consists of telling the team they should continue to do what they're doing. I have no doubt they're on the road to another winning season. They'll be conference champs again. They'll even go to State championships, hopefully bringing back the trophy for Spring Hill at the end. It's hard not to get caught up in it. For years, I sat by my brother at the dining room table and listened to it all. Listened to his every dream and wish, so even though he's not here, I want it for them. I want it for them because some of these guys probably have sisters they're sitting next to every night who hang on their every word, who want nothing but the best for them. And I want that little sister to have the satisfaction that their sibling did something. That they made it. Seeing dreams get accomplished can lead to a landslide of victories. One topples, then the next, and the next.

If my brother didn't succeed at football, I probably wouldn't have even tried for Valedictorian.

Once Coach leaves, the door opens and there are catcalls abound. I lean over the row of lockers and see Sasha sashaying in dressed in her cheerleading uniform. I roll my eyes and look away. From the sounds of it, this is a regular occurrence. I'm sure Reid loves the fact that Sasha waltzes right in with other guys half naked all around. To punctuate the point, Sasha coos, "Wrap up whatever you don't want seen, boys."

The guys all make inappropriate jokes at her, which I'm sure she lives for, until Reid clears his throat.

"You didn't kiss me after your win," I hear her saying.

Reid doesn't answer.

"Am I riding with you to your house? Or should I ride with Chelle?"

"Chelle," he finally says, but even from here and

not being able to see his face, I can tell he's curt. His words are punctuated and to the point.

Her voice softens, and even though it's as if she's trying to whisper what she says next, I also think she's just looking for attention. "I'm hoping we get some alone time later."

Again, nothing from Reid for a while until he says, "You need to replace Briar's outfit. The one you ruined today."

"What?" she scoffs. "No."

My ears perk up. I was already listening to what they were saying, but this suddenly got a lot more interesting.

"You heard me," he says.

The locker room quiets. Who knew a room full of boys could get so quiet? I thought testosterone basically prohibited that.

"What are you talking about?" Sasha whispers.

I smile at that. Suddenly, she's not that big of a fan of having an audience.

"I said," Reid replies, agitation lacing his voice. "Replace Briar's fucking outfit. The one you dumped gravy over earlier is ruined, and she's coming to the fucking party tonight and needs something to wear."

"I'm sure she can wear the dirty sweats that are probably all over her floor. They suit her."

A fist slamming into a locker makes me jump. "Don't test me, Sasha. Get her a fucking outfit. Tonight."

She growls in exasperation before I hear her footsteps scurry across the room and to the locker room door. I'm still wide-eyed, wondering what the hell just happened. Why should Reid care that she ruined my outfit? He's the one who had no trouble perusing me earlier as if I were on display. Also, who said I was going to the fucking after party? I want to go home. I want sleep. I want to text Ezra about meaningless shit before I drift off into the escape of dreaming.

Footsteps come near me. I glance up to find Cade there. "I'm not going to the party," I immediately say.

He laughs and then sighs happily. "You're too funny, Briar. I think you need to learn that your life isn't your own right now. It's ours."

I glare at him, which only makes him laugh louder. Fucking asshole.

Then, he pulls me to my feet. He's dressed in a completely different outfit. He's not in his shirt and tie, and he's not in his football jersey. He's in a tank top with large arm holes so that when he turns, I—and everyone else—can see his hard physique.

I flip through the images in my mind when I first walked in and try to think if I saw every bit of Cade.

Sadly, no. I would've remembered. Then, my mind automatically goes to Reid. No on that front, too. He had a towel around his waist, shower water dripping from his chestnut-colored hair. Just a brief glimpse before I slammed my eyes shut.

"So, you're making me go to the party?"

"We're making you go to the party. Come on. You can't pretend you didn't have fun in previous years."

I can't, really. I always had fun, but that was because my brother always included me in shit. He always watched over me to make sure I didn't go overboard, and the best part was, he didn't seem to mind. "You really want to babysit me, Cade Farmer?" I smile. I definitely have a plan now. This is going to be their big mistake. This is going to make them rethink their whole plan about making sure I do everything their way. "Let's go," I tell him, slipping my arm through his.

We emerge, and thankfully, everyone is dressed now. Reid watched us approach, his stare stuck on our linked hands. His jaw ticks when he looks away. He slams his locker shut. "Let's do this, boys. Briar's riding with me."

Cade slips his arm from mine with a small chuckle. My lips thin. I know this ride to Reid's house would be much better with one of the other guys. For one, Reid seems to despise me more than the others. My current choices seem to offend him most.

When Reid leaves the locker room, he doesn't even look back to see if I'm following him. All the way to the car, he's a few steps ahead of me. When we finally get to his Escape in the lot, he immediately goes to the driver's side and gets in. I feel like spinning around and taking off in the other direction, but I also know I'd just be delaying the inevitable. I have no doubt that Reid Parker would jump from the vehicle, chase me down, and forcibly place me in the passenger seat.

As it is, I get demoted to the backseat when one of his teammates says he needs a ride. Reid keeps checking on me through the rearview mirror, so I pull my cell phone out of my bookbag to ignore him. I smile when I notice I have a message from Ezra. **Missing you. Need more pics. Maybe something risqué...** He sends a winky emoji next. Just three short sentences, but my body heats immediately. I don't know what to say to that.

I bite my lip, thinking about it, then type out: **I'll probably be getting drunk tonight, so I might just have enough liquid courage to do it.** I also end mine with a winky face and wait to see his reaction.

Ezra and I haven't taken our online relationship

there yet. Don't get me wrong. I had high hopes that when we met in the city, we'd be doing all that and more, but it just didn't work out that way.

"Who are you texting?" Reid asks from the front seat.

"No one," I immediately answer. Right away, I know it's the wrong answer. His gaze slices through mine in the rearview mirror.

"Wrong, Briar. And before you say it's none of my business, you are my business now."

I roll my eyes for show. I know he means every word of it. "My mom, okay? Telling her I'm with you."

After that, I pretend like I get another text and then actually do send my mom a text telling her I'm with the guys in case she's wondering where I am. But I also send it because Reid might be crazy enough to check in with my mom to see if I'm telling the truth.

It doesn't take long to get to Reid's house. He lives in a relatively large house just on the outskirts of Spring Hill. It's literally on Spring Hill itself, at the top, overlooking the fields below. It's not that great of a view. Spring Hill isn't that tall, but they had to find something to name the town after and must be Waste of Space was taken.

When we get out of the car, the party is already in full swing. Every single light is on in the Parker household. I can hear the house music pumping away as we start up the walk toward the front door. I'm not unfamiliar with Reid's house. I've been here plenty of times. "Where are your parents?" I ask.

"Business trip," he says. His parents own an online fitness business, so they're gone a lot, meeting with various clients. If the guys don't party here, they party at Cade's family's camp, but that's a little further outside of town, so they prefer here.

As soon as we get in the house, a body flings itself at Reid. Reid catches Sasha, and she slides down his body, looking like a model from a music video. "I put an outfit for Briar up in the main bathroom."

I look down at my clothes, wondering why the hell I can't just wear this. It wasn't my decision to come here, and I doubt anyone will pay attention to me anyway.

Reid nods toward the stairs, then is vacuumed up by Sasha's lips, so I head that way. I have little hope for what Sasha has brought me to wear. It's probably a brown paper bag, but I can also raid Reid's mom's closet if I have to. I really want to make them pay for making me come here, and I know the guys will hate to babysit me, so that's my plan—making their lives miserable.

When I get to the bathroom, no one else is in there,

thankfully, so I pick the shirt up that's on top. I notice the gold glitter first. When I hold it in front of me, I see the word "skank" in big, block letters. I smile at that. Of course, Sasha would have a shirt that said that. It was probably a joke gift from one of her friends that she thought would be perfect for me. I don't even glance at the bottoms she left for me. There's no way in hell I'm putting anything on that may have touched her vajayjay.

I slip out of the bathroom, taking the skank shirt with me, and go directly to the Parkers' master suite. I close the door softly behind me, then turn on the overhead light. I've been in this room a time or two. Mrs. Parker always wanted a girl, so when I was little, she used to let me dress up in her clothes. I'm sure she wouldn't mind letting me in here right now for that very same purpose.

I look through the selection, and when I spot a black skirt, I stop. I can roll up the hem of the flare skirt and pair with the skank shirt, but not before I make one alteration.

After taking the skank shirt and Mrs. Parker's skirt, I slip down the stairs one more time and go to one of the side rooms. It's Mrs. Parker's craft room. It looks like she barely uses it anymore, but once upon a time, she fancied herself a crafter. I look through the cubby holes and the desk, and miraculously, I find just what I'm looking for. I thought she had tried to design their own t-shirts once, and I was right.

I lay the shirt out on the crafting table, and underneath 'skank', I write 'suck' then add an s to skank. I smile down at my masterpiece.

Skanks suck.

Who would disagree with that?

*A*fter dressing in Mrs. Parker's craft room, I walk out in my new outfit and make sure to immediately find Sasha. She's not attached to Reid anymore, but she is surrounded by all her bitchy friends out on the back deck, sitting next to the fireplace. I peek my head out. "Hey, thanks for the outfit, Sasha."

She does a double take, and I watch as her smile fades into a scowl.

"Hey, is that your shirt?" one of her friends asks.

I give them all a wave and then leave to go back into the house. The dining room is set up as a beer pong area. The living room couches are pulled back for a makeshift dance floor in the middle, and the kitchen is beer central.

I go there first to start my plan. After filling my cup from the keg, I down that immediately, and then fill up another one.

"Whoa," I hear a voice say.

I turn just as I top my cup off. The guy's eyes widen. "Holy shit. It's you."

I tilt my head. My first instinct is that he's probably realized I'm Brady's sister, but I don't think he'd have that smile on his face if he did.

He puts his hand over his heart. "You don't recognize me?"

My mind flits to Ezra, but that can't be it either. I've seen pictures of Ezra, and even though both him and the guy in front of me are super cute, this guy isn't Ezra. "Sorry, I don't," I say.

I try to maneuver around him, but he stops me. "Let's try this. Maybe if I walk away." He turns and struts away, picking up the back of his shirt as he does so, showing off his ass.

I laugh but shake my head anyway when he turns toward me.

He groans. "You're killing me. How about if I had Winthrop scrawled across the back of my football jersey?"

It clicks then. This is the wide receiver from the opposite team. The one who'd said he'd wished he'd caught that ball in front of me. Even though I get it now, I shake my head. "Sorry..."

He laughs. "Now you're just teasing."

I lift my shoulders. He'll never know. He'll definitely never know I checked his ass out when he walked back across the field. "So, you played for the other team today? Kind of ballsy coming here to party, isn't it?"

He leans against the counter. "I'm not a sore loser. I knew Spring Hill was going to kick our ass."

"Is that so?"

He drops his head. "You have more than a few players who are best in the state. Yeah, I'd say we had no chance whatsoever."

"Not confident, huh?"

A smirk plays over his lips. "Oh, I'm confident. Just not in the areas I know can be improved upon. Meaning..." He places his cup down on the counter and reaches for my hand. "You should come dance with me now."

My eyes widen at his invitation. I catch a glimpse of Lex looking at us. Ordinarily, I would've turned the guy down. Not because I'm not interested, but because I'm unsure of my dance moves at this point in my life, but I have a plan to execute.

I hold up a finger and then down the rest of the

beer in my cup. Hopefully I'll have a buzz by the time we get too into the song. I glance over at Lex as... Winthrop—I'll have to ask his first name—leads me into the living room. I hope Lex was paying attention to how much beer I just had. If these guys are hell bent on babysitting me, they can do just that.

The beer is sitting like a lead-weight in my stomach, but Winthrop—whose first name is Chad—knows just how to dance, so I'm not self-conscious. His hands stay on my hips. Sometimes they move to my lower back, but they always return to my hips where his touch isn't forceful but firm. We dance a few songs before he goes to get me another beer, then we sit out the next few, drinking, but are back on the dance floor after that. By this time, I don't have a care in the world.

Lex comes up to try to get me to dance with him, but I dismiss him, turning toward Chad. Chad looks up at Lex, but whatever happens, he looks back down at me shortly after Lex walked away. "Ex-boyfriend?"

I laugh in his face. "Um, no. Not at all. Friends with my brother."

"That explains the look then. Your brother isn't going to show up next, is he?"

Pain slices through my heart. I stumble on my feet and Chad has to catch me. "You know what? I think I need another drink," I tell him.

I turn toward the kitchen and walk toward the keg. Apparently, I haven't drunk enough to mute the pain. I stand there, filling cup after cup, until I've drunk at least another full three ones. Chad looks at me a little warily, but he doesn't say anything. I know what I must look like. I don't want to be a sloshy drunk person, but it's not my fault. He's the one who brought Brady up.

"Dance?" I ask.

He takes my hand again willingly, leading me out onto the dance floor again. This time, we dance even closer. His hands press into me harder, and when I turn into him, my ass sliding against his crotch, it's evident he's aroused. Hell, I am too.

His hot breath against my neck makes me shiver. He drags his tongue over it lightly, and I tremble in his arms. His fingers grip my hips. "Maybe we should go to a room?"

I have a choice to make now. Stay out here and stick to my plan of pissing the guys off, even though that doesn't seem to be working, or I can lose myself in Chad Winthrop like I've done with Lex in the past.

I nod, and his hand slides down my arm before curling his fingers into mine. We've only taken three steps when Cade Farmer steps in the way. His dark hair looks even darker in the low light. "Where are you two going?"

"A room," I say, smiling. "Just point me in the direction of one you haven't been to yet."

Cade smiles tightly and guilt creeps over me. That was a low blow. Instead of saying anything to me, he looks back at Chad. "Winthrop. How's it going?"

They do a bro shake that my hazy mind can't fathom right now. I tug on Chad's hand, but Cade steps ever so slightly in front of me again. He sends a warning glare at me as he talks to Chad about the game.

What the fuck? Cade Farmer can't seriously be cock blocking me right now.

I try to move around him again, but he puts his hand on my shoulder and leans over. "Don't make me embarrass you in front of Chad, Briar. He's a good guy."

"Then don't," I snap.

He sighs. "You don't want to do this."

"I think I do."

A throat clears behind us. "Is there something going on here I should know about?"

Cade looks up. "No, man. Just Briar is a good friend of mine."

I laugh at that. I can't keep it inside of me. It's the alcohol talking, but plus, I'm not wrong. He's not my friend. He was Brady's friend, and they've done nothing but fuck with me since I started school.

"Oh yeah?" Chad asks, sending me a winning smile. "She seems cool."

Cade's still giving me a dirty look in answer. I squeeze Chad's fingers. "I am cool. Thanks for noticing." After giving Cade a smile, I try to reason with him. "I'm good. Thanks for checking on me though."

I move around Cade, dragging Chad behind me as I move up the stairs. One of the spare rooms is slightly ajar, so I peek inside, then Chad and I walk in. He shuts the door behind us. "I think Cade Farmer has a thing for you."

I laugh at that. "I don't think so."

"Could've fooled me."

I turn, put my arms around him like we did when we were dancing, and start a slow rhythm that clashes with the music downstairs. He kisses my neck again, moaning when he gets to my ear, then tugs on my lobe with his teeth. I grip him, my head still fuzzy from the alcohol, but I know I want this. This moment of reprieve from the real me.

Chad inches ever so closer to my lips. The tip of his tongue slides up my neck, then he kisses me across my jaw. My hips are pressed into his, seeking that relief.

A loud knock comes on the door. "Briar?"

Chad lifts his mouth away from me. "Taken," he calls out. I don't know if he meant the room or me, but the next thing I know, the door handle is jiggling. Chad steps away, and we both turn toward the door.

"Open up the damn door!"

I know that voice. Chad starts to go toward the door, but I hold back on his arm. "He'll go away."

In the next instant, the door splinters open. I gasp as Lex walks through the door like it's nothing but cheap wood, Reid and Cade hot on his heels. Reid barges past all of them and goes right for Chad. He lifts his fist in the air. "Do you have any idea who that is?" he seethes.

Before Chad can even answer, Reid's fist connects with his cheek.

I scream, my hands moving up to cover my mouth.

Chad falls to the floor and Reid jumps on top of him, his fist already reared back for another punch. "Stop!" I yell.

"Jesus!" Cade rushes forward. He holds back on Reid's arm—his throwing arm—before he can get another shot in. He pulls him away while Lex drags Chad to his feet. The corner of his lip is bleeding.

He's scared, staring wide-eyed at all of us. Fuck, I would be frightened too. I move toward him. "I'm so sorry," I say.

He looks over at me. "I thought you didn't have a boyfriend."

"I don't," I say.

Reid wrangles himself out of Cade's grasp and fists his hand in Chad's collar. "That's Page's fucking sister, asshole. Touch her again, and I will fucking end you. Are we clear?"

Chad's eyes go even wider. "I didn't know, man."

Reid seems to relax a little then.

Chad holds his hands up and starts to slip by all of them. I reach out for him. "Chad?" My voice is slurred now. All that beer is catching up with me.

He looks at me and shakes his head before leaving the room. There's no way he's getting involved in this shit. I don't blame him. If I wasn't knee-deep in all this, I wouldn't want to be in it either. The crowd that gathered outside the room parts for him as he leaves.

"Goddamn you, Reid!" I lunge at him, my own fist raised in the air. I get a couple punches into his shoulder, which are more like hammer fists before Lex's arms come around me, pinning my own arms to my side.

Reid turns toward me, seething. "You were going to fuck him in my house?"

"It's none of your business," I scream back.

"You are my fucking business now." His loud voice

roars through the room. Almost the whole party goes silent then. At least the people watching shut right up. When Reid looks their way, they scatter. No one wants to be on the receiving end of his ire.

Reid shakes his hand out.

"Fuck, dude," Cade says. "We have to put some ice on that."

He nods, then looks at Lex. "Take her to my room. Lock her in if you have to."

"Lock me in? Are you insane?" I'm trying to sound coherent, but I'm pretty sure my words are all jumbled, drowsy with alcohol.

He doesn't bother responding. He walks out of the room with Cade, who glares at me. Lex, with his arm still around me, moves me forward until we hit Reid's room. It's on the exact opposite side of the house as his parents' suite, but it's not too shabby itself. It has an en suite even though the closets aren't as large as his parents' room.

When we get into Reid's room, Lex kicks the door closed. When he lets me go, I stumble forward, and he ends up righting me on my feet again before I pull away. I move to the bed, pull my knees up, and stay there with my head in my hands.

Shame washes over me. I'm so embarrassed. I thought they'd get exasperated watching me drink. I thought they'd say shit if I wanted to go into a room with a guy, but I never thought they'd barge in, telling him he couldn't do anything with me because I'm Brady's sister.

I rub my eyes, then my forehead, trying to make the memory disappear, but that's the thing about real life. Nothing disappears. Nothing dissipates. You can always still feel it in your heart.

"Why did you guys do that?" I ask. My voice cracks, and I clear my throat, trying to keep the emotion back.

"Why did you do that when you knew it would piss us off?"

"Why should me dancing and kissing a guy piss you off?" I counter.

Lex's jaw ticks. It takes him a while to answer, but eventually, he says, "Because none of this is you, Briar."

"You don't know that."

"You're wrong. We've all known you since you were little. We know you, whether you like it or not."

I sigh. "You only think you know me, Lex."

When I look up at him, his face falls. I must look so sad right now because he bridges the distance between us in two steps. He hesitates when he gets to me, but then he puts his hand on my shoulder. "We're trying stop you from being someone you're not. We're trying to stop Brady's death from turning you upside down, putting you on the wrong course. That's all we want."

I swallow hard. "I can do it myself."

His finger traces over my jaw. His dirty blond hair is all over the place. He moves toward me, his lips descending on mine. "You're so strong," he whispers.

My heart gets clogged in my throat. I've only kissed Lex once. I've let him kiss me down there, but not on the lips since that first night.

A loud knock comes on the door. Lex practically throws himself back from me before going to the door. He yanks it open, and Cade is there. "Reid needs your help calming Sasha down. She about lost her shit when she heard Reid punched Winthrop."

Lex nods and leaves without looking back.

Cade smiles at me, but then he pulls the door shut and locks it with him on the other side. I leap for the handle, but it's too late. It won't move. "Cade! Cade, what the fuck?"

"This is your punishment, Shortie. Next time don't try to screw a guy on our turf."

I pound my fist on the door. "I wasn't going to screw him, you fucker."

All I hear is Cade's laughter as he walks away.

I twist the knob on the door one more time, but it's useless. I wander back to the bed and throw myself down on it. My cell phone cuts into me. I pull it out. On habit, I bring up my conversation with Ezra and see his last message asking me to send him a risqué pic.

It might still be because I'm drunk, or maybe it's some sort of payback to the guys, but I lift my skank shirt, pull my bra down and cup my breast. I leave my fingers spaced apart, so you can see part of my nipple. Then, I hold the phone up, make sure my face doesn't show, and snap the picture. I hurry up and send it, so I don't overthink it.

Afterward, I lay on the bed waiting for my phone to buzz, but it never does. Eventually, my eyes drift closed, and I fall asleep on Reid Parker's bed.

11

I wake to the door banging against its hinges. I blink my eyes open and find my lashes wet, sticking to my bottom ones. The lights are out everywhere, so all I see is a huge, hulking form stumbling forward, cursing. I'd gone to bed with the sounds of the party below, but it's silent in the house now.

"Jesus fuck," a slurred voice says.

I have to peer hard through the dark, but I immediately recognize the form as Reid Parker. I sit up in the bed just in time to see him slam the door closed. Then, he stumbles backward before the back of his legs hit the bed and he falls over like a toppling domino. I have just enough time to move my legs and scoot out of the way before he lands right on top of me. Alcohol stench permeates the air. He's fucking hammered.

I growl in disgust and then get up, throwing the blankets over top of him. At least the door is unlocked now. I can get the fuck out of here. I'm sure my mom wouldn't be pissed if I called her to come get me from Reid's party.

Before I can get very far, a hand shoots out and wraps around my wrist. His grip has the effect of a rubber band, making me come back a step or two. "Just where do you think you're going?"

"Home. A different room. Somewhere you're not."

He laughs darkly. "Not going to happen. All the rooms are taken. No one's sober enough to drive you home and that would defeat the purpose of me coming in here, wouldn't it?"

At least, that's what I think Reid Parker said to me. His voice is still a bit slurred even though the grip on my wrist is pretty firm, drunken state or not. I try to wrestle my wrist from him, but he doesn't give. "What the hell, Reid? You make me come here. You lock me in your room practically all night."

"I'm saving you."

Now he's really pissing me off. I should definitely be able to get myself out of his drunk grip. I start hammer fisting his fingers that are wrapped tightly around me.

"Ow. Fuck, Briar." Finally, he releases me, but I don't get very far. Apparently, his athleticism doesn't fail him even when he's been drinking. He's up and on his feet, his hands around me. "I came in here because you were crying. Now lay the fuck down and get some sleep."

I lift my chin in the air. I can't even deny it. I wake myself up sometimes from crying in the middle of the night. It's not something I'm conscious of. "I don't need you to help me, Reid. Or save me. Have you noticed that you're, in fact, not helping me?"

He throws me down on the bed. A breath of air escapes me. "Stay there," he orders. "Sleep."

I can tell he's exhausted. He rubs his head, then his eyes. This is his own fault. "You're only making things worse."

"Oh, because I stopped you from losing your virginity to fucking Winthrop? That's making things worse?"

My cheeks burn. He just laid my truth out there without a conscious thought. "I wouldn't be losing my virginity. Asshole." I take one of the two pillows from his bed and throw it at him.

He laughs. Not just a slight chuckle, he full on

laughs. His face breaks out into a huge grin as he doubles over.

The more he laughs, the more the anger rises inside me. "What's so funny?"

"I know you're a virgin, Briar. Don't try to be something you're not."

I bite the inside of my cheek. Why does Reid Parker think he knows everything about me? He may be technically correct, but I've done other things. Hell, Lex can attest to that. "I am not a virgin," I tell him, still trying to argue the point.

I don't know why I care so much. It isn't as if I was going to let things get that far with Chad and me. Why does every guy think just because you want to have a moment with a guy it means you're going to have sex with him? Lex understood that. We had fun with foreplay. Well, I had fun with his foreplay. He never let me touch him.

I think what bothers me most is that Reid is laughing right now. Like there's no way I could have had sex already.

Reid stalks toward the bed. I have nowhere to go, so I plaster myself against the mattress as if I can dig right through it. "Who?" he asks.

"You—you don't know him," I say, thinking of Ezra.

He shakes his head. "I know everyone in Spring Hill, and I'd know if you gave it up, Briar."

"It wasn't with a guy in Spring Hill."

His eyes narrow at this. For a moment, I think I got him, but he just laughs. His eyes are clouded over, but he's pretty sure about this. "So, if I stuck my finger in your pussy right now, it'd be clear?"

I lift my chin and nod. I'm pretty sure no one can tell. That's a science thing, right? You can't actually tell if someone is a virgin or not. I've heard of the hymen, but I don't think it's something Reid would know where to find and say definitively that I was still a virgin if it was there. If anyone could do it, it would have to be a medical professional, even if such a thing can be done.

Reid reaches for my knees and forces them apart. I squeal, but he has a hold on them. The skirt I put on earlier is now wide open. He can definitely see my panties. For a second, he just stares down as if he can't believe he went that far either. My heart starts to pump harder inside my chest. I don't move. Not because I'm scared of what Reid might do to me, but because I'm secretly hoping he does.

I don't know where this came from.

His stare rakes over me, past my stomach where my shirt has pulled up, over my chest, then to my eyes. I raise an eyebrow at him. "Shall I take my panties off? Or will you?"

My stomach twists. I feel like I'm going to throw up with anticipation. His hands move down the insides of my thighs. He doesn't even have to keep my legs pressed open now. I'll freaking staple them to the bed to give him easier access.

"How was it?" he asks.

I blink up at him. Every muscle I have in my body is locked up. "Huh?"

"The sex? Was it good?"

He's hovering over the apex of my thighs. I'm creaming myself. If it wasn't so dark in here, he could probably tell. Hell, it's Reid Parker, he can probably tell now. He probably has a sixth sense about these things.

I nod.

"That's it?" he asks, his voice growing husky.

"I—I enjoyed it."

My intent is only on him. I'm answering with whatever comes to my mind first because I'm staring at his pointer finger, wishing it'll drop to my soaked panties, slip inside, and push between my folds.

"You're full of it, Briar Page," Reid says, dropping his hands to his sides, the moment leaving us just like that.

"No, I'm not," I say quickly. I grab my panties and start to pull down.

"Stop," he says. He reaches out, presses his palm against my lowering panties, which only puts pressure on my clit.

I exhale harshly at the contact. "Oh fuck."

His eyes blaze. He licks his lips as his chest heaves in front of him. "You liked that? Just that little touch?"

I bite down on my lip. I don't want him to know how much. I don't even want to admit to myself what my brother's best friend is doing to me right now.

"You want me to touch you, don't you, Briar?" His gaze rakes over me. Goosebumps sprout over my skin like waves coursing over the ocean surface, battering at the shores of my core. "I don't have a stop button, Briar. If I touched you, I'd keep going. I'd dive my fingers inside you, make you come around me, then rip your clothes from your body. I'd suck on your tits, pierce you with my cock until you scream my name. Is that something you want?"

I can barely get words out. With every description he uses, I picture the two of us together, connecting that way until my body vibrates with need for him. "Y-yes."

His face falters. He tears his hand away and then closes my legs. "None of that will bring your brother

133

back. You don't think I get sad, too. You don't think I want to set fire to the world and fuck everything else." He leans over me and grabs my chin. "None of that will bring Brady back, Briar. Start thinking with your head. What would your brother want you to do? Throw your whole life away because he died? Or get out there and do what he couldn't? You're not going to get that by fucking random guys at a party, and you're sure as hell not getting that with me.

All you're going to end up doing is adding shame on top of your grief. One day, you're going to come out of your bereaved stupor, even if it's ten, fifteen years later, and you're going to realize how badly you fucked up your life."

I went from being so completely turned on to being yelled at like I'm a little kid. "What's it to you? It's my life, Reid. Mine. I can do what I want with it."

"Not while I'm around."

I growl in frustration. "You're so fucking full of yourself. I want you to leave me alone. Cade and Lex, too. I've had enough. I'm not your puppet. I'm not your fan girl, and I'm certainly not your baby sister."

Reid lets my chin go and steps back. "I don't care what you want. You're doing things my way."

He yanks my skirt down, twists on his heel, and leaves the room. I hear the lock click behind him, and I know he's locked me in here again. He was right about one thing. Shame nudges me. My brother's best friend just touched me. It didn't bring Brady back. It didn't even make me forget for a little while. Now I'm just lying here staring at the red haze on the ceiling, the light from the alarm clock on Reid's dresser the only thing illuminating the room.

It all looks so ominous. It matches my mood.

I pull my skirt further down and then run my fingers through my hair. Reid's a prick. A hot prick, there's no doubt about that. He says some smart things though. Things that I grapple with. Things I know I should be doing, but I just can't bring myself to do them.

What's normal without Brady? That's what I want to know. But I'm also scared to find out.

What if I like it better?

What if I forget?

What if...? What if...? What if...?

My head starts to pound, and my dry eyes feel scratchy against my lids. I keep my eyes closed, trying to let sleep come to me. I'm certainly not getting out of here until Reid lets me out and it's not like I'm going to slip out of the second story window to walk home.

No, I'm stuck here. Just like my brother stuck me with these three when he left. I'm beginning to realize that just because I no longer want them in my life doesn't mean they're ever going to leave it. We're connected now in a way we might not have been before. We all lived through the same sadness. We all loved Brady like a brother, and we all lost him.

I don't know. I'm lost, and maybe I can admit that for the first time.

I'm sure Ms. Lyons will love to hear that on Monday.

12

When I get up the next morning, Reid's door is helpfully unlocked. I hear people talking downstairs, and since I'm too scared to jump out the second story window even if it is to avoid people I don't want to talk to, I decide to make use of Reid's en suite before heading down. It's a typical guy bathroom. Sparse with several pieces of clothing littering the floor. It's clean though. I find a fresh towel in the cabinet and drape it over the sink while I shower off the football game, the party, and even the moment with Reid.

I dreamed last night that he didn't stop, that we went all the way. Waking up in his bed was just a tease considering we didn't get near as far as we did in my dream. While I wash the shampoo out of my hair, I keep asking myself why the fascination with my brother's best friends now, but don't come up with any good answers.

Stepping out, I dry myself off, tie the towel around my body, then use the old brushing my teeth with my finger and toothpaste routine. At least it will help get the gunk taste from yesterday's beer out of my mouth. When I move back into Reid's room, I raid his closet. The skank shirt and skirt smells like the party, so there's no way I'm putting that on today. Miraculously, I find one of Reid's practice jerseys in the way, way back that looks like it's from his middle school days. I pull that on over my bra and then find a pair of athletic shorts in his drawer. I have to roll the hem up several times, but it's the best I can do right now.

After finger combing my hair, I walk downstairs. I blink as I take in the rooms. It looks completely different than it did yesterday. Everything is already back in order. There are no plastic cups all over the place, the keg is gone, and the furniture is where it used to be. I'm almost impressed. It's then that I see Lex coming in through the side door, wiping his hands on his shirt. When he glances up, his eyes meet mine. His eyes widen into spheres as he takes me in. I look down. I'm not slipping a nipple or anything, so I'm not sure what his problem is. "Breakfast?" I ask.

"There's cereal in the cupboards," he says after clearing his throat.

I head that way. "Are you the only one up?"

"No, we're all up. It's almost noon, you know."

"I must've lost all track of time when I was *locked* in a fucking room."

Footsteps sound from another direction. "Is that Shortie sounding so bitchy this morning?"

I look over my shoulder when his footsteps stop. He's in the mouth of the living room, just staring at me. When he sees me looking over, he chuckles and shakes his head. "This ought to be fun."

"If by fun you mean torture," Lex says.

Cade makes a non-committal sound and shrugs. "Whatever."

I shake my head. I have no idea what they're talking about and the only thing I can think about right now is food. My stomach growls, reminding me of my quest. I find some cereal and a bowl and fix it myself before sitting at the kitchen island. "Just where is Lucky Number Seven this morning?" I deadpan.

"Talking to Sasha out front. They had a bit of a fight last night."

"I can't imagine why." I roll my eyes. "And you guys say I'm a bitch."

"She's jealous," Cade says. "You should go out

there and let Reid know you're up. He wanted to know."

"No thanks. Reid doesn't need to know my whereabouts all the time."

"Aw, come on. It'll be fun. Plus, you'll probably be getting her back for dumping gravy all over you."

I lift my gaze to meet his. "How so?"

He smirks. "I don't think you understand how you look right now, Briar. Trust me, she'll want to kill you showing up in Reid's jersey like that."

A small smile flits across my face. I shouldn't be so petty...but I am. I finish my cereal up, wipe my lips with the back of my hand, and stand. "This look okay?" I ask the two of them.

"You have no idea what you're getting yourself into," Lex cautions.

I turn toward Cade. If he approves, I know I'm gold. "You look perfect, Shortie."

I strut toward the front door. I look through the glass and see that the two of them are talking a little way down the sidewalk. They're separated by about a foot, and I can only see their profiles. With a deep breath, I pull the front door open and lean out. "Hey, Reid."

They both turn. Sasha's face goes from surprise to fury within a nanosecond. After I'm satisfied with that reaction, I turn toward Reid to complete the reason for coming out here. His look takes my breath away. His stare is all consuming, eating me up from my head all the way to my toes.

I force words from my mouth. "The guys said you wanted to know when I was up, so...I'm up."

"What the hell is she still doing here?" Sasha cries.

Reid's already walking toward me. "Got to go," he calls out over his shoulder to his supposed girlfriend. "Talk to you later."

He moves inside, making me step back. Just before the door closes on Sasha, her mouth is open wide, and staring daggers at both Reid and me. Reid blinks as he locks the main house door behind him. I can feel the eyes of both Cade and Lex on us too.

"What the fuck are you wearing?" Reid asks.

I shrug. "I found the old jersey in your closet and the shorts in your dresser. The clothes I wore yesterday either smell like gravy or an ale factory. I didn't think you'd mind."

"He doesn't," Cade says.

"Fuck you," Reid spits back at him, glaring at his friend over his shoulder.

Then, Cade just laughs and slips back into the living and dining room. Lex stays there for a few moments longer. He shifts his weight from foot to foot until Reid gives him a look, then he swears and walks away, his neck splotchy red.

"I hear you and Sasha got into it last night," I say.

Reid just keeps staring at me, his eyes wide as he mostly zeroes in on the jersey of his I put on. I cross my arms in front of myself, trying to shield me from his stare. What's his problem?

He shakes his head. "Yeah. We did."

"Isn't she a little too bitchy for you? I mean, not that you're the King of Nice, but she's just... mean." This isn't a new thought for me. I've been thinking this ever since he and Sasha started dating. I know my brother was wary of her at first, too, but then I think that they'd all pretty much gotten use to her. He'd still complain about her from time-to-time, but not like in the beginning. She was just a necessary evil when she was around, but she was hardly around either. Not until Brady died. Now she seems like a permanent fixture at his hip.

"You need to take that jersey off, Briar."

I blink at him. "Why?"

"Now," he says, his voice hardening.

"Fine," I say. I pull the jersey over my head right there in the hallway and then throw it at him. "Happy? Jesus."

His eyes zero in on my chest. Typical male. He whips his shirt off and throws it at me. "Put this on."

His nostrils flare. I go to tug it over my head, and I'm suddenly doused with the smells of Reid Parker, a sweet, musky scent that makes me breathe in deep.

As soon as his shirt is pulled over me and draping toward my mid-thigh, I look up at him. I ogle his pecs up close, tugging on my bottom lip with my teeth. *Typical female.*

Reid is a specimen of athleticism. He's gorgeous, has the perfect body, with the attitude to match.

"Anything else you need me to do?" I ask, my voice cloaked in annoyance even though I'm anything but right now.

"Yeah, you wear a player's jersey like that, you suck his cock. That's the rule." He slinks forward until my back hits the hallway wall. "You got that."

My heart starts pounding like mad in my chest. He places one hand by my head and towers over me. I'm surrounded by his scent now. He's in front of me and on me. There's a feral nature to his eyes that send a yearning through my core. I don't know what Reid is thinking about behind those green eyes, but I like it. I like it a whole lot. "I-I didn't know."

His free hand moves between us. "I can tell. Should I make you? Now that you know, I mean?" He's not really asking me. He's asking himself, so I don't bother answering. His body starts to shift, and it's only then that I realize he's stroking himself right there in the hallway in front of me.

My pussy clenches. My eyes drift down, and I get a glimpse of him that makes my heart stutter.

"Eyes up here, Briar," he snaps.

I do as he says, squeezing my back against the wall some more and planting my palms on the wall as I stare into his eyes.

His breathing ratchets up, and his movements become more pronounced. He groans. "Oh, fuck."

I suck my lips between my teeth and groan with him. Every nerve ending I have in my body is fired up. Heat patches blaze all over my skin.

"The only way this would be better is if you were on your knees, your lips—"

"Around you?" I ask. "Taking your length inside my hot mouth."

All I see are his pupils. His eyes are like big, black circles. His body shutters a couple times with his climax, then his other palm grips the wall as he leans forward over me. "Next time you pay the price, Briar."

He leaves with that. I look down to see his cum spilled between my feet on the floor. I drop my head back against the wall. I think next time I'd enjoy paying the price. My entire body flushes red as I stare up at the ceiling.

Lex comes around the corner then. "You okay?"

I nod and swallow at the same time. "I'm good."

"Come on, I'll take you home."

"Briar's not going home," Reid calls from somewhere in the house. Then, he comes into view, drying his hands on a hand towel. "I believe someone has homework to catch up on and since I told her mother last night that we all stayed up late to help Briar do her work and then it got too late to take her home, I'm sure she doesn't want to make a liar out of me."

I've been wondering why my mother hadn't called freaking out. When I ran away before, I got calls from her almost every thirty minutes.

I look from him to the spilled cum. If my mother only knew about the boy trying to help her.

"Get your bag and get to work, Briar. No fucking excuses."

"Bag's already out on the kitchen island," Cade calls out.

I look both Lex and Reid in the eyes. Neither one of them is going to budge. I'm not getting out of here without their say. Walking forward, I step over Reid's release like it didn't even happen and push past him to sit in front of my bookbag. I can't believe the three

145

jocks are telling me to do my homework. Not that these three are the typical jocks you see on TV. They've always kept decent grades. The teachers don't have to mess with their grade books just to give them passing averages so they can play. No, they take their position on the team seriously. They make sure they have the right to play both academically and physically. They study, they do their homework, and they attend practices with workouts on top of that. I remember my brother coming over to Reid's house during the early summer for a makeshift football camp. They ran drills, upped their skill level. They pushed themselves to be this good by themselves.

With that thought, I crack open my first book and get to reading. A folder is slipped next to me. Lex nods. "I took the liberty of making sure you had every assignment you need to turn in."

For being only the third week of school, it's surprising how much there is to do. It's because I'm still on the accelerated track. I'm taking college level courses where the work is no joke.

Hours go by without me noticing. By the time I finish, I have a splitting headache and the guys are nowhere to be seen. I grab a bottle of water from the fridge and head out onto the back deck. They're all there, shirts drenched in sweat as they pour over game footage from the previous day. Coach must have sent it to them.

"Is that Winthrop?" Lex asks, pointing to the screen.

Reid grunts in agreement.

"I hate that fucker."

Reid glares over at him, but he catches me in his peripheral. He shuts the laptop, and I continue fully outside, his shirt still swimming halfway down my legs.

"You finished?" he asks.

"Yes." I sound ungrateful because I'm trying to sound that way, but in reality, I'm relieved to have all that work done. It was sitting like a weight on my shoulder. Despite my actions lately, I really do care about school. It's hard to just turn one-eighty and think something completely different no matter how hard I try. "Everything's done. I'm caught up."

"Was that so bad?" Cade asks.

I roll my eyes. "Don't fuck with me right now, Farmer. I have a headache."

Lex's chair scrapes across the concrete, and he slips past me through the back door. Reid watches him go and then turns toward me. "You actually did it? No fake answers? No writing anything down just to get it done?"

"You think it would've taken me that long if I just wrote random shit down?"

His gaze narrows like he's trying to tell if I'm being honest or not.

"You want to check it over?"

Lex comes back out on to the deck. "Here," he says. He holds out his palm. There are two white capsules there. "For your headache."

"Ugh, you're a lifesaver," I tell him. "Thank you."

I take both pills with the water bottle in my hand and then look up at all of them. Reid is still eyeing Lex suspiciously as he stands near me. "Can I go home now?"

Cade scratches his jaw. "Everyone's at the lake..." He's not looking at me. He's staring at Reid.

Reid shrugs. "Just keep Sasha away from me. I've had enough shit for today."

I look between the two of them. "Can you drop me off on the way at least?"

Reid shakes his head. "You're coming with us."

My whole body sags. "I don't want to be anywhere Sasha is." *Or you for that matter.*

"You're in luck." He stands and walks past me. When he gets to me, he leans down. "Neither do I."

I know what happens at the lake. A lot of drinking

and swimming. "I don't have a suit," I tell them, trying to think of any excuse.

"We'll figure something out," Cade says, patting me on the head. He's grinning from ear-to-ear. The lake is the place to be for someone like Cade Farmer. Half-naked girls everywhere. Wait, correct that. Half-naked, intoxicated girls everywhere.

Joy.

13

"The Lake" as everyone calls it is actually Lake Neavarro. It's about a quarter of an hour outside of Spring Hill. In the summer, it's filled with families and teenagers, everyone looking for relief from the summer heat. Now that school is back on, there's barely anyone here. When we pull into the public parking lot, there are more cars than normal, but I know it's probably just other students from SHH who heard that other people were going to be here today.

Brady loved it here.

He wanted a lake house when he grew up. Not here, of course, but somewhere else. A place he could escape to during the off-season of the NFL. A place he could fish, bring the family, just a place to relax from the rest of the world.

I had a stomachache all the way here because I wasn't sure how I would react being at the lake again, knowing it was one of Brady's favorite places and that he'd never be able to see it again. When we get out of the car, though, only the best of Brady's memories hit me in the chest. He and I as little kids playing frisbee by the water's edge. Coming here with these three knuckleheads as we got older. They started liking girls before I liked guys, so I didn't understand why they'd stop playing a game of volleyball right in the middle just because another cluster of girls walked by.

The thought makes me smile, looking out at the very spot the volleyball net is still located.

"Whoa, are you delirious, Briar?" Cade asks. "Because I could swear you're smiling, but you're not known to do that these days."

When I look up, I catch Reid's eye over the top of his car. Coincidentally, he's smiling, too, but when I see him, I drop my gaze and look away. "You're mistaken, Farmer."

"Of course. Can't let anyone see that you're happy," he deadpans.

He's not wrong. If people see that I'm happy, they're going to think I don't miss Brady and that's not true. I miss him so much it hurts. "Are we doing this or what?"

"You sure know how to have fun, don't you?"

"Fuck off."

He gestures toward me. "Exhibit A, Jury." He leans over, brushing his shoulder with mine. "Come on, Briar. It'll be fun, I promise. I'll swim with you out to the platform."

I smile again even though I don't mean to. There's a diving platform out toward the middle of the lake. The swimming area is sectioned off with buoys. The shallow area ends at about five feet, but when you keep going out, you can't touch at all. My parents would always get worried I wouldn't be able to make it, so that was there one rule: Brady, or one of the others, would have to swim out there with me. They usually would, but they always would if there happened to be a cute lifeguard on duty. "I don't think I need your help anymore, Cade, but thanks for offering."

I already texted my mother on the way here, letting her know I'd finished my work and that we were headed out to the lake. She told me to have a good time. I get the feeling she doesn't care where I am as long as I'm with these guys. If I were out by myself, then she'd be calling or texting every half hour making sure I'm not headed toward Calcutta—the big city where I'm bound to get raped and murdered and taken advantage of.

I lean back into the backseat of Reid's Escape. He threw together a bunch of beach towels in a bag his mom had. Lex takes it from me as we walk toward the sand. There's a little concession stand to our left along with a store where I'm hoping I can find a decent bathing suit. The guys didn't want to waste time to stop at my house, so I could find mine. Instead, I'll be buying a new one. When we find a good spot near some other football players with a huge cooler, I tell them I'm going to go to the little store.

"Cade," Reid says, motioning toward me with his head.

Cade sighs, then wraps his arm through mine. "Babysitting duty."

"I don't need you to go with me to the store."

Cade turns my head, and I find Sasha with her crew there. Sasha is glaring daggers at me, sitting there in her hot pink bikini. "If you want to be left alone, fine by me."

It's not that I can't handle Sasha by myself, but she's a ruthless bitch. She doesn't care about the scene she makes, and I know for a fact that when Cade or one of the other guys are with me, she won't be tempted to start her shit. "Fine," I tell him. "But please don't say babysit. I'm grown up now. I even showered by myself this morning."

"So I noticed."

We walk past the concession stand, the smells of grilled hamburgers and hot dogs assaulting us. I might have to get something to eat here sooner rather than later because I only had cereal so far today.

The little shop is exactly as I remember it. It's just big enough to sell towels, bathing suits, and beach toys. I head to the rack in the back with the sign that reads fifty percent off End of Summer Blowout Sale with a black Sharpie. There isn't a lot to choose from and even less so that matches my size, but I settle on a plain turquoise suit. It's a mix between a one piece and a two piece. The part connecting the bikini top from the bikini bottom is a flimsy see-through mesh. I take it into the very small room in the back that just has a curtain that you pull across to try it on. It's a little small on top for me. My breasts spill out a little, but it fits perfectly in every other way.

I walk out of the room wearing it, taking my clothes with me. Cade is talking the girl at the counter up. When I get to the register, he turns toward me, the little pout in his lips falling for a brief second. "Looks good."

I smile back at him and then pull the tag off the suit to show the girl. She rings me up, looking between Cade and me, probably trying to decide if we're together or not. I go to pay her, but Cade takes out his wallet instead, further confusing her because she most definitely thinks we're together now. "Thanks," I tell him, genuinely shocked. He didn't have to do that. When we walk out of the store arm-in-arm, I turn toward him. "You know she thinks you're with me now, right?"

Cade slides his Aviator-like glasses down his head and over his eyes. "She wasn't my type."

I smirk at that. "I'll pay you back," I tell him.

He shakes his head. "Don't bother. Just think of it as me paying for the price of admittance for all that's about to go down."

"What?" I ask, thoroughly confused.

He shrugs. "Don't worry about it, Shortie. The suit looks great on you, and you deserved to have it."

Reid and Lex both eye me as we walk up. Lex found me first because he was looking, but Reid was in mid-conversation with another football player when he saw me. I look down, making sure I'm not once again slipping a nip or anything, but I'm all put together, thankfully. I'm kind of worried about that with this suit.

"Look confident, Briar," Cade whispers to me. "You own that suit."

I do as he suggests as he walks me to the towels

155

they laid out. I find the sunblock in the bag and start to rub it all over my skin, even under the meshy part of the bathing suit because I'm not sure if the sun is able to get through that material or not. By the time I'm done, I lie down only to have a big shadow fall over me. I look up to find Reid there. "Yeah?"

"Volleyball?"

He knows I can't resist a good volleyball game. Brady used to tell me he was surprised I never took it up in high school. I could have. I was always just focused on my schoolwork rather than a sport. Reid holds his hand out and pulls me up when I take it. There are others walking toward the net too. A bunch of football players and some of their girlfriends. Every single one of them is from SHH. The last time I played volleyball here, it was a similar situation except Brady and Jules were playing too.

I take a deep breath, trying to relax into myself. Reid, Lex, and I end up on the same team while Cade ends up on the opposite side of the net. I fall into an easy rhythm when the game starts. Seeing the guys play another sport other than the one they excel at is comforting. They're not bad, not by any means, but the fact that I can keep up with them is promising. We play the best of three games, and the team Lex, Reid, and I are on cream the other team. Mostly because it looks like Cade is preoccupied with trying to get into a Sophomore's pants by the end of the day instead of on the game.

When we finish, it's high fives all around. Even Reid gives me one, along with a smile. I almost forgot what he could look like when he wasn't staring at me while pissed off. His look stops me in my tracks and throws me back in time. Maybe I always did have a soft spot for Reid Parker but kept it under wraps for the obvious reason that he was my brother's best friend. Then again, I had a soft spot for all of them. They were my...friends.

Lex hovers in the background and then turns in the sand as he heads back to our towels. I head that way, too, but instead of stopping where our stuff is, I keep going. Reid is rubbing sweat off the back of his neck when I pass while Lex is digging around for a beer in the cooler next to us. I keep going until my toes hit the water. The waves splash over my feet and up to my ankles, dousing me. It feels so good that I keep walking. When the water is up to my waist, I dive in, swimming under the surface until it feels like my lungs might burst. I come up around the buoy line that separates the shallow area from the deep end. I slip under the line and set my sights on the diving platform. There's only two other people out there at the moment, sunbathing.

I take my time, letting the water slip through my fingers before diving back under to swim, bubbles from my nose rising to the surface until my hands clasp onto the ladder. I heave myself out of the water and stand there. From here, the people on the beach are tiny. I can see Sasha and her friends who've avoided Reid all day. Looks like she wants to ignore him as much as he wants to ignore her. As I stand there, water sloshing off me, the two who were sunbathing decide to get up. I don't recognize them from school, even though they look like they could be my age. They must be dating because they hold hands and jump into the water at the same time.

I move over on the platform to even it out. The waves from the couple diving in rocks the platform for a moment or two before it evens out again. Another figure has passed from the shallow area to the deep area, and it doesn't take me long to figure out who it is. Before long, Lex appears at the base of the platform, pulling himself out of the water. His wide chest eclipses the ladder, making me laugh. He looks up, his head cocking to the side. His trunks slip lower and lower, so once he's on the platform, he hikes them up and ties them again. He shrugs when he looks over at me. "I swear I could hear your mother in my ear telling me to make sure you were okay out here."

The smile doesn't leave my face. "I remember."

After what happened between Lex and me, we haven't talked much. Since we're the only two out here, I take a seat on the platform, letting the sun's rays shine down on me. I sprawl out, leaning back on the palms of my hands, and he mimics my stance, sitting next to me in the same position. "I'm sorry all that happened," I say.

He must be thinking about the exact same thing. "Yeah," he says, jaw working.

I reach out to pat his hand. "I miss talking to you, Lex."

He looks over. Lake water is still dripping from his chin. It falls to his chest then traverses over the dips and hard planes of his abdomen until it slides right into his belly button. "I need to ask you something, Briar."

"Okay..."

"Or tell you something. I don't know. I guess I just need to get something off my chest. Something that doesn't seem right."

I cock my head at him.

His throat works for a second before he lifts his gaze to meet mine. His dirty blond hair is plastered to his forehead, giving him an almost boyish look. I swear we could throw ourselves back a decade and be in this same exact position. "Be careful around, Reid. He may look like he has everything together, but I—I don't know." He shakes his head. "I'm not sure he's in the right head space right now."

"You mean because he locked me in a room all night?" I tease.

"Yeah. Maybe," he says, trying to smile.

This is different. These three—used to be four—were untouchable. No one would dare say shit about one to another or they'd have hell to pay. "He seems... angrier than I remember," I say, almost whispering as if the lifeguard who is at least twenty yards away gives a shit about what we're saying.

He shakes his head. "That's not all I wanted to say either." He shifts up, placing his elbows on his knees, letting his hands dangle out in front of him. "I want you to know I don't regret anything we did. Not at all. I loved every second of it. What I do regret is that maybe you were doing it for the wrong reasons. Maybe that's why it made you sad." He runs a hand through his wet hair. When he looks over, he slides his hand over mine.

I don't have the ability to speak right now. I want to. I can see the need for me to say something in Lex's eyes, but nothing's coming out.

I open my mouth, but Lex is quick to jump in.

"Don't say anything until you're ready. You don't owe me anything. You don't owe anyone anything, so don't think you have to start something with me because of guilt. Or shame. I don't want that. I just wanted you to know how I truly felt about it."

Lex stands. He looks down at me and gives me a half smile.

"Wait," I say, just before he jumps in. "You—you like me?" Is that what he's trying to say? I really wish he would spell it out for me.

He nods once, then dives into the water. He doesn't come up again until he's halfway to the buoy line, and even when he does, there's still a stranglehold around my throat and my thought process.

The only thing that keeps whirring through my head is that Lexington Jones the Third just told me he likes me.

14

On Sunday, the guys must get sick of me because I spend the whole day at my house texting with Jules. Ezra still hasn't responded to my pic even though I can tell he's seen it. I agonize over what to do about it since things suddenly got awkward because of it. So, I end up messaging him that I was drunk, so he can delete the picture if he wants.

When Monday morning rolls around, I hear voices in the other room while I'm still lying in bed. I can pinpoint one voice intermixed with my mom and dad's. It's crazy that he's here this early in the morning. Usually, he'd send someone else, like Cade, to do his dirty work, but not today. His voice rouses me, forcing my feet to the floor. He completely ignored me at the beach after I got in from the diving platform. In fact, he completely ignored everybody. It's like his mood did a one-eighty, and when we left the lake, he dropped me home without a single word being said.

I had all day yesterday to think. I tried to read my textbooks, maybe even get ahead in class like I'm used to but going to the lake and then not having anyone to talk to right after about the mixed emotions flowing through me wasn't great for my mental state. Coupled with the fact that Ezra never messaged me back and that Jules was surprised I'd went to the guys' party, and I think hurt that I didn't tell her, made me slide into a deep yearning for Brady—for normalcy. Not some place where I have to "pay" because I wore a jersey I picked out of a closet.

I don't ever lock my door, but I walk toward my door now and flip the lock so Reid can't get in. Let's see how he likes being locked out instead of locking me in. Prick. There's something wrong with his head if he thinks doing that is normal. Then, I go to my closet, yank the doors open, and peruse what I got. I settle on an old t-shirt of my dad's that I used to sleep in. It's big, baggy, and has the name of some band I've never heard of scrawled across the front. Then, I find a pair of black leggings and throw them on. To me, everything else just takes too much effort.

A knock sounds on my door.

"Go away."

"Seriously?" I hear him mutter before he tries the door. The knob turns this way and that, and a sigh of frustration sounds. "Open up, Briar."

"No," I say simply. I'm facing the door with my hands on my hips, arguing with the door like I'd be arguing straight to his face. I feel like I was in another world for the last few days. I felt better sometimes and worse during other times, but it still brought me right back to here. *Why does everything always end with me feeling like this?*

He tries the door again like it's going to miraculously unlock itself. Not likely. "Goddamnit, Briar. Open this door."

"Yeah, I don't think so," I say, calling out over my shoulder. "I'll meet you at school."

"Not happening. I'm taking you to school."

"Don't need you," I remind him as I pull my hair up in a high ponytail. It still has lake water in it and doesn't smell the best, but I'm not concerned.

"You do," he says, arguing with me, "because your parents just left."

I sigh. Of course, they did. Are they just relying on the guys to bring me up now? What the hell is wrong with them? I bet even if I told my mom that Reid jerked himself off in front of me, she'd probably come up with some excuse for him. "I'll walk."

"I don't think your parents will like it if I break this fucking door down. You're going to school."

I fucking know he will, too, but if he does that, he'll just be shooting himself in the foot. "Have at it, Lucky Number Seven," I deadpan.

Footsteps stalk away. I roll my eyes, but he's back before I can think of what to do next. If I have to walk to school, I should really go now. I can always go out the window...

A drilling sound revs through the air. "What the...?" I move closer to the door and lean toward it. Sure enough, Reid Parker is taking the doorknob off my bedroom door. Fucking Asshole. I scramble toward my desk for my bookbag and then head for the window. I take the screen out, throw the window up, then hear several noises behind me. With one leg out of the house, a hand clamps around my shoulder.

"Briar, get your ass back in this house."

"I thought I told you to leave me alone?"

Reid gives me a tug, taking my bookbag right off my shoulder, then pulling me back through the window and into my room before replacing the screen. He looks me up and down once he turns. "You're not wearing that and look at your hair. Get in the shower."

I step up to him. "Leave me alone, Reid. I'm going to school, and I don't need you or your *help*."

Reid sits down on my bed and leans back, his hands behind his head like he owns the place. He leaves his scent in the air between us. "I'll wait here."

"You'll be waiting a long time."

"Don't test me, Briar."

"Test you?" I laugh darkly. "I'm one moment away from telling my parents what you did to me in the hallway of your house. You think they love you now? Just wait."

Reid moves so fast I don't realize what he's doing at first. Before I know it, I'm hiked over his shoulder and he's striding out of my bedroom.

"Reid!"

His hand clamps around my back as he takes me into the bathroom. He turns on the showerhead while I'm trying to wiggle out of his grip.

"Stop!"

He tries to deposit me in the shower, but I hold on for dear life. I'm doing anything to make this harder on him. Tears of frustration gather behind my eyes. I know I'm acting like a bitch and a baby. I know this isn't normal behavior for me, but I just want everyone to leave me alone. Is that too much to ask?

Reid curses sharply under his breath, then he kicks

his shoes and socks off before stepping into the shower with me. I gasp when the water runs down my back, instantly soaking my shirt and falling down my hair. In that instant, he deposits me on my feet and turns me around, then pushes me back until my head is under the spray. In the commotion with him, my hair pulled out of the hair tie, so my dark hair is long down my back and now completely soaked through like the rest of me.

I just stand there and glare at him as the shower-head does what it was created to do, except I'm also in clothes. "Happy?" he asks.

I don't answer. My jaw clamps shut, and I'm still fighting against the emotion threatening to pour out of me.

Reid sighs. He lets me go long enough to grab the shampoo and put some in the palm of his hand. Then, he turns me around and starts to wash my hair. I'm too stunned to say or do anything. His fingers work over my scalp, and I grab the shower walls to steady myself from his thorough work. He slides his hands up my neck and into the back of my hair. My eyelids flutter closed. I don't know how long he does it for, but I'm so caught up in the moment that when he jerks me back around to put me under the water again, I go willingly. He tilts my head back by lifting my chin, then slides his fingers through my hair again as the soap runs over my clothes and to the drain.

"You've always been just—" He swallows. "—a classic beauty. Like Julia Roberts or Marilyn Monroe. I don't know why you do this to yourself. It doesn't make you fit in, Briar. All it does is make you stand out more."

My breath hitches in my throat. I'm staring into his green eyes the entire time he talks. There's so much depth of feeling in his stare right now that I don't know what to focus on first. There's sadness there, making me believe he's thinking about Brady, but there's a lot more there, too. Concern, and lust maybe? I don't know how well all those feelings go together, but they're all there.

He brings me out of the spray and squeezes the water out of my hair. "Do you use conditioner?"

I push his hands away. "I can do it."

He quirks his brow, but he must believe me because he steps out of the shower. He doesn't go anywhere. He hops up onto the counter and stares at me through the glass. He's distorted, so I can't see his look anymore, only his general shape.

Since I'm already in the shower and soaked, I decide I might as well finish what he started. I pull my leggings and panties off and deposit them at the end of the shower. Then, I peel my shirt over my head before dropping it with the rest of them. I hear a groan even over the shower noise. I look down when I unhook my bra and notice I was wearing a red one, something I'm sure shows up really well even through the glass shower distortion.

So, I was right about the lust I saw in Reid's eyes.

I pull the strap from my arms and toss it on top of the other soaked clothes at the end of the shower stall before rubbing conditioner through my hair. My legs are next. I shave from ankle to thigh, casually shifting my gaze to Reid every now and then. He hasn't taken his eyes off me the entire time. I use the Bath & Body Works shower gel I have next, soaping me up good and filling the whole bathroom with the sweet scent before washing everything off. The soap, the conditioner, and what's left of the shaving cream from my legs. After I squeeze the excess water out of my hair, I shut the shower off and turn toward the door. "I'm ready to come out now," I say, a little breathless. I feel like we've just ran through the best foreplay without touching ever.

I know Reid has a girlfriend, and besides the fact that she's just a terrible person, they aren't right for each other either. I'm probably not right for someone like Reid either. Too much history. Too much...I don't know. Everything.

I grab hold of the shower door and roll it open. I stand there, naked, in front of Reid while his gaze devours me from head to toe. He's hard. His cock is pressing against his khaki shorts, but I remind myself that guys Reid's age get hard over everything. I could probably be a middle-aged mother of three standing in front of him and he'd still probably want to bend me over. It doesn't mean anything. It's sex. It's not love. It's not all those feelings I think I'm missing now more than anything.

I reach for a towel in the open shelving, but Reid beats me to it. He lets it drape open then comes closer. He reaches it out toward me, his hands sliding from my collarbone down. When he hits the swell of my breasts, he hesitates a moment before sliding further, then cupping me through the towel, taking his fill.

My heart stutters, and my knees feel weak.

The top of the towel falls open, revealing the swell of my breasts as he cups me. "I have no fucking willpower," he growls. "I need a taste."

He bends his head, his own hands offering my breasts up to him. They feel round and full due to his attention, but when his mouth clamps over my nipple, a surge of pleasure shoots through me. My hands reaches out to steady myself, and I cry out.

"Oh fuck," his muffled words sound around a mouthful of my breast. He wraps the towel around me and then carries me back to my bedroom. He sets me on the edge of the bed and then climbs over me. My legs automatically open for him. I'm wet and not just from the shower. I want him to touch me. He ravishes my breast while I writhe on the bed. I lift my hips in search of him, of something, and rub against his erection. He groans hard, forcing his hips down to grind against me. "Fucking hell, Briar."

He throws the towel out of the way, his hands moving up my inner thigh. He touches me the way he did Friday night, his palm resting against my clit before he moves lower, his fingers swirling through my hair until they're at my entrance. I can barely think. "Oh, God."

"Mmm," he murmurs, his lips still worshiping my breast. "You want this?"

"Yes," I say, nodding.

His finger swirls over me, and I buck into him. He moans in approval. "No lying this time, Briar. Has anyone done this to you?" He slips his finger inside me until I cry out.

Our gazes meet, and my heart catapults against my

chest. He moves his finger out and in once, his eyebrow rising, waiting for me to answer. "Yes," I nod.

He stops, his expression tightening. "Who?"

"Reid, really?" I ask. *He wants to talk about this now?* All I want him to do is to continue what he's doing. Not because of the way I feel but because of the way *he's* making me feel.

He pumps his finger inside me a couple of times, making me forget what we were even talking about, but then he stops. "Who, Briar?"

"Please don't stop," I tell him, moving my hips to force his finger inside me again.

He watches me closely but holds my hips to the bed. The way his eyes bear into mine, I have no choice but to tell him. "Lex," I say breathlessly, then I move into him again.

His eyes widen, and I know in that instant, I've made a terrible mistake. He pulls his finger from me. "Lex touched you like this?" I nod, reaching out for him, but he sits up. "When?"

"After—after Brady. We used to talk, and then it turned into more, but it wasn't right, so we stopped."

Reid's eyes glaze over. His jaw tenses. He runs his hands through his hair. "Motherfucker."

I sit up while he starts to pace the room. "Don't get mad." His head spins, and the look he gives me makes me shrink inside myself. "He—he likes me. He told me on Saturday."

This makes him stop pacing. He moves forward. "Do you like him, Briar?" I feel like there's an inherent choice in that question even though he didn't outright give me one. Do you like me? Or do you like Lex?

"I don't know," I say honestly.

I don't know if it's because I tilt my chin in the air afterward, but Reid swears again, then he tells me to get fucking dressed. Even as he says it, he goes to my closet. He flips through the different outfits hanging up, then takes one out and throws it down on the bed next to me, the dress covering my bare ankles. I stand up, my legs still a little weary. I went from being the most turned on I've ever been to now. Reid Parker had a mouthful of my breasts. His finger pumped inside me.

I see his toes next to mine before I look up. He cups my cheek. "I don't share, Briar Page. You got that?"

I nod.

"Did you—?" He looks away. "Did he fuck you?"

I shake my head. "We didn't even kiss. Once maybe."

"Oral?"

My jaw hardens. I don't want to say. This is less

about me and Reid now or me and Lex. Reid seems genuinely angry. I'm worried for them, for their friendship, even though I don't know why Reid would be this mad if I was just an easy opportunity. "On me," I say. "That's all."

"That's all?" he asks, his eyebrow sharp and his eyes fierce as he stares straight inside me. "That's not *all*, Briar. That's too fucking much."

15

*T*he drive to school is filled with tension. I don't know what to say or do, but the amount of anger seeping out of Reid seems catastrophic.

"It's not Lex's fault."

"Don't talk to me about my friend. I know what is and isn't his fault."

I shake my head. "This is utterly ridiculous, Reid. At least Lex fucking likes me. I'm just some game to you. You didn't care about me until you saw me as a charity case. Until you could somehow be a fill-in for Brady, and let me tell you, you're a poor stand-in for my brother. You think he'd want you to touch me like you just did?"

A growl rips through the car. "Stop fucking talking."

"No," I growl right back. "You think these clothes will somehow make me feel normal again. They'll make me forget the huge hole I have in my heart. You think if I dye my hair back, I'll go back to being the person I was before Brady died... Well, I fucking won't. I won't ever be the same again. It's nice that you can just continue on with your life like nothing fucking happened, but that's not me."

The car swerves to the side of the road and the brakes lock. I brace myself on the dashboard. Reid throws the car into Park and glares at me. "You think I'm the fucking same? You're not looking close enough. It's not all about you. Yes, you were his sister, but I was like his fucking brother. All of us were, so don't act like you're more broken up than me, Briar. I just knew I had to grow the fuck up and realize he wasn't coming back, and even though I want to bury my head in the sand, even though it sometimes kills me to pick up a fucking football, I know I have to do it because not doing it isn't going to bring him back."

By the time he finishes, he's shouting. My skin sprouts in goosebumps.

"He's gone," Reid says, his voice lowering. It's half

disbelief, half resolute. It's like we know it, but we also can't believe it at the same time. "Making your parents work extra hard to try to comfort you isn't helping anyone, Briar," he says. All of the hardness has left his voice. "Running away won't help. Making other people worry won't help." His hands turn to fists on the steering wheel. "I'm just trying to get you to see that you can be the same person you were and the world won't end. It doesn't matter if you go to school wearing black with dirty hair or if you try to make yourself feel nice, your brother still won't be there at the end of the day when the last bell rings. I get all that. But one way, you feel good about yourself, and the other, you're just... depriving the rest of us of that light we're so used to seeing, even if you don't see it inside yourself right now.

"One of the things I hate most about not having Brady around is seeing the change in you." He shakes his head. "It infuriates me," he spits. "It makes me want to yell at someone—anyone—for seeing this. And no, I'm not your brother or your parents. I'm not going to coddle your ass." He turns back toward the road and puts the car in Drive. He pulls away from the side of the road a little less abruptly then how we got here, but he still swerves.

Tears track down my face. I'm angry at Reid for

yelling at me. I'm angry at Brady for dying. I'm angry at myself.

When we pull into a parking space by the school, I step out of the car and start walking away. "That's great, Briar," Reid calls out after me. "Keep running away."

I walk faster, my bookbag banging against my back as I go.

"I'm still going to be there when you turn around, and Brady still won't be."

My foot catches on a loose crack in the pavement, but I keep going. I want to put as much distance between Reid and myself as possible. When I get inside, I head toward my locker only to find Lex there. He cocks his head when he sees me. "Are you okay?" He doesn't wait until I get to him, he pushes off the lockers. "You didn't answer your phone."

I swallow, trying to get my bearings. All I can choke out is Reid before we hear the culprit behind us.

"You motherfucker."

Lex's head snaps up. "Dude, why the fuck is Briar crying like this?"

Reid comes up and pushes Lex into the lockers beside us.

My stomach drops. The boys don't fight. They just don't. Not for real. Not like this.

"You fucking asshole," Reid breathes. "I can't believe you'd do this to me."

Lex's gaze flicks from me to Reid. He looks resigned, which only spurs Reid on.

"You touched her." He gets in his face. Lex is huge, but Reid has him on height. "You know—" Reid slams his fist into the locker behind Lex's head, cutting himself off.

We've drawn the attention of the entire hallway crowd now. Looking around, we must've come into school between periods.

"The hell?" I hear Cade say behind me.

He runs up, and I grab his hand. "Make them stop." The world is just so topsy turvy right now.

Reid's breathing down Lex's neck, a scowl twisted in betrayal.

Lex swallows. "You know I wouldn't do anything to hurt you, brother."

"You touched her," he says again. "Do I need to spell it out for you?"

Cade turns, his eyes wide. "Alright, everyone. Get to fucking class." He starts to urge the crowd back, but no one's budging. This is fucking juicy. This is juicier than Reid making me stand and turn in a circle so he can approve my outfit. When that doesn't work, Cade turns to his best friends, "Guys, we need to take this elsewhere."

When they don't move, Cade physically moves them to a classroom that happens to be empty. I try to turn away, go to my next class or something, but he grabs my hand and yanks me inside too. I can't even look at Reid, but there's really nothing else to look at.

"Let's just talk this over, okay?" Cade starts.

Reid runs his hands through his hair. "Sure, let's talk this over. Let's talk about, oh, I don't know. How did she taste, Lex? Huh?"

Cade's eyes round once more, then he looks from me to Lex. I can see the questions flaring in his eyes, and in the next second, him making the connection.

"Answer me!" Reid roars.

Lex shakes his head. "I'm not doing that, man. I'm sorry you're pissed, but I couldn't help myself."

Reid pulls his fist back and punches Lex in the mouth.

Lex's head snaps back, and I gasp.

"And she says you like her? You told her that?"

"Guys!" Cade says, placing himself between Lex and Reid before Reid can take another shot at him. I can tell he's as disturbed by this as I am. My mouth dropped when Reid punched Lex and it's still hanging open at this moment, wondering what world I'm living in now.

Lex looks over at me. I feel so guilty for saying something to Reid. "I I didn't know," I say to him. I feel like I need to apologize for Reid's outburst. I had no idea he would react that way. Now he's getting punched because I didn't keep what we did between us.

"It's okay," he says with a small smile. "I should've told him before this."

"You're damn right you should've," Reid says, pushing against Cade to get to Lex.

I lunge forward. I've been staying out of it until now, but the tears dried on my face a long time ago. "Stop," I shout, holding back on Reid's arm. "Please. This isn't you. This isn't all of you."

My touch on Reid's arm does something to him, and he steps back. That doesn't mean he likes it. He pulls his arm out of my grip and then wipes at his face. "Yeah, how does it feel to have someone you know act completely out of character? I told you you weren't the only one suffering."

"Leave her alone," Lex says.

Reid points a finger at him. "Don't you dare fucking act like she's yours to defend."

My head explodes. The fucking testosterone in this

room is too much. "I'm none of yours!" I scream. "I ran away to leave all this behind, and I'd gladly still be there. If you want to punch each other, fight with one another, be my guest, just leave me the hell out of it."

I turn on my heel and leave the room. Oddly, there are only a few people still outside the classroom, and when I open it, they take huge steps back, giving me as much room as I need. I grab my bookbag that's still sitting at the base of my locker, and I head toward my next class. I have to check the time to figure out where I should be, and I don't even know how late I am because my brain completely skipped over the bell ringing overhead or maybe I couldn't hear it over the shouting.

When I walk in, the teacher gives me a look at the front of the room. "Pass?" he asks.

I blow him off, stalking my way to the back row and finding a place to sit. Classmates stare at me like I have three heads in the process, but that's nothing new. The teacher continues on with his lecture while I sit in the back, trying to piece myself back together.

What the hell is going on now? Both Lex and Reid like me? Or just want to fuck me? Because from what I can tell, there wasn't any difference. Only Lex gave me a proclamation of his feelings for me the other day and it had nothing to do with any of this happening today. I don't know what to do with any of that. They were both tormenting me just a few days ago.

My head snaps up when the door at the front of the class opens again. The teacher sighs, then stands up straight. I barely glance up then want to flee the class when I see Lex walk in.

"You're not in this class, Jones."

"I know," Lex says. When he spots me at the back of the classroom, he sits next to me.

I try to crawl into my desk further to get away from him, but there's only so far I can go.

The teacher opens his hands up at the front of the class in an "Are you kidding me?" gesture, but Lex isn't even looking at him, he's staring at me while I'm making a point to look everywhere else but at him.

The whole class goes by like this. My body is boiling just under the surface. My thoughts went round and round in circles, mostly centering on Lex because he wouldn't take his eyes off me. When the teacher dismisses the class, I grab my work from this class that I did over the weekend and head toward the desk at the front of the classroom. Lex is right behind me. I can feel his presence.

The teacher sits and crosses his hands in front of his chest.

I place the worksheets down on his desk. "This is

the work I haven't turned in yet. Grade it or not, I just wanted to show you that I did it."

He nods, then looks behind me. "Please don't come in this class again, Lex, unless you're supposed to be here."

"I can't promise that, Sir," Lex says from behind me.

He says it in such a way that he's going against the teacher's wishes, but he's also very polite about it. How is the teacher supposed to say anything to that?

He doesn't. He just shrugs and both of us leave the room. He follows me to my next class, and the next class after that until we're at lunch. I'm about to sit with Jules when I notice Jules is at the football table again. When I glare at her, she lifts her shoulders, and I notice that Cade has a hand on her upper arm, making her stay in place. "I take it I'm going there," I ask behind my shoulder to Lex.

"We would prefer it."

I'm so tired. I'm too tired to argue.

Reid is nowhere to be seen, which means Sasha isn't at the table either. She's a few over. When I glance at her, she's talking happily with one of her friends. Who knows what's going on? I don't know if anyone picked up on what was going on earlier, but I would've thought news like Reid punching Lex over me would've gotten to Sasha already. Maybe everyone thought it was about her. No one probably even noticed me there.

Classic beauty, I think as Reid's words come back to me.

My stomach twists at the same time Cade looks up. "You going to sit down, Shortie, so Lex can sit too? I don't think he's going anywhere without you."

I fall into the seat across from Jules. We just stare at each other until Cade eventually gets up. He nods at Lex and then heads off toward the lunch line. I'm starving, which I've only realized right this moment. I didn't eat any breakfast, so it's unsurprising.

"Where's Reid?" I ask.

"Taking a breather," Lex says.

I glance toward him. His brown eyes are on me and his dirty blond hair is still a little disheveled from the fight this morning. There's also a red welt on his cheek. My eyes won't move away from it. "I'm really sorry, Lex."

He shrugs. "It's my fault."

"I'm pretty sure it was Reid's fault."

"Reid's got...some issues to deal with," Lex finally says. He's talking about his friend like nothing happened between them this morning. Like they're still the same people who never fought.

I blink at him. "You don't say?"

Cade comes back with two lunch trays after that and sets them down in front of Jules and me. "On the house, ladies. Don't say I never did anything for you."

"What about me?" Lex asks.

"Eat a bag of dicks, big guy."

I blink up at them. Oddly, inexplicably, I'm transported to a time before Brady's death interrupted our lives. Cade and Lex joke. Jules and I laugh. Even through all the shit that's been happening, they can still draw life out of me.

16

*R*eid keeps his distance from me the rest of the week. Not physically. Never that. He still shows up at my house every morning to make sure I'm dressed and decent for school, and I don't give him a hard time. He hasn't once dropped my ass in the shower again or had to pick out my clothes. My parents sit back, drinking coffee with him every morning until I come out of my room. He had a point about making their lives more difficult. I'm not fucking telling him that to his face, but I can admit I'm being a brat. Hell, I feel it in the moment I do it, but I just can't stop myself.

On Friday, he shows up in a suit and tie. It's homecoming. There will be a pep rally in the gym during school, a dance tonight, then the big game tomorrow against SHH's archrivals—the Red Raiders. Actually, they're just the closest town to us, which in and of itself makes us enemies, I guess. However they got to be our homecoming foes, they're still going down. Spring Hill has a streak to uphold.

My mom gets misty-eyed when we leave for school. She even makes us stand next to each other so she can take a picture. I stand there awkwardly, and Reid does, too. In this moment, it kind of does feel like she's replacing Brady with Reid. As soon as she's done taking the picture, we both step away from one another as quick as we can. The awkwardness doesn't stop there though. It gathers around us like BO, staying pungent in the air until I want to choke on it. He hasn't said one word to me in the car during our trips to school other than, "Is this station okay?" or "Are you too cold?" He certainly doesn't bring up what happened on Monday with me even though things between him and Lex are fine now.

This morning is a different story. We're about halfway to school when something in the air shifts. He twists in his seat, which usually wouldn't draw my attention, but I swear I can feel his eyes on me too. It makes my hair stand on end. I'm aware there's going to be a huge divide, namely Brady's death, between Reid and I for the rest of forever. I can admit that I was stupid to push my brother's friends away. Maybe because I was their friend too. Just because they were always classified as "Brady's friends" didn't mean I wasn't always around them or included in everything they did.

I hear Reid half muttering to himself when he finally says, "Briar..." More twisting in his seat like he can't quite get comfortable. I don't know if he can't think of what words he wants to say or if he's just uncomfortable in general now around me. "I want you to come to the game tomorrow." He swallows. "Will you?"

I raise my eyebrow at that before I look over at him. He actually asked. He didn't just show up and demand it of me.

He lets out a breath that erases some of the tension in the car. "I was talking about it with your parents. They don't know if they're ready yet, but I'd really like you to be there. We're going to dedicate the game to Brady, so I thought you might want to see that."

My stomach drops. "Oh." I hadn't quite expected that though I don't know why. Of course they would want to pay some sort of homage to him.

"Nothing over the top. I promise."

Considering just Brady's name makes me sad right now, I can't imagine what something "over the top" would do.

Now I'm the one squirming in my seat. The shorts I'm wearing feel like they're riding up my ass even though they come below dress code level, so that's definitely not it. My skin just feels itchy like we shouldn't be having this conversation. I close my eyes and count to five. Even though my first reaction is to shy away from this conversation, I know I have to have it and many more just like it because Brady isn't here, and he isn't coming back.

I need to get comfortable with the uncomfortable.

"Yeah," I force out through the closing of my throat. "I'll come."

Reid expels a breath from his chest that sounds as if he's been holding it in for ages. We don't talk the rest of the way to the school, just that, but already things feel a little lighter between us. When we pull into the parking lot, Jules is there waiting for us. Well, not really for us, she's actually waiting there for me. I filled her in on everything that went down with Lex and Reid. Well, most everything. I kept some of the sexy stuff to myself, but not all of it. She knows now that Lex and I were having a fling or whatever it was, and she knows Reid flipped his shit over it. She was kind of shocked by everything at first, but she's pretty sure I have a decision to make. She thinks both Lex and Reid like me. Like, really like me. Not just want to jump my bones, or make sure I'm okay because I'm their dead best friend's sister.

I can't even think about any of that right now. As far as I'm aware, Lex is the only one who has feelings like that for me. And despite the fact that he's told me, he hasn't acted much differently. I don't know how long that will last. He's caring and a sweetheart, so he'll probably give me all the time I need to figure things out. That sounds just like something Lexington Jones the Third would do.

Unlike Reid Parker.

This whole week has been insanity. I'm reminded of that when a bunch of guys who are completely decked out in our school colors jump all over Reid in the parking lot, growling like warriors. They have a semi mosh pit thing going on until Reid emerges from it, his tie askew and his hair all over the place. He looks over to find me. Jules and I haven't waited for him, but he watches me with hawk eyes until I'm in the building.

"Still no communication?" Jules asks.

"Not much. Though, he did ask me to go to the football game tomorrow?"

Jules' eyebrows raise, eyes widening into saucers. "The homecoming game? *The* game?"

"Oh, is that what game it is?" I deadpan. "I wouldn't know it from all the shit hanging up in the halls." I tear a streamer down from the ceiling as we walk by and wrap it around Jules like a scarf.

She shakes her head. "No, it's just—" She stops in the hallway, making me turn toward her. "Usually when a football player asks a girl to come to the homecoming game, it's a big deal."

"Ha," I choke out. The sound more of disbelief than of amusement.

"I'm serious," Jules says. She holds onto her books more tightly as she stares at me.

"In case you haven't noticed," I tell my friend. "Reid's still dating the bitch supreme of SHH. I saw them kiss the other day." I did, too, and my gut twisted at the sight. I mean, I usually want to throw up when I see Sasha, but this was different. She laid an ardent kiss on him, and honestly, it was hard to tell if he was kissing her back, or if she was just all over him. They haven't been talking much. That I know of anyway.

Not that I've been paying attention or anything.

"She's an evil bitch." Jules says. "How long was that going to last anyway?"

I laugh, then we both laugh. The look in my eyes is —I'm sure—screaming about the fact that they've been with each other since middle school. That's a hell of a long time. And weird. Especially for the head jock and cheerleader of the school. Like, they have to be good at everything else *and* be in a long-term relationship with each other? So not fair.

I see Jules's gaze wander off. She taps her fingers against her books, her frown lines deepening into her forehead. Today's going to be a hard day for the both of us. And tomorrow. I walk forward and grab her hand. "Well, will you go to the game with me then? If either one of us cry, we won't have to ask the other why. Or if we don't talk, it won't be weird. Or if we just tell stories about Brady the whole time, we—"

"Yes," Jules says, interrupting every reasoning I could think of to try to get her to go to the big game. "This doesn't change the fact that Reid Parker asked you to go to his homecoming game though."

I shrug. I think Jules's grief have taken over parts of her body. She wants to find happily ever after's everywhere she looks just like she and Brady had. "You're off your rocker."

"I guess we'll see, won't we?"

I guess so...

———

THE PEP RALLY IS AN EPIC DISASTER.

Not for the football team, the school, or the cheer-leaders. Unfortunately, Sasha didn't trip and ruin her face during one of the routines. It wasn't that at all. It was just everything combined. Jules and I sat next to one another, squeezing the life out of one another's hands like we were both about to get shots in the arm and needed the other's support.

When Reid is asked to say a few words about the game, her fingernails dig into me. He gets the crowd up and on their feet with all the "annihilate the Red Raiders" talk, but at the end, he looks up to the gym ceiling and points to the sky. "This is for you, buddy." And I swear Reid has the GPS coordinates to wher-ever I am in the room because his eyes find mine and linger there until he's swept away into a heap of bro hugs.

The cheerleaders get up and perform another routine before the principal moves back in front of the mic. He talks to us about the behavior that's expected of us at the game tomorrow and then dismisses the school. It's a madhouse to get to one of the gym doors right now, so Jules and I stay seated, our hands still wrapped tightly around one another.

Tears have gathered in the corners of Jules's eyes. "I wonder when this pain will stop."

"Probably never," I tell her, saying it optimistically, tacking on a tight smile to the end.

"Yeah, you're right," she says. "Not that I want it to," she quickly adds on. "It's just, you know, I don't know how much heartbreak I can take."

And that's what I love about Jules. Right there. She knows exactly what I'm feeling, and I don't even have to say it out loud. I pull her to me and give her a hug. "It'll fade," I tell her. "It'll always rise up, but it won't always be hovering at the surface." I use the words Ms. Lyons has been telling me. "Eventually, you'll find someone again. A prince, probably, because you're definitely princess material. You'll move to some exotic country where you'll rule the land and you'll only think about Brady on his birthday."

"Or when I watch football," she says, sniffling.

"They won't have football in this magical kingdom."

She half laughs into my shoulder, tugging me to her for dear life. "Fine. Then every time I see the stars."

I close my eyes tight together. Jules told me all about her and Brady's first date, camping out under the stars. "That I can't do anything about. The stars will always be out, whether we want them to be or not."

"It's okay," she says. "I think I'll like staring up at them and remembering him no matter where I'm at." She pulls away from me and wipes at her eyes. Again, she says exactly what I'm thinking. "Now, if only I had a dollar for every time I've cried in school this year. I'd be rich enough to be my own princess."

"I fucking love you," I tell her.

"I fucking love you too."

"Hey now," Cade says, approaching cautiously, but with a shit-eating grin on his face. "If there's going to be some loving going on between you two, I want in on it."

The top buttons on his pressed shirt are undone and his tie is stuffed into the back pocket of his nice dress pants. He actually looks like he could've just gotten done with a threesome. "Eat dirt, Farmer," I say, then smile to myself because that actually made sense. *Farmer. Dirt. Get it?*

He shakes his head at me, then gets serious for a moment. "You two planning on going to the dance tonight?"

I groan inwardly. Last year, I was so excited to go to this dance. I wanted Peter to ask me, and when he didn't, Lex and Cade danced with me all night just to make up for it. Reid was too busy with Sasha and Jules and Brady were all over one another, so it was just us three.

"I see that look on your face," Cade says, drilling me with his panty-melting smile. "Don't act like we didn't have a great time last year."

Jules sits up straighter and makes her shoulders go back. "Yes. Yes, we're going. We'll meet you guys there tonight."

"Really?" Cade asks, his eyebrows practically in his hair line. I understand his reaction because I'm looking at Jules the same way. Just, why? Why would we go?

"Definitely," she says, eyes flaring. She pulls me to my feet and down the bleachers, leaving Cade there with the same look still on his face. She yanks me right out the main doors and to her car. "Okay, we need dresses. Makeup. Shoes. Hair."

"Have you lost your freaking mind?"

She laughs, then pumps my hand a couple of times. "I think—I think your brother would want us to go, Briar. Let's just go have a great time. I'm serious. We can do this. Especially on the backs of retail therapy. Come on, we don't have much time."

I shake my head at Jules as she climbs behind the wheel. We may have been forced together based on the fact that she dated my brother, but I'm not sure I could've picked out a better best friend myself.

Images of Reid, Lex, and Cade pop up, and my stomach twists in a high school crush kind of way. I have to grip the handle to the car door hard as realization sinks in. Brady left me with an amazing support group. I didn't pick any of these people for my life, but they're here anyway. And I'm right, I couldn't have chosen better for myself if I tried.

17

don't know how we pull it off, but we do. Jules and I look fucking fantastic. Newly purchased dresses, shoes we had in our own closets, and we decided to do each other's hair and makeup because we were running out of time, but by the time we head out into my living room after getting all glammed up, we look seriously hot.

When we walk out, my mother does a double take. "Whoa, you two. You look great." For the second time today, she insists on taking a picture, so Jules and I hug each other on the same wall Mom took Reid's and my picture this morning. Though, this picture is way less awkward. "Have fun," my mom calls out to us on our way out the door.

A niggle of excitement starts to spark in my lower

stomach. It's been a long time since I've been excited about anything, but I can't help myself. Remembering how Lex and Cade treated me last year makes me want to go this year despite the fact that I'll probably be missing my brother more than anything. Maybe I can spin it and remember how much fun we had last year instead of thinking about losing him.

Jules parks in the parking lot as a bunch of students make their way into the school in droves. It looks like we got here just in time for the dance to start. We link arms and walk in. The gym is bright with purple and yellow streamers and balloons. In the center of the gym stands the football team. They've gathered together in a cluster, all of them still wearing their suits from school today and flanked by our school colors. They look like a posh pack of athletes, easy enough to distinguish from the rest of the male classmates who've decided to go a little less fancy for this dance.

Reid is in the center of everything. It might be his height that makes him stick out initially, but he just has a way about him, like hot guy sonar that immediately draws attention. Of course, after I see him, my stomach twists because there's a Grade A Bitch hanging off his arm, smiling and laughing like nothing happened between them at the party the other day.

My teeth immediately grind together. He's an

asshole. Seeing him with her makes me feel like a toy he's been playing with on the side. Sure, he doesn't really have anything to defend himself for. We didn't actually take it too far, but there were definite moments of connection. There's something here. And the way he got so fucking jealous over Lex liking me?

I tried to talk myself out of the fact that Reid Parker might have a thing for me, but maybe part of me hopes he does. From the way I feel right now, I can tell I secretly held a candle for him, which just makes me feel so fucking stupid because the sight in front of me screams the opposite.

I hesitate while Jules keeps walking. My elbow around hers makes her stop. She follows my gaze and frowns. When she turns back to me, her face drops. "I knew you liked him, Briar. You should stop trying to fool yourself and go after what you want."

I shake my head. "Yeah, and risk being torn down again by the most popular guy at school? I don't think so. I have enough on my plate to worry about this year."

Jules looks me straight in the face, eyes commanding my attention. "You know Reid's a good guy." The look I give her tells her I'm not so sure of that, but she keeps talking anyway. "Think about how much we're suffering. Don't you think he's probably suffering, too? He's probably confused and lost, and

Sasha is just there. She always has been. Old habits are hard to give up."

Earlier, my subconscious reminded me that Reid's birthday is tomorrow. I wasn't allowed to go out with my brother and the guys for his annual party before. Now that it's coupled with the football game, I'm sure they'll be doing some major partying after the game tomorrow, especially if they win. It's weird that no one's mentioned his birthday yet though. Then again, their practices have been crazy difficult to prepare for the important game. They are missing one of their most important players after all.

My eyes flick over the rest of the people surrounding Reid. Lex is there, of course. He's looking especially sharp and swaying side to side with the music. As far as Cade goes, he always just has this swagger that draws people in. I must've repressed the idea of my brother's best friends being so freaking hot out of respect for my brother. It isn't as if I never noticed how good looking they were, but I knew there could never be anything between us, so I shoved it down until I only saw them as good friends. And yes, maybe I have—and had—a sort of brotherly affection for them too.

Those three guys would do anything for me. I know that now more than ever. I may not agree with their tactics, especially Reid with his caveman type style of "just do what I say, or I'll make you do what I say", but that's just the way he is. And now, standing back from all that, I have to admit that it's a little hot. In a way. A weird way, possibly.

"Are we just going to stand here all night?" Jules asks. "We look really good, so we should try to enjoy some of it."

I cock my head at her. Jules is in no way ready to start dating again, and I honestly don't think that's her intention here either. Forgetting for a bit, maybe. Hell, I can relate to that. I just hope she doesn't do something she'll regret.

She gives me a small tug on my hand, and I relent. We walk toward the huge circle of football players and step inside. After Brady died, it felt weird to do this, but now I know it's not. It was dumb to try to fight it. I belong with these guys. Not as a fangirl outsider who drools over them like over half the girls in the school, but as friends at the very least. And whether or not anything comes from these new feelings that are sprouting, they're still my people.

"Sexy ladies," Cade says as soon as we make our appearance. There's a hip-hop song on with a hard beat. He dances over to us, fake grinding in the way only he can do. He accomplishes what he set out to do, though, he gets us moving, laughing, and enjoying ourselves.

In all my life, I'm not sure I've ever felt so carefree as I do in this moment. There are so many thoughts and feelings that want to try to anchor me down, but for tonight, I'm determined to put a brave and happy face on for Jules. We dance together, uncaring if anyone looks at us funny or wonders what the hell we're doing. Maybe that comes from the knowledge that the worst thing has already happened, so what else could possibly go wrong? Oh, someone thinks we look stupid? Who freaking cares?

There's more than one pair of discerning eyes on me though. I ignore them as best I can. I don't engage with either Lex or Reid. One of the football players steps behind Jules to try to dance with her, and she locks up. Cade immediately comes to the rescue, hip checking his teammate out of the way before I can even say anything. I'm sure whatever was going to come out of my mouth was a lot harsher than Cade moving him along. My dark-haired friend looks up and winks at me. A part of me melts inside. For him to notice what happened, he had to have been paying attention. People can say whatever they want about Cade sleeping around, but he's a genuinely good person. So what if he likes sex? What people our age don't?

"Decided to come out of the goth phase?"

My stomach sinks as I look up into Sasha's twisted gaze. She's so conniving and evil. Her eyes are almost black, and I'm not just saying that for effect. It's true.

She leans over. "I've heard whispers about you and Reid. It's never going to happen, Skank. I have him by the balls."

"How endearing," I counter. "I'm sure he gets all kinds of turned on with that dirty talk."

Her eyes flash. "Just know that while he's playing Save the Princess for you, he's in my bed at night."

Not every night, I think. But I'm not going to throw Reid under the bus. Sasha definitely isn't worth my time.

"Stay in your lane, and we won't have any problems. Do you understand?"

"Ooh, you're threatening me now. The gravy wasn't enough. Or the skank shirt, or any of your other little petty tactics." She's growing angrier and angrier by the second. "Just stay away from me, Sasha."

"You'll see," she says. "Reid won't always be coming to your rescue once he finds out some things about you."

I roll my eyes. There's nothing she could possibly have on me. I'm literally an open book. What? Is she going to tell him that I lost my shit after my brother died? I'm pretty sure he had a front row seat for that.

"Plus, you can't satisfy him like I can, so you should just back off now."

I fake frown. "Did you just call yourself a slut? I'm not sure."

"You fucking bitch," her hand raises like she's going to slap me, but Lex steps his huge body between us.

His brown eyes capture mine right away. "Don't engage with her, Briar. She's petty and spiteful, and you're better than that."

I bite my lip while I look up at him. Every rational thought decides to run away in that moment, so I just end up staring at him slack-jawed. I can't believe he just said those things about Sasha for anyone to hear. She makes an annoyed sound behind him, but we both ignore her. His sleeves are rolled up to his elbows again, which instantaneously makes him five times hotter. The whole sleeve thing is something I wish more guys knew. Then again, they may not be able to pull it off like Lex.

He leans over me. "Did you hear me?" Concern flickers in his eyes.

I nod, then I groan inwardly. How loquacious of me.

He smiles down and places the flowing curls Jules

was able to give me with a curling iron around my ear. "I'm trying not to bring it up again, but have you thought about what I said to you at the diving platform?"

My tongue feels too swollen to make words. I lick my lips. "A little," I tell him.

He keeps his eyes on me. Not a hint of disappointment darkens his gaze. "I know you have a lot on your mind. It's okay."

I reach up to grab his forearm when it looks like he's going to turn away. "Are you and Reid okay? We didn't get a chance to talk about what happened at school on Monday."

His gaze flicks to where I'm holding him, then back to my face. "We're good, Briar. We'll always be good. You don't have to worry about that."

I nod, but there's no way I won't worry about that. When Reid punched Lex, it was like the world as I knew it began to crumble. It was then that I realized I had basically set my life up around these guys. Then, when the world felt like it was going to shit around me after Brady's death, I tried to block them out. It made everything worse. I should've realized sooner they were staples in my life.

Lex cups my cheek, sending my heart racing. "That goes for us, too. If you decide we're better off like this, I'll still be here. You don't have to worry about that. I don't want you to worry about anything."

I give his arm a squeeze.

Loud cheers erupt around us, making me jump. When I look over at what's caught everyone's attention, I see Sasha and Reid going at it on the dance floor. Sasha is all over him, causing my hackles to rise. She dances to the floor, sashaying her hips. Her head is aligned with his junk, and I swear to God her tongue darts from her mouth, licking the bottom of his fly to the top of his belt while she dances back up his body.

And she somehow calls me the skank?

Lex mutters under his breath. Reid looks blissed out of his mind, his head tilted toward the ceiling, his eyes closed. "Is he drunk?" I ask.

"No," Lex says adamantly. "He'd never drink the night before a game."

I thought so too, but he clearly looks high on something.

He dips her afterward, then follows, kissing the copious amounts of cleavage the dress she's wearing today displays.

I look away after that, and Lex notices. "He's..." Lex trails off. "He's...healing, Briar. In a different way than all of us."

I can't believe Lex is standing in front of me

explaining away Reid's actions. It's like he wants me to know that Reid doesn't really like Sasha. Why would he do that if there's a little bit of competition between the two for me?

Maybe I read everything wrong.

Or, maybe Lex is just that good of a guy.

The song switches to a slow one, causing several of the football players to groan that their free show with Sasha and Reid is over. "Do you want to dance?" I ask Lex.

I look over and see that Cade is already dancing with Jules, even though there's about three feet between them and it looks awkward as fuck, almost like they're at a middle school dance.

When I look back at Lex, he's still staring at me. He leans down, pressing a chaste kiss to my lips. It's like he's thanking me for asking him. I blink after he pulls away. I was so not expecting that. Then, he leads me further into the circle near where Cade and Jules are dancing and holds me to him, his hands around my waist. His thumbs make tiny circles against the fabric of my dress, making my nerves pitch higher and higher. I start with my hands on his shoulders, but then I wrap my hands around his neck as we turn in slow circles.

My gaze happens to lift at the same time I'm facing Reid and Sasha. Reid's glaring our way while Sasha has her head leaned away across his shoulders. His stare is hard, and it makes me swallow some guilt down. Lex said nothing would come between him and Reid, but why does it feel like he's lying to me? At least from Reid's point of view because he seriously looks like he could kill Lex right now and be okay with it.

I turn away from Reid. Lex holds me closer to him. I'm betting it's because he felt the slight difference in my posture, from relaxed to stiff, while meeting Reid's gaze. He rubs my back for a moment then settles back on my hips, but I still can't get Reid's gaze out of my head.

18

he day starts out with a group text from Reid that includes Jules and me, and Lex and Cade. He's telling Jules and I that he secured a place for us to sit, front and center, in the stands tonight during the homecoming game. It's roped off, apparently.

I nibble on my lip while reading it. My parents have decided not to come, which is fine. To each their own. Jules seems excited for it, so even if I didn't want to go, I'd go to support her. Us girls have to stick together. But the main reason why his text has me on edge is because I know I need to tell him happy birthday, but I also don't want to do it through text. That seems like a copout. I also don't want him to think I forgot about him.

I go back and forth on it all morning, sometimes picking my cell up to just send him a text already, but then putting it back down without a word being written. We may not agree on the way Reid got me out of my funk, but I know his heart was in the right place. I mean, I'm pretty sure it was. With Reid, it's a fifty-fifty chance, but I like my odds.

Deciding I'll tell him in person, I get myself ready for the game. Since the guys are busy, my dad drops me off at the school. He blows out a breath when he sees the line of cars and the pop of purple and yellow as people make their way to the small stadium. "You could come," I suggest.

He shakes his head. "I'm waiting for your mother." He looks over at me, a small smile spreading his lips. "I'm...really proud of the way you've turned around lately, Briar. I know it's not easy since we lost Brady, but I think you're headed in the right direction. Finally."

I smooth my SHH t-shirt down, avoiding his eyes. "Thanks, Dad." I could tell him I'm sorry for running away. I could apologize to him for a lot of things, but I'm not sure I actually am sorry for them. Not a lot of people would understand, but it felt like I needed to do those things. "I'm working on it."

He rubs my shoulder briefly, then I get out of the car. I walk toward the field by myself after shooting Jules a quick text that I'll wait for her by the main gate. My phone buzzes in my pocket. Thinking it's a response from Jules, I pull it out. It's not. It's a message from Ezra. Finally. **Sorry. I've been crazy busy. You're fucking hot.**

I narrow my eyes at the message. It took him that long to respond, and *that's* what he said. I shake my head. I'm thinking it was definitely stupid to try to meet Ezra in Calcutta, but I'm not going to lie and say I didn't like the time away from everything. I know I worried everyone to death, but while I was there, by myself, I was able to work a lot of things out in my head, too. I don't know. Maybe that's one thing I could thank Ezra for. It's certainly not going to be him telling me that I'm "fucking hot" weeks after I sent him a tittie pic.

Jesus. What the fuck was I thinking? I blame it on the booze. And on wanting to just feel like someone liked me. It's stupid and, yeah, maybe a little shallow, but losing Brady left a big hole in my heart, and I have to fill it up somehow. At least, that's what I'm beginning to understand.

While I'm waiting for Jules to show, I see the guys

exit out of the locker room. I run over to the path they always take to get to the field, the same one I actually ran myself when Reid took me out of detention. A few of the guys greet me as they run past, but I'm waiting for one in particular who has a birthday message coming to him. Cade approaches me first. His eyes are glassy, taking me a little off-guard. He throws his arms around me, which is slightly uncomfortable with all the pads he has on. I squeeze him tight, matching the ferocity of his hug, and it reminds me of when Brady used to hug me while he was still in his gear. "Hey, Shortie. Thanks for coming."

"Where else would I be?" I say, trying to keep myself in check. I don't know what they have in mind for dedicating the game to him, but I'm hoping I can get through it without waterworks.

He pulls away and cups my cheek. "I haven't said this to your face yet, but I'm really proud of you. I... uh...can't imagine what it's like, and all in all, you were — You just— Fuck."

I laugh at that, and he looks at me with his deep brown eyes mixed with shards of black that match his hair. "I know," I say to him.

He leans over and kisses me on the cheek.

I blink when he runs away from me. The spot

where he kissed tingles, but I can't dwell on that fact because Lex is in front of me. He pulls my hands up and kisses my knuckles once on each hand. He smiles then. "Remember when we used to call you our lucky charm?"

My smile grows bigger at the memory. It started when they were in middle school. I happened to be watching them practice once when Reid threw this amazing pass to Brady. It was super long, and Brady caught it effortlessly. After celebrating in the end zone like a bunch of middle school kids, they turned toward me, insistent that it was all my doing because Reid had never thrown a pass that far yet, and Brady hadn't made a touchdown off a Hail Mary before either. They explained to me after that that I was expected at all their games, home or away. No excuses. It was fun at the time. It made me feel special. "Yeah, I do," I tell him. They haven't called me that in years, but the memory, instead of making me sad, makes me smile.

He runs his thumb over my lower lip. "I'm glad you're here."

"Me too," I tell him, and I know in my heart I'm not lying. There really is no other place I'd rather be right now. "Good luck, Big Man," I tell him, using the phrase I coined around that same time.

After Lex runs away, Reid is next. He saunters up to me after patiently waiting his turn. I feel like things are a mess between us right now. I don't know quite how to feel when I look at him. Turned on? Conflicted? But I do know what I want to say to him. "I came over here because I wanted to tell you happy birthday." I tack on a smile when I look up at him.

His eyes widen. "You remembered my birthday?"

I shrug. It's not like I haven't been celebrating it with him for years. He shouldn't be that surprised. "Well, yeah. Of course."

His chest inflates in front of me. The shoulder pads he has on makes him that much bigger than me. He has black lines under his eyes to help keep the sun out while he reads the field during plays. "We're all celebrating tonight, whether we win or lose," he tells me. "You and Jules should come. It feels...better when you guys are there." I nod. I know what he means. He starts to turn away, but he stops himself. "Thanks, Briar." His gaze drags over me, setting my skin on fire.

His throat works. He shifts away, then back to me. He opens his mouth like he's about to say something, but a throat clears behind him. We both look back and see Coach Jackson waiting there.

"Sorry, Coach," he says immediately before taking off and running onto the field.

I give Coach Jackson an apologetic smile and go to turn away from him, but he stops me. "Briar," he calls out. When I shift back to him, he says, "I was actually waiting to talk to you." I stand up straight, not knowing what's going to be said, but wanting to be prepared for anything he might say. "Reid told you that we're doing a little something for Brady at the beginning of the game. I wondered if you could follow me, so you can accept the dedication?"

"The dedication?"

My lips feel numb, and my head spins.

"Yeah. It's a plaque. Reid told me he discussed it with your parents and they weren't ready to be here yet, but I was hoping you would do it. If not, Reid will, but..." He looks up, and I follow his gaze. Reid has one hand on the gate, getting ready to go out onto the field, but he's looking back at us like he's waiting for my answer too. "...we were all kind of hoping you would."

I nod before he even making the conscious decision that I'd do it. Eventually, I say yes and follow Coach Jackson to the field and the Spring Hill sidelines. Brady's teammates accept me there, pulling me into their folds. Not just his best friends, but every single one of them, even the ones I've seen naked—acciden-tally. They clap me on the back, most of them looking contrite and sad. I don't know what was said in the locker room, but it must've been something about Brady that has them all thinking about him right now. Not surprising since they're going to be doing something for him before the game starts, but my heart feels full and about ten seconds from bursting.

Quickly, I pull out my phone and text Jules that she'll have to sit without me in the beginning because they want me to accept a plaque on behalf of Brady. She sends me a few crying emojis, but then tells me her parents decided to come with her anyway, so they'll be in the spot Reid picked out for us when I'm done.

I watch from the sidelines as the football goes through their warm-up exercises. Spring Hill is on one side of the field while the Red Raiders are on the other. Nerves tighten the muscles in my stomach. I'm usually not so nervous for the football games because of how amazing our team is, but this time, I am. Maybe it's because of all the other emotions swirling around and how much I know the team will want to win this one for Brady.

When the officials walk onto the field, I plant my feet and bob up and down on my tiptoes. The cheerleaders start a cheer to get the crowd revved up, and it's at the end of that when the announcer from the top of the stands calls everyone's attention to the middle of the field for a tribute to Brady Page. My feet feel stuck in place. I had no idea they were going to get right to it like this. A few of the players pull me in close, and then we all lock hands around each other's backs while Cade, Lex, and Reid make their way to center field where Coach Jackson already is.

My heart is in my throat when he starts to talk. There's also a damn news camera in my face, reminding me how it was right after Brady suffered his aneurysm. The damn newspapers and television stations called my parents every day and even showed up at his funeral. I suck in a breath just like I did back then, avoiding them. I don't know why the news is so fascinated by grief that they always want to put it right in everyone's faces.

I block them out as best I can and focus on Coach Jackson. "As many of you know, we lost not only a great player last year, but also just a terrific human... Brady Page. I'm going to ask his sister, Briar, to step out here and accept this plaque, commemorating the dedication of the new flag staff outside of the football field to Brady. That way, for years to come, others will know his love and dedication to not only this game but to Spring Hill."

The players next to me step away, and suddenly, I feel like I can't do this. Everyone is staring at me, and I don't have anyone to lean on. Someone puts his hand on my back and whispers to me that I can do it, but I'm stuck. I can't fucking move. I hear the people in the stands clapping. On the other side of the field, people have risen to their feet, so I can only imagine what it looks like behind me, but all there is is a deafening buzz.

Coach Jackson is smiling at me, clapping his hands in a slow rhythm. The guys are clapping, too, but when they see I'm not moving, they step toward me, like their thoughts were all aligned. One brief hesitation, and they're right there. Like always. Like they were before when I didn't even realize it. Getting me out of bed, making me take a shower. Going to school. Hell, I probably needed a little hard talk like Reid gave me.

The rest of the team steps back as Reid, Lex, and Cade approach. It might just be my imagination, but I swear the crowd claps even louder. Even the players on the other team are showing their respect. It's not surprising. With the small town that Spring Hill is, everyone knows these three boys and Brady. They know they grew up together, inseparable and unstoppable.

I'm afraid I might ugly cry when Cade, Lex, and Reid get to me, wrap their arms around me and each other and walk me out to the fifty yard line, but instead, I gather some of Brady's courage and tamp the torrent of emotions that threaten to take me down.

When we get to the middle of the field, Coach Jackson hands me the plaque. I accept it, hands shaking, and turn toward the SHH stands. I was right. The sight would make anyone want to cry. There's such an outpouring of love that it chisels away at the armor I put up when we first got the phone call from Coach saying Brady was rushed to the hospital. Tears track down my face, and I hold the plaque to me. Behind me, the guys all take the microphone for a few words. Words that make me want to hug each and every one of them for loving my brother so much. For making the short time he had here on Earth worth it. It's like the eulogies from his funeral all over again. It's been months and months since I've felt that much love.

When Coach offers the microphone to me, Reid tries to intercede, but I'm okay, actually. I really am. I smile at him gratefully and take it, turning back toward the crowd. "On behalf of Brady, I just want to thank everyone for this thoughtful gesture. My brother would love every second of this." I smile through the pain tearing at my heart. Sometimes grief is just that. A happy memory mixed with desperation because you know you'll never get to make memories like that again. "He'd probably walk around the house for days like he won the lottery." The crowd laughs, but most importantly, the richness of the three distinguishable deep chuckles that come from behind me matter most. I turn around. "Thank you to everyone who's supported my family over the past year, but most importantly, the three players standing in front of us right now. I don't think my family could've gotten through it without you. You already know Brady loved you guys, but in case you need to hear it again, he did. So much."

My voice breaks then, and even though there's still so much more I want—no, need—to say, I give the microphone up and hand it back to Coach Jackson. I have time to tell these guys exactly how I feel. I don't need to say it all here in front of everyone.

We all walk off, and the crowd cheers again. I stop once more, Brady's plaque in hand, in the team's huddle and smile. "I guess it's about that time that Brady would be wanting you to kick this team's ass."

I walk away to several pats on the back and shoulder, blinking away my tear fractured vision so I can make my way to Jules now, but Reid catches up to me. He spins me around and hovers over me. The look in his eyes pins me in place. His throat works. He wants to say something, I can tell it's killing him that he can't get his brain and mouth to work together in this very moment. Coach calls him back to the huddle, so I just nod. "I know, Reid. You got this."

He runs his hand over my head, clutches my hair at the nape of my neck, and then squeezes my shoulder before running back to his teammates.

Sometimes, a touch says everything.

19

I walk up to the bleachers, expecting to see Jules front and center just like Reid said. Instead, I see a stuffy man and woman who are dressed over the top for the occasion. It's a high school football game for crying out loud and they're dressed as if they're headed into important business meetings. When Sasha calls out and waves to them, making sure I notice, I get it. She placed her parents there. I don't know why I didn't recognize them in the first place.

Bitch.

All I really wanted was to climb the bleachers and throw my arms around Jules and show her the plaque. I see her sitting just behind them. When she catches my gaze, she shrugs. Ordinarily, I wouldn't care. I probably really shouldn't care, but I'm sick of Sasha and her bullshit. This day is supposed to be about Brady and his friends and family, and here she puts her family front and center. I have no doubt Reid told her it was supposed to be for us. This is a move on her part to tell me she doesn't give a fuck.

I walk right up to her mid-cheer. She glares at me, only stopping her cheer once I make it impossible for her to move even though her team continues around her. "What the fuck do you think you're doing?" I ask.

She gives me a half grin. Oh, she knows. She knows exactly what she's doing. "You can't be here right now, Skank. In case you haven't noticed, this is the cheer-leading area."

"In case you haven't noticed, though I'm sure you have because you have to be smarter than you look, your parents are sitting in the area Reid roped off for Jules and I."

She fake draws a breath in and puts a hand over her mouth. "Was that what that was? Oops?"

I want to tell her I'll march right up to Reid now and tell him what she's done, even though there's no way I would do that. It would be just a bluff, one that might work, but I'll handle this myself. I turn on my heel and make a beeline straight toward her parents instead. "Mr. and Mrs. Pontine? You probably don't know me. I'm Briar Page."

"Oh, yes, dear. We're so sorry about your brother."

I force a smile out. "Thank you. Listen—"

Someone stomps up the bleachers behind me. "What are you doing?"

I ignore Sasha's screech. "Your daughter was mistaken when she sat you here. Reid blocked this area off for us." I point behind them to Jules. "My brother's girlfriend and I, so that we could watch this important game from these seats. I'm sure you understand."

Sasha nudges me out of the way. "Mom, Dad, you don't have to move."

I tilt my chin in the air. "Yeah, they do."

Jules's mother looks positively embarrassed, and yeah, I know this whole thing is petty and that I can just sit next to Jules in the seats above these ones, but you know what? Sasha could've just put her parents there too. I'm not going to let her bitch ass win anymore.

"We weren't aware," Mr. Pontine says stiffly. His throat is all red. People are staring now. A few people are whispering, which I can tell he hates. He looks around, his skin growing ashier.

Someone yells from behind them, "Let the sister sit there!"

I smile up at them and give a short wave before turning back around.

"It's just a seat, my dear," Mrs. Pontine says, and I can tell already where Sasha gets her fucking bitchiness from. "But if it means that much to you."

"It does," I say sweetly.

Her parents look at each other while Sasha scoffs behind me. "Don't move," she tells her parents.

They're not about to turn this into a big thing though. It's something Sasha should learn. Right behind them, I see Jules whispering something to her parents, hopefully telling them that there's a reason I'm doing this.

In front of me, Sasha's parents stand at the same time and move into the aisle. I plop my butt down just as content as can be, but Sasha grabs my shirt and yanks me toward her, whispering harshly in my ear. "You need to learn that Reid doesn't own this school. I do. Fucking with my parents is the wrong move."

When she lets me go, I brush my shoulder off. Loudly, I say, "I'm so sorry you think you're more important than everyone else."

People are still looking, and what I've said causes even more whispering and dirty looks their way. Sasha's father turns her around on the stairs and gives her a slight shove, telling her to get her ass moving and stop making a scene. She gives a withering look over her shoulder at me.

Jules climbs down to sit next to me, her eyebrows raised. "Dude. That was spectacular."

I smile at her and then look over my shoulder, prepared to apologize to Jules's parents, but her mother is already shaking her head. "No need, Briar. Jules told us how that cheerleader is bullying you at school."

People gasp around us, and I swear I see the muscles of Mr. and Mrs. Pontine lock up as they walk down the bleachers. There are no more available seats in the crowd. Too bad. I see them stand near the gate for a little while, but eventually, they leave. I happen to be looking at Sasha when she realizes they're gone, and if she didn't turn a look of death toward me right afterward, I might have felt sorry for her. Might have. It's just so difficult to feel badly for someone who's such a terrible person.

After the drama at the beginning of the game recedes, the drama is left on the field where it should be. Spring Hill High is playing their hearts out. Since the last game I watched, everything seems more intense. The plays Reid calls out are short and curt with the ferocity of a tiger growl behind them. I have no idea what they mean individually, but I do know RHH is doing a great job because when the buzzer sounds for half time, we're winning by two touchdowns. The game would be perfect if I could just drown the cheerleaders out.

Jules's dad goes to the concession stand during halftime and brings back a bunch of food for us to enjoy. While he's gone, Jules knocks my knee with her own. "That ceremony was really nice. I was thinking that if they let us, maybe we could plant flowers next to the flag staff, kind of like a memorial garden."

"Yeah, we should definitely do that," I tell her.

Her eyes are a little glassy as she nods. "Jeez, Brady really loved game days, didn't he?" She smiles, but it's like a camera flash, one second it's there, the next, it's disappeared.

"Yeah, he really did."

Jules's mom starts to rub her back, so I pull her head onto my shoulder, and then place mine on top of hers while I squeeze her hand. Lex happens to look up from the sidelines. He's pouring sweat, his hair soaked against his head like he just got out of the shower. He gives us a small smile and then turns to Cade and Reid as they all suck water down from green bottles. I don't know what he says to them, but the guys look up after that, nodding to themselves.

"Such good boys," Jules's mom says. "They always have been."

I snicker at that, but I hide it. They are good guys;

however, they can be bad too. They have faults like everyone else. They also have a whole lot of love between them too. A brotherhood that somehow, I think I just managed to squeak into from a young age. They can't get rid of me now. "I think we're going to win this one," I say.

"Think?" Jules asks. "We got this one in the bag."

The next half, we devour the food Jules's father brings us and cheer our team on like our lives depend on it. This second half is a little back and forth from the beginning. The other team is trying to fight back, but they don't have what we have. At the end, SHH pulls away again, putting an exclamation point on their seventeen-point win.

Because so much of the crowd are students, they rush the field. Jules and I hang back. We've never been "rush the field" type of people. I notice Sasha takes off though, trying to get to Reid no doubt. I tell myself not to look even though I find myself looking to see what happens. The guys deserve this moment. They played tremendously.

The team hikes Reid up on their shoulders, and I laugh as they try to keep him up there. He's a big dude, but the players holding him up are big dudes, too, so it's probably a piece of cake for them. He whips his helmet off while he's up there and holds it in the air with a cry of triumph. Eventually, he's let down, and I see a bright purple bow approach him from the top of Sasha's head. Someone jumps in the way of my prying eyes, so I don't see everything that happens, but I do see the rest of the players envelop Cade, Lex, and Reid, leaving poor little Sasha behind.

I turn toward Jules, needing to look away for a moment. "Reid invited us to go to his birthday celebration. Are you in?"

Her face pales. "Shoot," she says. "I forgot it was Reid's birthday. I'll have to send him a text." She lowers her voice for this next part. "Are you sure he invited me, too? Or just you?"

She winks, and I roll my eyes. "He invited you, but even if he didn't, I am and that's all that matters."

She smiles, but instantly rubs her face. "I don't think I'm up to it, but I want you to go and have fun. You can tell me all about it afterward."

"You sure?" I'm torn. I wish she would go with me, but I also don't want to force her either.

She nods. "A hundred percent."

She stands, and her parents follow her lead. I give her a hug and tell her I'll text her for sure. I say goodbye to her parents and then wait a few minutes, watching the celebration before following the crowd out the front gate. With the new plaque in hand, I head toward the flag staff. There, just outside the field is a little stone memorial with garden accents. The circular brick outline is filled with mulch but could easily look really nice with some planted flowers. I'll have to talk to the principal to see what Jules and I can do about that. We can make it our little project, changing out the flowers for each season.

"Thought we might find you here," a voice says.

I jump because I really wasn't expecting anyone to come over this way. Once the voice registers, though, I know exactly who it is. Cade Farmer.

I turn toward the sound of his voice and see all three approaching me with their football jerseys still on. "You guys did great," I say. "Congratulations on the win."

They shrug like it's no big deal, even though I can tell from their flushed faces that they're on cloud nine right now.

"Are you coming with us tonight?" Reid asks.

"Wouldn't miss it," I tell him. "Jules went home though."

They nod knowingly, and then we all look down at the stone marker with Brady's name on it. Instead of making me want to cry, I smile, feeling pride seep into me that I'm this guy's sister. This guy who was special enough to warrant a dedication near the school's football field.

"I think I'm lucky," I tell them. Or maybe I'm not even telling them. I'm just voicing my thoughts aloud. "To have had Brady as my brother, I mean."

Lex puts his arm around my shoulders and squeezes me to him. It's a little uncomfortable with his huge pads, but it's normal, so I don't balk at it. "We were all lucky, Briar."

We stay there for a little while longer until we turn as a unit and head toward the locker room entrance. When we walk in, I look up briefly only to groan and cover my eyes again. "So many penises. Why? Every freaking time."

Cade chuckles low. "That's what you get for going into the boys' locker room, Shortie. As many dicks as you—"

"If you say want, I'll throat punch your ass," Reid says.

Cade laughs once again as Lex releases my shoulder. "I would never say that to my best friend's little sister. You're the ones who want to fuck her."

And just like that, the locker room miraculously quiets as if the universe is determined to make me want to get swallowed up and die.

I hear a voice I don't recognize and can't tell who it

came from because my eyes are still shielded by my hand. "Can anyone put their hats into the ring?"

The room goes eerily silent. I look through a space between my fingers and see a glimpse of the look Reid is giving the guy. No wonder why no one laughed at that. They're probably really worried about pissing Reid the fuck off. "In case it isn't clear," Reid says. "Briar's off limits."

Someone else chuckles. "I wonder what Sasha will think of that."

A low growl comes from the back of Reid's throat. The sound of it sends a mix of perverse pleasure through me, like I can feel it right in my core. I feel ridiculous just standing there with my hands over my eyes, so I say, "Is someone going to walk me to a place to sit or do you really want me to stare at all the dick while you guys change?"

This elicits a round of laughter from the other players, but a firm grip grabs me by the forearm and navigates me away from the other guys. This is starting to feel normal now, hanging out with these guys, having them make comments about me. It never would've flown if Brady were alive. No way in hell I would be in this locker room right now if he were still on the football team. He'd be furious, but I guess this is just one of the ways life is changing without him. I actually quite like being in the locker room, knowing what's just beyond the row of purple lockers in front of me.

When I blink my eyes open after someone maneuvers me to a sitting position, I see Cade walking away backwards. He winks and mouths, "Call me". I roll my eyes at him and smile.

"Don't take too long," I quip back.

"Ooh, mouthy. I like it."

"Farmer," Reid snaps. Then, the whole room erupts into laughter again.

Yeah, the guys are having a ball with this. It's just good fun though. Reid is their leader. There's no way anyone would do anything to piss him off on purpose. That's just not how it works here at SHH.

20

*A*fter the guys get dressed, all the players split up into cars in the parking lot and we head out of town. It isn't until we're a few miles out that I think to ask where we're going. I just assumed we'd be going to Reid's house since it's his birthday, but we're headed in the other direction.

"One of the guys on the team, his uncle just bought a cabin out on the lake, so we're headed there," Cade says from the driver's seat. Lex is sitting next to him in the passenger seat and Reid is sitting in the back with me.

"Oh," I say. That's a surprise.

"Don't worry," Lex says. "I grabbed your suit if you want it. You left it in the car from the other day when we went to the beach."

I smile at him through the rearview mirror. As I do, Reid's phone goes off. He swears and pulls it out, sighing when he sees the name on the screen. "What?" he answers.

Yikes. I wouldn't want to be the person on the other end of the line.

"We're on our way to the cabin." He pauses, and I hear a high, tinny voice. "No, we're not turning around to get you. Aren't you getting a ride with Chelle or something?"

I look away, out the window. It's definitely Sasha on the other end of this phone conversation.

He hangs up after that, not even bothering to say goodbye. Lex turns his head. "You have to do something about that."

Even though Lex is speaking clearly, I'm not sure what he's trying to tell Reid to do about his girlfriend. It's on the tip of my tongue to tell these guys what she did to the area Reid roped off for us, but I don't. I handled it. "Do something about what?" I ask. I figure if they're going to talk about it in front of me, they can at least give me the courtesy of telling me what it is. Also, I'm nosy. Especially if it has something to do with Reid and Sasha.

He's so much better than her.

I look up to him, hoping to convey what I'm

thinking with my eyes, but he avoids my stare. "That's my business, Lex."

Lex just shrugs and turns back around in the seat. The car is pretty quiet after that. Cade doesn't even turn the radio on, but my heart starts beating in my ears when I feel Reid touch my hand that's pressed against the seat. It's just a whisper of a touch, but it doesn't stop. I look down, trying to avoid any sudden movements. Sure enough, Reid is pressing his pinky into mine. I swallow, the butterflies in my stomach threatening to shoot right out.

He turns my palm over and drags his fingers across me. I sit there, motionless, definitely speechless, as he touches me. He's flirting with me. Coming on to me even. When I do sneak a peek his way, he's not looking at me either. He's glancing casually out the window like playing his rough fingertips over my hand is just something he does.

Holy shit.

He plays with my hand the whole way to this cabin on the lake, which, by the way, isn't a cabin at all. It's freaking humongous with several bedrooms, a game room, copious living areas, and a huge dock out the back that leads right out onto the lake. When we get there, people are already inside partying. The guy at the door is taking five-dollar bills, so he can get the place cleaned after we leave. That's actually a great idea.

I pull out my wallet to pay, but Reid puts his hand over mine, grabs a twenty out of his own wallet and pays for all of us as we walk in even though the guy tries to tell him he doesn't have to pay. Disregarding the guy's objections, Reid puts the twenty in his hand and doesn't look back. We follow after him as he heads straight for the kitchen for a beer. It's late afternoon now, and the sun is hanging low in the sky. The back room is all windows with sliding glass doors, so it's easy to see the beautiful horizon with its orange and pink hues. It's going to be a spectacular sunset out tonight. I really wish Jules had wanted to come. She was so confident and had fun at the dance, but maybe that alongside the game just took it out of her. In a way, I can't blame her. A month ago, I would've pitched a fit if the guys told me they wanted me to come to this. I would've done everything I could to get out of it, including wearing the rattiest clothes I own.

They saw through that shit though.

The party is really fun for about forty-five minutes while we play beer pong out on the back deck. I'm actually pretty good at it which shocks the shit out of the guys. In a way, I get better the more I drink. I think it's because my inhibitions are crumbling. I'm not wondering what other people are thinking of me, which I tend to do a lot even though I act like I don't. However, the party starts to get shitty for me as soon as Sasha shows up. She marches right up to Reid and chastises him about not giving her a ride. He ignores her as we play. Right now, we're on opposite teams, and with the way we're both being super competitive about it, you would think there's something else at stake.

"Jeez, lay off him," Cade says. "It's the guy's birthday."

"I know," she snaps. "And I had something planned I don't want him to miss."

I take a huge gulp of my beer after that. She hasn't even acknowledged my existence, which is fine by me. If she kept ignoring me, that would be fantastic. In fact, if she let Reid go, that would be even better.

Eventually, when Reid ignores her enough, she grabs her friend Chelle's hand and announces that they're going to go get drunk, so that they can pull off what she has planned later. Lex lifts his eyebrows after they're gone. "What exactly does she have planned?"

"Fuck if I know," Reid says.

His gaze meets mine. There are sparks there. Definitely. He makes my lower stomach heat. I know he's with Sasha. Technically. I guess there's no technically about it when a couple is boyfriend and girlfriend, but what about the fact that they are two people who shouldn't be together? What about if I think the guy who has a girlfriend wants to be with me?

I line up my shot, take it, and drop it in the front cup. I throw my hands in the air. "Winner, bitches."

I'm teamed up with another guy from the team. He and I slap hands as we watch Cade and Reid down the rest of the cups left over.

"We brought a ringer to the fucking party and didn't even know it," Cade says grudgingly.

"I guess I am pretty good." My face lights up with fake enthusiasm. "Who knew sports were my thing? Maybe I should play football."

The guys all stare at me, wide eyed. "Bad idea, Shortie," Cade says. "You're too...petite."

I scoff at him. "You didn't hear about the girl a few towns over who helped the all-boys basketball team win state?"

Lex smirks. "Quintessa Dale? Who didn't hear about that? It was all over the fucking news."

"Not gonna lie, I'd tap that," Cade says.

The guy next to me laughs. "Are you kidding me, the whole team is probably already tapping that."

I narrow my gaze at him, and he lifts his hands in surrender. I have no idea who the girl's dating, or if she's dating at all, but just because she's on the team with a bunch of guys doesn't mean she's fucking all of them. How misogynistic.

Though if she were, more power to her.

"Keep it up," Lex says. "Briar won't want to be your partner and you're shit without her."

Their teammate playfully gets down on his hands and knees and steeples his hands in front of him. "Forgive me?"

"Get your ass off the floor," Reid says, voice strained.

The guy gets to his feet, chuckling. Cade downs the last cup, and then Reid sits one out so Lex can join in. I try to tell them I'll bow out of this one, but they insist I keep playing. I'm a little worse this game because I feel Reid's eyes on me the entire time. He doesn't let up. It makes me nervous with the way he watches without words. I want to know what he's thinking. Why he flirted with me in the car, why he punched Lex in the school classroom that day. All these things should be obvious, but I want them to be spelled out for me. He's a hard read. Especially since he has a girlfriend, and as much as I hate Sasha, I'm not going beyond those boundaries.

While we continue to play, Sasha comes over with Chelle and a few other friends in tow. "Are you ready for your birthday present?" she asks. She's standing in front of him in a rose gold silk bathrobe. I lift my eyebrows at her over the brim of my cup as I take another drink. Something tells me I'm going to need a lot of alcohol to get through this night.

Reid's gaze rakes up and down her. "What are you doing?" he growls under his breath.

She smiles wide then spins to address everyone on the deck. "Attention, everyone. In case you didn't know it, it's our quarterback's birthday today!"

The crowd that's outside starts cheering, and a few people begin to gather around. It's my turn to shoot, but I can't tear my eyes off of what's going on.

"Are you ready, baby?" she asks. "Here's your birthday present. Boys," she says, nodding to two guys. The two guys, linebackers on the team, I think, take the ends of the bench Reid is sitting on and turn it toward her.

He's scowling. I can tell he hates this. His face is growing red, crimson splotches creeping up his neck, escalating even moreso as Chelle starts playing a song from her phone. The first few beats of the music play and on a bass drop, Sasha drops her robe.

My mouth drops to the fucking deck. She's dressed in a thong and a skimpy, sequined bra top with SHH colors. She walks toward him with what's supposed to be a sexy walk in her high heels. She dances up close to him, practically shoving her tits into his face before she saunters off, climbs up on the nearby pool table and drops her ass practically to the ground like there's a stripper pole in front of her.

Guys cat call her. I see a few girls roll their eyes, but her little bitch crew is smiling and clapping to the music. They probably all choreographed this. Even though my eyes wander there, they go right back to Reid. He's glaring at Sasha like I've never seen him do before. He's fuming, and every time a guy calls out something, I see his hands clench to fists.

Eventually, he gets up and walks away, completely averting his eyes from the scene before him. Sasha's mouth drops as she undulates on top of the pool table. She stands up. "Reid?!"

He walks inside the house. Lex appears next to me and lowers his voice even though no one is paying attention to us. "This isn't going to be pretty."

Sasha jumps down from the pool table and almost turns an ankle on her super high high heels. Chelle struggles with the phone, trying to turn the sexy music off. Cade and Lex take off after them, so of course I follow. It seems like everyone else does too. "Reid Parker!" Sasha snaps. "Stop!"

Reid turns suddenly, and she runs right into him.

She sputters at the angry glint in his eye. "What

are you doing? I'm giving you your birthday present. That was rude," she says, finally realizing there's a crowd of people around them now.

"A strip tease?" he seethes. He steps away from her. "That wasn't for me. That was for you because you just love being the center of attention. You love having every guy in here want to fuck you. Well, congratulations, they can fuck you because I won't anymore."

Her head snaps back like he's punched her. A few of the onlookers gasp, but everyone is straight up gawking at what's going on. "You don't mean that."

He shakes his head. "I should've done this a long time ago. You're selfish, self-centered, and you think I don't know you fucked that guy at that party right after Brady died last year. I know. I've known this entire time."

"Oh, shit," someone says.

I have to agree. *Holy shit.*

Sasha looks around, noticing the crowd that's gathered are now scowling at her. Even though there are tears in her eyes, she sticks her chin in the air. "You're just weak. I only fucked him because you couldn't get it up."

"My fucking best friend *just* died!"

An uneasiness starts in my chest. I stare at Reid. I feel terrible for him. I knew Sasha didn't give a fuck

245

about me when it came to Brady's death, but I thought for sure she was somewhat remorseful for Reid's sake.

I move forward because Reid looks like he's going to lose it. Cade and Lex flank me like we're running a football play. I place my hand on his chest. "Hey." His eyes burn into me, and his face softens.

I see Reid's growing reaction before I feel or hear anything. "You bitch," Sasha snarls. She grabs my hair and yanks my head back. Cade and Lex are right there, freeing me, but it doesn't help Sasha from spewing her hate. "Are you fucking her? You have a lot of nerve, talking shit about me fucking someone when you're fucking your best friend's sister."

I spin around after they free me, but Reid maneuvers between us, blocking me. "I'm not fucking her, but I want to be. You want power and prestige, and money and makeup, but you're missing the point of life. You should want to help people and be brave and not use your fucking body or your family to get whatever the fuck you want."

"You're nothing," she seethes. "*She's* fucking nothing." She shakes her head. The tears, which were probably fake anyway, are already dry on her face. Replaced there is a mask of fury that just makes her that much uglier. "You'll see, Reid. I hope you know what you're doing. Actually," she laughs. "I don't. I hope you go fucking down." She leans around him to glare at me. "And I think you'll find Briar isn't the perfect person you think she is."

He shifts to move in front of her again. "I know exactly what I'm doing. Leave us alone. If it wasn't clear before, we're done. Don't call me anymore. I mean it this time. Don't blow up my phone like you usually do after I try to break up with you."

She lets out a scream of rage and lunges at him, but Cade and Lex have her under control. The guy who was at the door collecting five-dollar bills comes up behind them. "Okay, enough." He throws Sasha over his shoulder and starts to carry her almost naked ass toward the front door. "Here's my birthday present to you, Cap," he says, calling out over his shoulder.

There's a smattering of applause, but mostly people are still in shock that the king and queen of SHH just had a very public meltdown. This is going to be all over the place on Monday.

Reid storms outside. I try to follow him, but Lex and Cade hold me back. "Just give him a minute," Lex explains. "He needs to blow off some steam."

I look into his eyes. When he meets my stare, there's a resignation there I haven't seen before. My lips thin. Maybe he even knew it before I did. I don't know.

*T*he celebratory party starts back up quickly after the show is over. My partner wants to keep playing beer pong, but I escape as soon as Lex and Cade turn their backs. I know they say to give Reid some time, but I feel like he needs someone right now even if he thinks he doesn't.

Plus, I'm being a little selfish too. I feel like I was definitely a part of their breakup somehow, which means Reid owes me some answers finally.

I walk outside, past the firepit and immediately spot him at the end of the dock. He would be hard to miss anywhere, but with the sun setting behind him, he's lit up like a halo of light with his hands in his pockets, staring out at the water.

He hears my footsteps as I approach. His back

stiffens at the intrusion. Then, he says, "I'm not in the fucking mood."

"I know," I say.

He tenses even more then, twisting his head to look over his shoulder at me. I have to bite my lip because of how perfect he looks right now. Cut muscles, tailored waist, and angular face to die for. I must have been ultra-oblivious when Brady was alive. How could all three of my brother's best friends be this hot and it just never occurred to me to crush on them? He glares at me. "It's not a good idea for you to be out here right now. Around me."

I step closer, disregarding his warning. A muscle ticks in his jaw. "Why's that, Superstar?"

"I just told the whole party I want to fuck you, and you still have to ask me that question?"

A fierce longing strangles me. This is more than before. A lot more than what I felt with Lex, and the things that happened previously with Reid? This feeling makes those seem like a tease, a precursor to this overwhelming heat enveloping me right now. "I don't have a lot of practice, but I think we have to start somewhere first before we just jump into fucking."

His eyebrow cocks, questioning me like I've just laid down a challenge. "Not necessarily."

"I lied to you once." I'm side by side with him now.

He tilts his head at me. "I haven't actually had sex before."

He smirks. "No shit, Briar. You weren't fooling anyone with that."

I narrow my eyes at him. I don't know why I'm getting mad, I'm actually a really terrible liar. Plus, I'd forgotten that these guys pretty much know everything about me. They would know if I'd had sex, unless of course, I did it while I'd been a runaway. They have no idea what happened in those days of my life. They're just for me. "I probably could've fooled someone," I insist. "Peter Phillips maybe."

He shakes his head. "No one who really knows you though."

"I think I forgot about that fact," I tell him. This is the moment for me to be completely honest about everything. I pushed these guys away. I pretty much ensured that they'd battle their way back into my life. "I forgot how well you guys knew me. I know now. In my head, I believed you were just Brady's friends, but maybe..." I hesitate because if I'm wrong about this, it might break me. "Maybe you were my friends too?"

He turns toward me. He reaches his hand out, pulling me by the shoulder into an embrace that warms me from the inside. I feel the brush of his lips on the top of my head, and I shiver. "You were *always* our friend too." He pulls away, but he doesn't get very far and not just because my hands are around his waist now. I don't want to let him go. He slides his hands through the hair above my ear and cups the back of my head. "I have something to confess." Pausing for a moment, he looks away, but when he faces me fully again, his green gaze is hard, confident and sexy as hell. "I wanted to be more than a friend, Briar." He takes a deep breath, brushing his chest over my mine. My nipples harden at the contact. "It started late Freshman year. You just...grew up. I don't know if it's because you were all of a sudden in the same grade as us, but you weren't the little sister anymore. You weren't even one of us to me, you were more."

My lips tingle. He keeps glancing at them, making me acutely aware that they're there and ready for him to claim. The feeling spreads, and my whole body buzzes with anticipation. I think Reid fucking Parker is going to kiss me out here under the prettiest sunset I've seen in a while. Although, I haven't been looking for the pretty in my life lately. Maybe that's all about to change right now.

He grips me hard. "God, I want you." He shifts his hips closer to me, and I can feel how much he means that. He's rock hard, and with just that motion, he's already fanning the embers in my core.

I lick my lips in preparation to say something, but how do you tell the guy you've been friends with your whole life that you'd like to see if there's something more there? Reid seems to be going with the straight on approach, but I just can't seem to get the words to come out of my mouth.

He curses low under his breath. His fingers keep moving over my hair like he's cherishing me. "I should tell you though." He licks his lips and stares down at me hesitantly. "Your brother didn't want me to pursue you."

I stare into his green eyes, feeling their pull. *Wait. What?*

Reid swallows. "I would hate myself forever if I didn't tell you that."

"Brady knew? He knew you liked me?"

Reid nods. "I wasn't going to move on his sister without telling him first. That'd be a dick move."

"And he said no." I don't even pose it as a question because I can see Brady saying that. I don't know his reasons. I'll never know his reasons, but when Brady was adamant about something, he stuck to his guns no matter what. He was a bit stubborn in that way. I guess our whole family is.

"Why?"

His jaw hardens. "Look at me," he says. "I'm not

good enough for you. You're super smart. You're going to college to pull off some Bill Gates shit, and the only reason I'd be getting out of Spring Hill is because I'm a muscle head."

"That's what Brady said?" I ask, disbelieving. Brady loved Reid. There's no way he'd put him down like that.

He shakes his head. "Not in so many words. He actually wouldn't really say why, just that he didn't think it was a good idea."

I pull him toward me. "It was probably just an older brother thing then. Maybe he didn't want to lose you to me."

Reid dismisses that idea with a quick shake of his head. "We'll never know, I guess. I dropped it after that, even though he watched me like a hawk around you. I didn't mean to fall into it with you again, Briar, I swear. But when you were so lonely, so broken up and you needed somebody, I couldn't stay away."

My hands move up his sides. "I'm glad you didn't." I don't want to think about where the hell I'd be if Lex, Reid, and Cade hadn't forced themselves back into my life.

He shakes his head and steps away. He's clearly still stuck on something. "I've been thinking about it. I've even talked to Lex about it. You should just be with him. He likes you. Really likes you, and we all know he's the better person out of all of us. Hell, he's like Mother Theresa in football pads."

Bile rises in my throat. It tastes like slow boiling anger. "Maybe I'll go be with Cade," I offer.

Reid practically growls at that, but he's not fazing me anymore. Shrugging, he says, "He's probably better for you than me too."

This is just so surreal. "How can the most popular guy at SHH have such a terrible opinion of himself?"

Reid lets go of me and forcibly steps back. "I have football, that's it."

"That's it? It's only the most important thing in Spring Hill, Reid. You're acting like you're some dumb jock, but you're not. You're a leader. You're—."

"Stop," he snarls at me.

He turns to walk away, but I walk up to him and shove him in the back. I'm not one for physical violence, but this all stems from when we were kids. I used to like to play rough with them, which sounds dirtier than it is. Sometimes you just have to do what you have to do to get their attention. He stumbles a few steps, probably only because he was taken off guard. He turns around slowly. I place my hands on my hips. "You're loyal. You're smart. You loved my brother so much that you made sure I was fine, even when I pushed back and pushed back. You have real talent, Reid. Not just Spring Hill talent, but you could go so far. Being gifted at a sport is impressive."

He walks straight toward me and gets in my face. "Then why does none of that seem to matter if my best friend couldn't even trust me with his sister?"

I suck in a breath. There's betrayal in his eyes. Wow. Brady really hurt him. I'm gathering that all this happened a long time ago, but it hurts Reid to this day, and now look. Reid will never get his answers. He'll never know why Brady said no.

"I trust you," I say. I move forward pressing my lips to his. It's an awkward exchange of pressed lips until Reid takes over. His resolve seems to crumble after a moment of hesitation. Then, he wraps his arms around me and pulls me closer, angling his head to deepen the kiss. His skilled tongue passes over the seam of my lips until I open for him. It's a free-for-all then. Our kiss seems to mimic Reid's inner turmoil. One second, it's passionate and all-out, kissing me with months of pent-up feelings. Then, it's slower, more cautious, like he thinks this will be our last kiss and he just wants to savor it while he can, imprinting it on his memory.

If I have anything to say about it, it definitely won't be our last kiss. This was what I was missing these past two years? Each pass of his tongue stokes the fire inside of me until I'm breathing so heavy I can barely scrape in breaths. Everywhere his hands glide over me, my skin sparks like it's a live wire. I moan into his mouth, my fingers creep up his neck until I lace my fingers behind him, making him stay in place, feeding my soul with his kiss. But it's more than that too. I'm feeding my soul with the fire inside Reid that makes him Reid Parker.

We kiss for minutes upon minutes. When he finally pulls away, my lips are swollen and satiated, and I'm light-headed on my feet. "Christ, Briar," he groans.

My first thought is to tell him I'm so glad he broke up with Sasha, but I tamp down that word vomit and smile instead. No need to bring up that name to ruin the moment. "You can say that again."

He stares at me, taking in every little nuance of my face. "When your brother first told me he didn't think you and I were a good idea, I had a brief thought about sneaking around with you, but I didn't think it would be worth losing my friendship with Brady over. After that kiss, it would've been fucking worth it. Worth *anything*." He plays with my hair again, tangling the darker tresses in his fingers. "What stopped me is that you never gave me any indication that you felt the same way. No lingering looks. No flirtations. Not anything."

He implores me with his green eyes like he needs

me to put an end to his suffering over this one point. Reid Parker doesn't look like the star quarterback right now. He's tense and unsure. He needs me right now instead of the other way around.

I give him a small smirk. "I've been wondering what world I was living in not to notice that my brother's three best friends were super hot. It's probably a good thing I didn't because there's no way Brady would've let me hang out with you guys if I was always drooling over one of you."

Reid's face temporarily pinches, but he brushes it off in the next second. He studies me, taking me in like I'm a world-renowned painting. "You're fucking perfect." His fingers tease over my collarbone, move to the center of my chest to trace down my cleavage, and stop just above my belly button. "I wish this whole party would fall away, and then it could be just you and me. I'd get you naked right here on this dock."

I peek around. There are people everywhere outside the house. Some are even wading into the water at the base of the dock we're standing on. We're nowhere near being alone, but I can't pretend my heart doesn't skip a few beats at his words. "Mmm, voyeurism."

He shakes his head. "Not my style. No one gets what I have, not even a look."

It suddenly makes sense why he gets so upset with Sasha. I thought the whole stripping for him thing was stupid myself because who wants to see her strip tease? But it went beyond that for Reid. He's territorial, which is probably why he punched Lex when he found out about us. I swallow. "You can't fight with Lex anymore."

Shadows cross over his face. "You have no idea how much I want to throttle him for touching you."

"It wasn't his fault."

"Funny. He told me it wasn't your fault. He says he took advantage of you while you were grieving. He feels sick about it."

I shake my head. "It was a mutual decision, but neither of us was in our right minds. I just wanted to forget. Don't...don't tell him that though." The last thing I want to do is hurt Lex.

Reid kisses my forehead. "He already knows, baby." He keeps his lips there, eyes closed. "He told me it wouldn't work between you two. Not that he wasn't hell-bent on trying."

"It wasn't one of my finer moments," I confess. Shame washes over me at the fact that he and I did that. "Lex is too nice. He didn't..." I trail off. I don't know exactly where to go with that. "If I'd known he actually liked me, I wouldn't have done any of that." I blow out a hard breath. "Which I guess makes me sound like the skank Sasha keeps telling me I am."

Reid turns my head toward him. "The fact that you're questioning whether it makes you sound easy means you're anything but."

I let that sink in, but I only half believe him. I think Reid Parker would pretty much do or say anything to make me feel better.

22

The next few weeks are a blur of schoolwork, football games, and Reid's kisses. We've only ever gone as far as some heavy makeout sessions. Hell, we did more when I didn't know he liked me like this. It's been frustrating, but what Brady said must've gotten into his head because it's not like I haven't been ready and waiting for more.

Things with Lex are fine even though we try not to be affectionate in front of him. Hell, we aren't affectionate at all in school. Jules still doesn't know what's going on, and I think, in a way, Reid is trying to save me from all the Sasha shit, so the only time we have together where we can act like a couple is when he comes to pick me up in the mornings or if either one of us ends up at the other's house after practice.

After pulling my grades back up to where they were in Freshman year, I've been begging my parents for a car. It's been pretty much non-stop, but I feel like they're giving in. It's a Monday morning, and Reid hasn't gotten here to pick me up yet, so I sit down with Mom and Dad for breakfast. Things seem more comfortable around here now that I feel like a human being again. "So..." Dad starts, his usually punchy early morning voice a bit reserved. My ears perk up, hoping this is the part where he tells me they're going to take me car shopping, but the conversation doesn't go that way at all. "Your mom and I have decided to go away for a little while. A couple's retreat."

I tilt my head at them. They're both making their morning coffees. Even though I absolutely love the smell of coffee, I just can't bring myself to drink it. I think it was all that talk about it stunting my growth when I was younger. "Yeah?" I ask, surprised at the sudden turn of events. We've only ever gone on family vacations before.

"For a week or so," Dad explains. He comes down to sit at the table with me while I eat my Cheerios. "Now that it looks like you're finally back on track, we'd just like to take a little time for ourselves."

"If you don't mind," Mom tacks on.

She's swirling the creamer in her coffee, but her

261

eyes are plastered to mine. "No...I don't mind," I say. Listen, I know what it's like to need something after someone's gone from your life, and I think if my parents need this time, they should take it. No questions asked.

Mom looks a little relieved at my statement. Now that I look at her, she has more lines by her eyes than she ever had. "We're hesitant to leave you here."

"I'll be fine," I tell them, trying to relieve any worries they have about doing this for themselves.

"Not just that, but physically leaving you here alone," Dad says, clarifying my mother's statement.

"Oh," I say. I didn't really think about that. I look around the house we've lived in my whole life. It will feel so empty without them here now that Brady's gone. "Um..."

"We were thinking," Dad says. "You can try to stay here if you want. It's a lot of trust that we're willing to give you because of how well you've been doing recently. Or, if you're not up to it, we'll talk to the Parkers to see if you can stay there. I know you've always gotten along really well with Mrs. Parker."

This should probably be the moment where I tell my parents that I kinda, sorta, might be dating Reid Parker, but I'm certainly not opening my mouth about that right now. "Oh, okay. Yeah, I mean, I've stayed there before," I say, trying to sound calm, even though on the inside I'm bursting at the seams.

Mom frowns. "I just hate to impose on the Parkers again," she says. "Reid has been so good to Briar since Brady... Since Brady," she says with finality. My mother's words have piqued my interest. Could I have been that self-absorbed not to notice that my mother can't even bring herself to say that her son's dead?

There's a short knock on the door and then Reid lets himself in. My stomach does that twisty thing it always does when I see him now. I don't know how my parents haven't noticed that I'm different around him. They definitely need this break more than I thought.

"Well, here's Reid now," Dad says. "Let's ask him."

"Ask me what?" Reid says. He turns to me and gives me a sly wink.

I don't know how anyone can look like utter perfection in the morning, but he does. Always. Now that he and Sasha had such a public break up, the girls have been coming out of the woodwork, and since we aren't official yet, I've had to stand by and watch all the flirtations sent his way. I like the mornings the best because that's when I get him to myself.

"Well, Pam and I were talking, and we'd like to go away for a week or so. Recharge. That kind of thing.

We just don't know what to do with our baby girl here." Dad reaches over and ruffles my hair.

"So..." Reid starts, looking somehow cute and confused all at the same time. I wouldn't normally use the word cute to describe Reid Parker, but I think he's showing a new side of himself to me.

"If it's too lonely for Briar here at the house, I was going to call up your parents to see if she could stay at your place."

Reid's green eyes light. He turns toward me, a real and true smile on his face. "I'm sure they would love to have her. My mom's always thought of Briar as her only daughter."

I'm sure that's not exactly what Reid is thinking. I'm sure he's thinking much more dirtier things to himself. I know I am.

———

JUST AS MY PARENTS SAID, THEY LEFT FOR THE airport that Friday while I was at school. I kissed them goodbye that morning, telling them to text me with pictures and updates on what they're doing. I'm nervous as hell about staying at the Parker house, but I'm also a little sad to see my parents go. I know I actually ran away to put distance between us over the summer, but it's been a long time since I felt that need. I could tell the same idea was going through my mother's head when she left because she gave Reid the biggest hug and told him not to let me out of his sight. I swear she even asked him to send her updates in regard to me instead of asking for them from me.

I tried to reassure her I wasn't going to go anywhere, but once trust is gone, it takes a lot to repair. The fact that they were even going to let me stay home by myself tells me that they're trying to rebuild that foundation, the one I shook down to its core.

School flies by. I was on autopilot through most of it, writing down notes without thinking, collecting the homework sheets like a robot. It was an out-of-body experience day. I'll probably look through my bookbag later and think, "We did that in school today?"

It just so happens that this weekend is an off week for the football team. I stayed after school to watch the guys practice and then Reid loaded me up in his car and we took off for his house. Ever since he found out my parents said I could stay at his place, he didn't even ask me if I'd rather stay home. I'm not sure if it's because he knows me and knows I would've been lonely there or if it's because he wasn't going to give me an option anyway. He wanted me here. With him.

Maybe he's got a little bit of trust issues too.

We walk in through the front door. His house is eerily quiet. I look around. "Where's your mom?" She's usually buzzing through the house somewhere looking fit, like she's prepared to make an online video for their clients at any moment.

"I kind of have a surprise for you about that."

I cock my head at him. "Which is?"

"Mom said to take really good care of you this weekend because...her and Dad are out of town too."

"You're kidding," I say.

He shakes his head. "One of their clients needed them. A fitness emergency of some sort."

My stomach tumbles over itself. I thought at least I would get a grace period. Some time to acclimate myself to the Parker house again with his parents being home. Instead, my mind is already latching onto the fact that we have this whole house to ourselves. *Ourselves.* For the entire weekend.

I can think of a lot of shit I want to do.

But I'm also terrified to do any of it.

He smiles, cupping my cheek. "Relax, Briar. I'm not going to throw you over the couch right this minute."

I think all the color drains from my face as Reid laughs. What if I wanted him to throw me over the couch right now?

"Then again..." He darts forward, claiming my lips for his. He backs me up until I'm pressed against the sofa and he's kissing the crap out of me. He pulls away a minute later. "I don't know why I did that. I'm just teasing myself." He lifts his gaze to meet mine. "Just know, that by the end of the weekend, I plan on burying myself so deep inside you I'll never want to come back up for air, Briar Page."

My legs quiver. I keep telling myself that having sex isn't a big deal, but I'm not very convincing, even to myself. It feels like a huge deal when it concerns Reid Parker. Trust me, it's a step I want to take, but it also feels like it's a milestone. A life changing marker that denotes I'll never be the same again.

Who knew I could wax so poetic?

The thing is, Reid is a force. I already know I'll be a goner after this, but I kind of want to do it on my terms. I lift to my tiptoes and give him a solid smack on the lips. "Well, Reid Parker, we'll see if you can win me."

He blinks. "I've already won."

Jesus. This guy.

He steps away from me, tangling his fingers in mine while he walks us past their formal living room and into a living room in the back of the house with a big screen TV and surround sound. "I think you'll love the movie line-up I have planned," he says, turning the

TV on. "I've also got a pizza coming, and my parents stocked up the snack cupboard for the weekend. If we play it right, we might not even have to leave the house."

The brush of butterfly wings flap around my heart. It feels as if the most important muscle I have is going to take flight right there in my chest with nowhere to go.

Finally, Reid goes to the stand and holds up three DVD's that instantly put a smile on my face. *The Great Outdoors, The Monster Squad,* and *The Goonies.* Reid's dad is like an eighties freak. He has so much memorabilia from this time period that it was always readily available for our consumption. He introduced us to these three movies, and many more, when we were just kids. These three films just happen to be my favorite. I haven't seen them in so long.

"You're kidding?"

He shakes his head. "Which one first?"

I cringe. *Oh no, I have to pick? This is so not right.* "Um.... *The Monster Squad.*"

As a little kid, I had such a crush on Sean and Patrick, two of the main characters from the movie, even though I couldn't fathom the way they were dressed.

Right after Reid puts the movie in, the doorbell

rings. He jogs off to pay for the pizza, and when he comes back in, he places it on the coffee table in front of us along with a couple of cans of soda. We each take a slice as the opening credits come up. The younger me can't believe I'm a teenager right now, having kissed Reid, and sitting in his house all alone...without Brady. I sigh. "Brady loved this movie too."

Reid slides his arm around me, pulling me close. I wasn't in any danger of falling into a sour mood with that thought, but he's right there anyway, making sure I won't. It actually just felt good to talk about him. I'm sure the sadness will always be there, but that doesn't mean I can't look at the things we did together and remember them fondly. I smile as we settle in, watching Dracula recover Frankenstein who just so happened to drop in a swamp right by where a group of kids have a monster fan club.

Perfection.

Halfway through the movie, Reid and I have obliterated the pizza and the soda. I stand, asking him to pause it so I can excuse myself to the bathroom. I take the pizza box as I go, placing it in the recycle bin inside their garage and then head toward the downstairs bathroom. I take a moment to check my teeth, making sure there aren't any stuck pieces of pepperoni or anything like that in there. Even though there's nothing there, I even take the time to find their toothpaste in one of the drawers and swish it around my mouth. I scrunch up my hair, which has pretty much already faded from the midnight black back to my brown color.

When I step back into the room, Reid's moved the coffee table back and put up the leg rest on the couch. As I come around the back side, I realize that's not all he did either. He's lying there bare-chested, having taken off his shirt. I stop, and he gives me a lopsided smile. "Hi, baby."

"Hi," I say, not recognizing the tightness in my own voice. "What...are you doing?"

"I thought we could play a game." He opens his arms, and I go willing into them, sitting just to his side with my head on his chest. "I'm letting you have the upper hand."

I raise my eyebrow at him. This should be interesting.

"I think..." he says, clearly enjoying this. "Every time someone says 'virgin', we should shed an article of clothing." I replay the whole movie in my head and realize we're going to be so naked by the end of this movie. So, so naked.

Bring it on, Lucky Number Seven.

23

I wasn't underestimating the tally.

But I did overestimate how much resolve I'd have to have not to stare at Reid while he took his clothes off. He paused the movie each time. Him shedding his article first, then me. The socks were no big deal. Relatively speaking, the pants weren't all that bad either. I've already been in front of them with a bathing suit on, so it felt a lot like that. Plus, there was that incident with Reid in the bath towel.

Since he started with his shirt already off, he was the first to reveal his...well, his major package. He stripped his boxers off, revealing his already semi-hard dick while I tried not to gawk.

With his hands on his hips, he waits for my turn.

I take a deep breath, unable to really tear my gaze

away from him. He is perfection in the best way. His physique is so defined I'm suddenly super nervous to be revealing myself. I'll probably come up short compared to him. "You need help?" he asks, dropping his gaze to my fingers which are wrapped around the hem of my shirt.

I shake my head. A bathing suit is one thing, but bra and panties are so much more intimate. Also, I just can't believe he's going to be sitting naked next to me for the rest of the movie. I close my eyes briefly and start to lift, my heart in my throat. When I drop my shirt on the floor between us, his gaze takes me in appreciatively, making my nipples harden with only the thin, silky fabric of my bra to hide them. I sit down on the edge of the couch tentatively and he sits next to me, putting his arm around my shoulders and pulling me toward him again. When he presses Play on the movie, his fingers dip down swirling over the swell of my breasts, making me squirm.

If he can play that game...

Now that I'm held captive against him, I splay my fingers over his chest. His muscles tighten underneath me. I work them down and down until my palm is covering his belly button. His cock is one hundred percent hard now. The bad thing about this is, I'm not paying attention to the movie. So, when Reid pauses it, announcing that they've said "virgin" again, I have to take his word for it. He peels me off him, and I stand in front, my body vibrating with a hundred different emotions. Fear, lust, anticipation. He reaches down to rearrange himself, drawing my attention. When he jerked off in front of me a couple of weeks ago, I never looked down. Not once. Now, I take my fill. He squeezes his base, and I have to bite the inside of my cheek to stop from groaning.

Reaching behind my back, I undo my bra clasps, then stand there with my hands at my sides for a few more moments. My breasts feel heavy, and my nipples are straining, waiting for Reid's touch. First, I drop one strap down, then the other. I peel the cups away from my breasts and let my bra drop to the floor. Reid, whose hand is still around his cock, squeezes it tighter. "I hope you're as turned on as I am," he chokes out.

I can already feel the dampness in my panties. He'll notice as soon as I drop them to the floor. Hell, this is Reid. He probably already knows.

He beckons me forward, then holds out his hand. I put mine in his and he spins me around, pulling me against his chest. He spreads my legs using his own. His cock peeks out between my legs as his hands dig into my hips. His fingers slowly move up my body until I'm breathing hard. He cups me, almost like he's testing the weight of my breasts, before the coarse pads of his thumbs pass over my nipples.

I buck, and Reid hisses. "I can feel how wet your panties are right now, Briar. Can you feel it?"

I nod.

"Tell me."

I nod again, trying to regain control over my own voice. "I can feel it."

His teeth bite into my shoulder. "I've wanted this for so fucking long."

I feel like I'm about to come apart at the seams. I move against him, and he pinches my nipples until I yelp. It hurts at first, but now there's an explosion of want, making me rock my ass back into him.

"We started a game, Briar. When I start a game, I finish it. Understand?" he warns.

I settle back down onto him. He presses Play on the remote again. The characters' lips start moving on the screen. I swear I try to pay attention, but Reid's body and scent is all around me. I watch my childhood crushes act on the screen and realize they don't hold a candle to the guy I'm currently entwined with now. How did I not see it before?

Unfortunately, there's such a long gap between the last "virgin" and the one that removes my panties. It hasn't even come yet. The tension stays at disaster level, making my pulse thump at my wrist. Reid keeps exploring my body like it's a lazy Sunday afternoon and he doesn't have anything better to do. All it docs is ratchet me up, though, until I'm so in tune with his touches I'm practically vibrating.

Reid's fingers sneak between my legs, sweeping up my panties. My mouth opens in a silent scream at the barely there touch. "Just checking," he says.

I'm so slick. I already know.

His thumb passes over the line of my panties until he's gripping the crotch fabric in his fist, groaning happily into my ear. "Wet, wet, Briar."

I lift my hips into his thumb. I'm so hypersensitive, I groan at the contact. "Fuck, Reid."

He presses my hips back down again. "I want to take my time with you."

"What if I just want you inside me? Like right now?"

His thumb flicks over my clit. I half scream into the air, and my body tightens right along with it.

"You are so ready, aren't you?"

"Please."

"You want to stop playing the game? Are you forfeiting?"

"I—"

As if by some divine miracle, I hear the word "virgin" from the Surround Sound.

Reid chuckles into my ear, nipping it, before he splays his hands over my stomach. He moves down, taking the fabric of my drenched panties with him until I squeeze my knees together and kick them off. They land on the coffee table, the crotch completely wet.

"Look at you. All of you," he says, running his fingers over the seam between my legs. "You're perfect. All this has been off-limits to me for years. Then, you've literally hidden it away from me for months."

He says it in a way that I feel like I should apologize. If I'd known something like this would happen, I wouldn't have hidden myself under layers of baggy clothes and dark hair.

Reid Fucking Parker.

He spreads me wide again and tucks my head on his shoulder before tracing my clit with the tip of his finger. One hand comes across my waist, barricading me in while his other finger pushes inside me. My first instinct is to buck, but his arm over my hips prevents me from that. I'm trapped as he coaxes his finger in and out of me. Then, on one withdrawal, I feel him shift. The next time he pushes inside me, there are two fingers. "Christ, Reid!"

"A whole week of this," he says, pressing inside me and hooking his fingers. "Whenever we want."

I make a strangled cry. While still keeping me in place, Reid lifts his other hand until his thumb flicks over my nipple. Sensations course through me until I'm practically shaking on his chest. My fingers dig into the couch as he whispers huskily into my ear over and over again about what he wants to do to me. When I groan and move against him, he picks up the pace until I'm so close to reaching the climax I know is coming. "Reid," I cry out, as soon as it starts to hit, and then my mouth is open in another scream as my body takes over, throwing me into the throes of intense pleasure. Waves and waves hit me like aftershocks until I start to come back to my body.

His fingers slow, then eventually pull out, leaving me with an empty feeling. I take a deep breath, letting my body finally relax against his. He kisses my shoulder. I think I hear him say "Forgive me", but then I'm moving in the air, landing with my back against the seat cushions with him hovering over me. He's stroking himself near my entrance, an almost pained expression on his face.

Now that I see him above me, it feels right. It feels like what I've wanted for a long time. He inches closer.

I feel the head of his cock rub against me, and I inhale sharply. "Condom, Reid. Condom."

He narrows his eyes at me, but then it must dawn on him.

Yeah, I am so not on birth control. This is my first time.

He pauses for a brief moment, but then gets off the couch. "One second," he says.

He strides away, the muscles in his ass on display for me, but then I hear him run through the house, all the way up the stairs, then back down again before he stops and strides right back into the room, catching me staring at the ceiling smiling. I haven't moved an inch since he left, and he smiles predatorily at me.

"I'm sorry," he says, shaking his head. "I should have thought of that."

I return the gesture, then watch as he rips the package open and runs the condom down his length, stroking himself more while he leans over me. He kisses the tip of my nose, and I feel him at my entrance again, this time with the rubber securely fastened.

"Ready?"

I nod, bracing myself on the couch when I feel the head of his cock push inside. Then there's more of him. More and more until he presses hard once, and my head drops back at the feel of him inside me.

"Are you okay?" he asks.

I moan. There was a slight pinch, but in reality, I feel filled. I feel...wow. Reid's inside me. I nod. "It's good. I'm good."

He starts to move cautiously, but his face is strained. He keeps a slow rhythm until his body starts to shake. Then, he kicks it up a few hundred notches, slamming into me. "Fuck, Briar." He does it again and again.

My hands slide up his back, then down to his ass where my fingers grab hold, moving with him, even encouraging him to go faster. Seeing him struggle to restrain himself sends a wicked heat through me.

"Fucking tight."

I glance up while he moves over me. As I watch, he tries to smooth his face out, but fails. His body takes over. He trembles and shakes, several moans passing from his lips before his cock jerks inside me. He stops and presses into me, then with a few, short pumps, he collapses on top of me, his breath rattling out of him. I've seen Reid play football games all his life and have barely seen him out of breath, but right now, today, over this, he's sucking in air. When his breathing returns to a somewhat normal state, his lips capture mine, needy and hot. He kisses me thoroughly, a clash of tongues and lips that has us breathing hard against one another.

He pulls out of me and sits up. I pull my legs out from under him, resting my knees against the couch to look him in the eyes. When he can barely meet my gaze for longer than a few seconds, I reach out and grab his hand that's resting on my knee. "What's wrong?"

He shakes his head.

"Don't lie to me," I tell him.

His throat works. "It's just Brady, I guess. He told me not to."

I sit up, holding his hand to my chest, clasped securely between my own. "Don't do that," I say. "He would've been fine with it. I swear."

"I hope so," he says, then he does meet my stare head-on. "Because I'm not letting you go, Briar Page. You're mine."

Heat whips through me like an electric shock. That was just my first time, and I have no idea if I'll be sore, but right now, with the look he's giving me, I feel like I could go again.

On the TV, the corny hip hop song comes on, signaling the end of the film. Reid reaches over and stops the movie before pulling the condom off and throwing it on top of one of the empty cans of soda on the coffee table. He switches out the movies, then returns, sliding in behind me on the couch and pulling me to his chest while *The Goonies* starts.

I don't last very long. I don't know if it's Reid's strong arms around me or just the peacefulness that surrounds me after what we've done, but I only get through the opening of the movie before my eyes drift shut and I'm lulled asleep by the steady rhythm of Reid's heart behind me.

24

---

*T*he next couple of days are spent exploring one another on a whole other level. I've been through a great deal of emotions with Reid since I've known him. Brotherly love, friendship, and yes, even hate, but this, this right here is by far the best. I didn't know someone who wasn't family could become so important to me. That I would literally want to hold onto him every chance I got. The best part about it is that I'm not trying to do it to recover from Brady's death. No, this is something else entirely. Being with Reid is making me feel so much more than just "better".

I blink awake Monday morning. At first, I don't realize what woke me. My hair is mussed over my face, and my legs are tangled up in his sheets and his legs.

We tried yet another different position last night as Reid continues to give me a crash course in sex, "bringing me up to speed" as he calls it. I can't say I mind, but I do mind being woken up from a peaceful sleep.

"Reid," I hear. "Up. Now."

My heart sinks. It's Mrs. Parker. Holy shit. I'm so fucking naked right now.

She must kick the edge of the mattress because the whole bed moves. "Reid. Now. I told you I didn't want her in our house."

I gasp as Reid lazily lifts his head, peeking back at his mom. I try to crawl into a hole. I just want to fade away into the background because this has got to be the most embarrassing thing ever.

"Shit, Mom. I'm sorry."

"You're going to be sorry," she spits. "Get her the hell out of here, I mean it."

"Mom," he says, pulling the sheets around his waist, but also trying to hide me as well.

"Reid Jeffrey Parker," she says. "Do as I say!"

She exits the room and then slams the door closed. I finally lift my head to meet Reid's eyes. His are down-turned. I've never heard his mom so mad before. I thought she liked me. I thought— Well, I'm sure any parent doesn't want to find their kid in bed with someone else when it's so clearly blatant that they've been having sex, but it's me. When he sees the look on my face, he cups my cheek. He then stretches his long legs out of the bed and finds a pair of shorts to put on before walking to the room and stepping out.

"And where's Briar?" she immediately starts in. "I can't believe you brought her here with Briar. You know we're supposed to be looking after her. Where is she? Her mother's going to kill me. Is she okay? I tried texting her, but she's not answering."

I cringe. I'm pretty sure I left my cell downstairs after Reid carried me up to his room last night like I weighed nothing.

"And I don't know how many times I have to tell you I do not want Sasha here, Reid. You know I don't like her."

"Mom," Reid tries again. I can tell she's way past listening to him though.

"I'm going to try Briar again."

I pull myself to a sitting position on the bed, hugging my knees to my chest as I listen to what's going on in the hallway. Relief floods me when I realize she thought Sasha was in the bed with him and not me. So, at least there's that.

"Mom, you don't have to." The door swings open once more, and Reid points inside. "Briar's right there."

I glare at Reid, then look over to meet his mother's eyes. I smile and give her a small wave. "I'm so sorry, Mrs. Parker. I didn't— I wasn't thinking."

Reid drops his head to the side like he's disappointed in me and then pulls the door shut again, capturing his mother's shocked face on the other side with him. I scramble around the room and throw on clothes while there's still silence out in the hall.

"Mom?" Reid asks, his voice softer now.

"Was that Briar Page? In your bed?"

"Yeah, Mom. There's something I need to tell you."

She squeals. I just pull my shirt down over my head, completing dressing myself when the door opens again and Mrs. Parker barges in. She throws her arms around me. "Oh, Briar. It's you." For as small as Mrs. Parker is, she's got some strength in her. She holds on to me so fiercely that the initial shock wears off, and I hug her back, both our arms clasped tightly around one another. "This is great news."

"Jeffrey! Get up here!"

"Mom!" Reid says.

"Oh, right. Right." She pulls away from me and smiles.

A hesitant smile pulls at my own lips. "I'm sorry about this," I say, gesturing toward the bed.

Her face finally reddens. "Well, I can't say that I'm

— I'm sure you guys were safe. Right? Oh honey," she says, cupping my cheek. Tears spring to her eyes. "I'm so happy."

Thunderous footsteps sound on the staircase leading up to the second floor. Reid swears under his breath. "Mom, can Briar and I please have some privacy for a minute?"

"Oh, of course," she says. "I'm making breakfast. We'll talk more about this down there. We'll have to have ground rules or something. Your dad and I will talk." Even though the words coming out of her mouth sound so adult, the smile she's holding on her face tells me she's pleased.

As soon as Reid ushers her out the door and shuts it, he leans against the other side, sighing. Mr. and Mrs. Parker are whispering out in the hall. Reid shakes his head and comes forward.

"They weren't fans of Sasha, I take it," I say.

He shakes his head. "Not at all. My mom has never liked her."

"So, you used to bring her here?"

Reid entwines his fingers with mine. "Not for a long time, but yes." He blinks once. His hair is still sleep-mussed, making him look adorable right now. "Are you jealous?"

I'm trying not to be, but hell yes, I am. Reid Parker's mine. I'm almost positive we've claimed each other in any way we can over this past weekend.

Reid tilts my chin in the air and kisses me, making me forget all about being embarrassed and jealous, wrapping me up in him until he pulls away. "Do we have to go to school today?" I ask, blinking my eyes open as if these past couple of days have been a dream.

"I'm afraid so," he says. "I've got practice tonight, getting ready for the game this weekend." He squeezes my ass. "Why don't you take a shower? I'll drop the clothes you brought in here, and I'll go downstairs to try to head off all the questions we're about to get."

"Your mom," I say, smiling. "She didn't seem to mind that I was in your bed."

"If I'd known I wouldn't get in trouble for having sex in the house, I would've brought you here earlier."

I laugh at that, but then he nudges me toward the shower.

I hurry through my morning routine, not wanting Reid to have to brave his parents for too long by himself. I pull on a pair of jean shorts and a nice t-shirt, throw on a layer of foundation and some mascara before padding downstairs. I peek around the archway to find Reid huddled over a plate of pancakes, the steam rising from the stack going out and over his tousled hair.

"You were safe?" I hear Mr. Parker ask.

"Yeah, Dad," Reid says. And the funny thing is, he doesn't even sound embarrassed or exasperated. "Though, Briar will have to be put on birth control now."

"You were her first?" Mrs. Parker asks, excitement clear in her voice.

"Shh, Mom," Reid chastises. "The shower turned off. She'll be coming downstairs any minute now. I doubt she'll want you talking about that."

He's right. My face is already all sorts of red right now.

"It's just so sweet," she says. "Ugh, I just knew you two would be perfect together."

Sweet? I think. Her son can be far from sweet, especially when we're talking about sex. But we'll just let her think there were candles and roses involved instead of a game where we stripped naked in front of one another.

I clear my throat and decide to walk in. Reid shouldn't have to deal with this alone. Next to him, there's already another plate filled with pancakes. "Hi, Mr. Parker," I say when his dad rises to his feet to greet me. "I'm so sorry—"

Mrs. Parker says. "No need for that," at the same time Reid says, "Would you quit saying that?"

I shoot him a look. His dad looks thoroughly uncomfortable now, so I just sit down at the table, and his parents follow suit. None of us say anything for a long while because I'm sure what's on all our minds is the fact that Reid and I are fucking. I know it's on my mind, and I'm sure as hell not going to bring it up.

I'm about halfway done with my pancakes when Mrs. Parker says, "You do things your way, Briar, but I think your parents need to know what's going on. They're probably going to feel differently about having you stay here now that you and um...you and Reid had sex—are dating? You two *are* dating, aren't you?"

My heart lodges in my throat. I peek over at Reid, wanting to see his reaction. He's annoyed. I can't tell if it's because of the question or because his mom is asking the question. He looks up. "I'm sure Briar will tell her mom when she's comfortable."

Briar sure as hell is not saying shit to her mom.

Mrs. Parker worries over her lip. I can tell she doesn't want to misuse my parents' trust.

Reid stands, his chair scraping against the floor as he takes in his mother. "Oh, Jesus. I'll stay away from her for the rest of the week. Okay? I don't want to piss off the Pages either."

I watch as Reid walks to the sink to rinse off his plate. Mr. and Mrs. Parker both relax with that sentiment. In fact, everyone else in the room seems calm now, but not me. I don't agree with this staying away from each other bit. When Reid and I get in his car so he can drive us to school, I tell him that.

He side-eyes me, then winks. "I'm sure we can find ways."

He pulls my hand to his mouth and brushes a kiss against my knuckles while still watching the road.

He takes a right into the parking lot and pulls into the closest parking space to the front entrance. I go to get out, but he stops me. "Once people realize we're together, rumors will spread everywhere. Sasha won't be happy but leave her to me. If you need anything, go to me, Cade, or Lex...or hell, any of the guys on the football team for that matter. We'll all be there for you."

"People are going to know?" I ask. This is a lot different conversation than we had last week.

His mouth twitches. "I think they're going to realize when I can't keep my hands off you."

That makes me smile. "So, we're going to make it official?"

He gives me an inquisitive glance. "As far as I'm concerned, it was official as soon as I was free. My hearts been yours for a while, Briar, even when you didn't know it, and even when it was trapped."

Speaking of hearts, mine's melting right here in the car. For everything Reid Parker is and has been, he just etched his place onto my heart. No matter what happens, he'll always be there.

"You ready?" he asks.

I take a deep breath and stare up at the school. I've come a long way from the girl a month ago who didn't want to go to classes, who felt like no one was by her side, and who didn't care about anything anymore. But somehow, I'm getting a lot of the same feelings. The school looms intimidatingly and nerves strike inside me. But when Reid meets me out in front of the car, slipping his fingers between mine before walking to the school with me, I leave all that shit behind.

I'm not going at it alone anymore.

25

*I*t feels as if from the very moment Reid and I make things official at school, Ezra starts messaging me again like some sort of cosmic practical joke. He seems off, too. Not like the guy I poured everything out to, but some incessant gnat that won't go away no matter how many times he gets swat at.

Pic? He sends on Wednesday morning before school. I have to hide my phone screen away from Reid while we're eating breakfast together with his mom staring at the two of us. It shouldn't matter that I had an online relationship with someone, but at the same time, I see how territorial Reid is, and I honestly don't want him to know Ezra is part of the reason why I ran away. I wanted to meet him. I feel so differently now though. Now, I don't even want to answer him. On the way to school, he sends another message. **You used to send me pics all the time.**

I'm getting frustrated now. I've already told Ezra I'm dating someone not through a cell phone screen, but he won't take the hint. I feel bad for wanting to block him because he did so much for me, but I don't know if I have another alternative right now. I'll probably try to talk to him at least one more time, see if I can't get him to back off.

"Who's that?" Reid asks.

"Um, Jules," I say before turning the screen off and putting my cell in the front pocket of my bookbag. I hate lying to him, but the alternative is to get into a huge and lengthy conversation this early in the morning. I'm also embarrassed. I don't want Reid to know about Ezra, and I especially don't want Lex to know about Ezra. He'd be so hurt considering I was talking with Ezra at the same time I was doing things with him.

Surprisingly, Lex has been okay about Reid and me. He'll look away when Reid kisses me at lunch and other things, but he's hanging in there, which I appreciate. I didn't realize how much I needed these three boys in my life. Yes, Cade too. All six-foot ridiculousness of him. His thing now is telling me that it's only right he and I have a sexual encounter since I've done things with both Lex and Reid. Reid doesn't find this funny at all. For that matter, neither does Lex. Cade's usually the only one who laughs, which is fine by him. He's busy sticking his dick into one of Sasha's friends to be serious at all about screwing me anyway. Not that he would. He would never jeopardize his relationship with Reid for sex. He just likes to get under people's skin.

Jules has also adjusted well to mine and Reid's new relationship. When we walked into school that first day, she couldn't keep a smile off her face. I tried to ask her if Brady ever said something about not wanting me to be with Reid, but she couldn't think of anything. The only thing she commented on was how fiercely protective Brady was of me.

Pretty much the only one who hasn't taken Reid and mine's new relationship well is Sasha, but I'm not shocked about that. The skank comments have significantly increased as well as the rank faces she throws my way. It's amazing how someone so pretty can twist their face into something so awful. None of the guys on the football team will touch her after what happened at the party following the homecoming game, so instead, she's dating someone from the lacrosse team, though she seems too preoccupied with Reid to even bother to pay attention to her boyfriend. It's sad, really. The guy is cute, and he seems nice. It just makes me wonder how long that relationship is going to last.

After school, I walk out to the bleachers like normal and watch the football team practice. I'm not the only person who does this. There's usually a steady stream of admirers. I swear the guys could jog off the field, pick a girl, and bang them just like that. Since I've always been so close to the team because of my brother, I've never really seen the appeal. I do now though. I wonder if any of these girls have gotten a taste of someone like him. Maybe they've fucked Cade. Maybe they wait at the edge of the fence to see if he'll even remember their name. I think I would. If Reid left me... I'd wait at the gate. I'd follow him after school. I'd text his phone. It all seems so needy, and it is. I need him. We've gone so far past the realm of friendship that I would never want to go back, which scares the shit out of me. When I think about it, my chest constricts. But when I stare into his eyes, I can see he feels the same way. Whatever hold we have on each other is overpowering for both of us.

Like I'd hoped, we haven't paid attention to his parents' warnings about not having sex in the house. We've just been extremely secretive about it. Either him or I sneak into the other's room at night, testing the boundaries with one another. When I have to go back to sleeping in my own house, I'm going to be so lonely. I don't ever want to go away. I want to be trapped in Reid's embrace forever.

I'm sitting on the bleachers thinking about that, my foot tapping against the seats in front of me when a figure sits down next to me. I see the ribbed colors of the cheerleading skirt first, then hear the rustle of pom-poms. It doesn't take a rocket scientist to figure out that Sasha just found her way to me. I sigh and look over. She's staring ahead at the field, her lips thin.

"What do you want?" I ask her.

"I want Reid back."

My hackles rise. For her to even think she could get him back boils my blood. "Not happening."

A vicious scowl parts her lips. "You underestimated me. So did Reid."

I shake my head at her. "I see you watching him still," I say. "Why would you even want him back? He clearly doesn't want you."

"You don't know that."

I shrug. I think I would know considering it's obvious he wants to be with me, but I'm not going to turn this into a bitch fest. "Let's say for argument's sake that he doesn't. Sasha, you can have any guy at school." I look around her, seeing if her boyfriend is anywhere near. "You got that new guy."

She makes a disgusted sound in the back of her throat. "He's a baby."

I'm pretty sure the guy is only a year younger than us. Actually, that would make him my age, so what does it matter? I look away, obviously trying to reason with her isn't working, and I'm not going to fight with her either.

Like I've just been sitting here musing, Reid and I are meant to be. I can feel it deep in my bones, and when we're together, it just feels so freaking right.

"I don't know how you got your hooks in him, but you need to give him up. Break up with Reid."

"Not happening," I tell her, a shocked laugh forcing my lips apart

"Oh, you will," she says, a small smile playing over her ever-present scowl.

I turn toward her. All the petty shit that's happened with her since Brady died rushes over me. "You know, you'd think I'd get some sort of reprieve from the likes of you after the year I've had. You never once sounded sorry about Brady. Not once. Hell, Reid told the whole school you fucked someone else because he couldn't do it."

"So, because someone dies, I'm supposed to not go after what I want?" Her eyebrows pull together. "As far as I saw it, Brady only hindered

Reid and me. He never liked me," she says, her voice hard.

Can't imagine why. But I've heard this story before. Brady didn't like Sasha, and when she and Reid first got together, he was opposed to it. I know he and Reid got into several arguments because of her. I'm not sure what happened, but eventually, it died down and Reid and Sasha had their own thing.

Maybe that's why Sasha doesn't like me? Because she sees me as being connected to my brother. She probably despises the fact that Reid is with me moreso than if he'd gone after someone else.

"Your brother was never any concern to me," she says, straightening her shoulders. "But Reid is."

"Why?" I ask, not getting it. The way I see it, she could still have pretty much any guy she wants. I'm sure a lot of them would be thrilled to get a striptease from her for their birthday. Reid's just not it.

I say as much to her and she turns toward me with almost black eyes. "He is though, and you're going to break up with him, or I'm going to make sure he breaks up with you."

My heart starts thundering in my chest. "You're insane."

She smiles politely. "Recognize this?" she asks. She pulls her cell phone out and shows me a picture. The color drains from my face. It's the same picture I sent to Ezra, the one with my fingers covering most of my breast, but not all of it.

"Where the hell did you get that?" I try to snatch her phone away, but she pulls it out of reach. "Did you hack me?"

She turns the screen off, hiding the picture away. I could take her phone right now and smash it, but that wouldn't do any good. If she hacked me, all she'd have to do is log on to her online storage somewhere else. I'm sure she has it saved in a bunch of places.

My face heats up. To think that Sasha has seen that picture, probably all of her fucking cheerleader friends too. My stomach drops and then twists when I think that she may have read my messages too. All that grief. All that bare pain just laid out there, and she's read it. She seems that maniacal to have planned all this out.

"I'm going to show Reid this picture. You know what he thinks about his girl showing themselves off…"

It dawns on me now what she said at the party. How I'm not the girl he thinks I am.

Shame washes over me. She's had that picture for so long. My eyes track over to where Reid, Cade, and Lex are. They're oblivious to what's going on up here, but I feel like the world is coming down on me now. I should never have taken that. I should never have sent it. It was in a fit of despair, of truly feeling low and needing someone to fill me up. That's not really how it works though. Someone else can't fill you up. Someone else can't take your pain away. If that was the case, all the help Reid and the guys tried to give me in the beginning would've been enough, but it wasn't. It wasn't until I started to accept it, until I started to turn myself around that I finally was able to let them in.

"If you don't do it, I'll make sure the whole school sees this picture," Sasha taunts.

"You wouldn't," I say, glaring at her.

She shrugs. "Test me. If you think Reid didn't like it when I stripped in front of a few people at a party, how do you think he's going to take it when everyone sees you like this?"

"You can't even tell it's me," I say.

She laughs. "You think this is the only picture I took? I have screenshots of everything you said to your boyfriend. I can prove it's you." She stands, her pom-poms rustling as she places her hands behind her back. "By tomorrow, Reid will come into school alone, without your skank ass in tow, or I'm sending it to everyone."

"He doesn't want you," I say through clenched teeth. Why is she even bothering? What's the point?

Why want someone who doesn't want anything to do with you?

"He'll want you even less soon," she says, shrugging. She skips down the bleacher steps, the purple and yellow of her pom-poms trailing behind her.

I want to go after her. I want to punch her in the face, make her pay for what she's doing to me right now. I had a few blissful days of finally feeling okay again, but it's gone.

Just like that, it's gone.

26

*S*asha's only giving me until tomorrow to figure this shit out, so I don't waste any time. Reid expects me to be there after practice, so I am, sitting in the grass by the Brady Page dedicated flagpole. *It's just a picture*, I keep telling myself, but it doesn't feel that way, even to me. It feels like a direct representation of a sad, lost girl. It feels like if I tell Reid what I did, I'll be laying myself bare to him. Or even worse, if Sasha shows the picture to the school, she'll be laying me bare to everyone. I'll no longer be able to keep quiet and just be Brady's little sister or Reid's girlfriend, I'll be someone. They'll have a memory peg to remember me by, so even when it's our ten-year reunion, they'll be saying, "Briar Page? Yeah, you remember, she's the girl who got caught sexting a picture of her breast."

I spy Reid, Cade, and Lex walking from the locker room and turn away. All three of them. Wonderful. So many times, the sight of all three of them used to bring me happiness, but now, it feels like a weight on my shoulder. Even if I tell Reid privately, he'll just tell them. They're all about to know what happens when a sad girl has very little self-esteem and no one to turn to.

How fucking embarrassing.

"Hey," Cade says. He kicks the underside of my shoes playfully. "Did you see that run?"

I lift my gaze to meet his and shake my head. He tilts his head to the side, but it's Lex who's immediately there. He crouches next to me, taking my hand in his. "What's wrong?"

I can't stop the tears from falling over then. I'd been trying to blink them away, but sometimes it feels like grief is an unstoppable force. I can't just hold it back, deal with it when it's a more opportune time for me.

Reid nudges Lex, and Lex has to put his hand out before he falls to the ground. "Briar," he says. My name on Reid's lips make the tears come faster. "Jesus," he says. He picks me up, cradles me to him, and walks me to his car. He whispers to me the whole time. Such sweet words that make me wonder what it's going to feel like to lose all this.

There's no fucking way on this earth I'm breaking up with Reid though. Sasha was stupid if she thought that something like this would make me do something so brash. I'm worried it's Reid who won't be able to tolerate me now though. Sasha said something at the party, something that stuck with me and I wasn't sure why. She told Reid I wouldn't be an innocent in his eyes soon. She was right. She had a backup plan this whole time.

"What's going on?" Cade asks. His voice is laced in a compassion I haven't heard from him before. "Is it Brady?"

I shake my head. Sasha's hatred might be rooted in Brady, but it's grown from there.

"Parker," a voice shouts.

Reid moves in front of me, blocking me from the owner of the voice.

"What are you guys up to? Pizza at the Shack?"

"Sorry, dude," Reid calls out. "I've got like a shitton of homework."

The guys all surround me. It makes my heart swell, but really all it does is make me feel worse. Why couldn't I love myself as much as these guys wanted me to?

They turn back around once I hear a car start up a few rows behind us. Reid grabs my hands in his. "Talk to me, Briar. Do you want us to be alone? Do you—?"

I shake my head. The sight of his beautiful face is fractured before me, the tears still gathering even though I wipe then away. Right now, he looks so worried and affectionate. When I look into his eyes, there's a warmth there, but I'm wondering how long that's going to last. I can't even really be mad at Sasha for this? It was me. I was the one who was dumb.

While I waited for the guys after practice, I sent Ezra a text, telling him I'd been hacked and that our conversations weren't safe. I told him I was sorry. The only thing I didn't tell him about was Sasha's threat. She doesn't care about him. She only cares about making me miserable enough to break up with someone she wants.

I don't understand why she can't see she has no claim on him. Reid Parker isn't like a horse she can tame. Or someone she can buy off or convince that he likes her when he doesn't. She's all smoke and mirrors dressed up in Barbie doll outfits.

"You're going to be so mad," I tell Reid, looking him in his gorgeous green eyes.

He tilts his head. "It can't be that bad."

The heat from the car hood feels warm against my

bottom. I take my phone out that's been clutched in my hands. I want to tell him what I did first, then tell him Sasha's involvement. How she wanted to make me suffer so bad she broke into my social media to make a Sunday special out of me. I can see it now. *The dangers of online sexting.*

I turn the screen on and angle it toward me so I'm the only one who can see it at first. "When Brady died, you know I made a lot of misguided decisions." I give Lex a small frown. I hate lumping him into that category, but it's true.

His lips thin, and he looks away.

"There was also one more that I didn't tell you about. It didn't seem relevant until...well, until now. I sort of, kind of had this relationship with a guy I met online."

Reid's gaze narrows. "What kind of relationship?"

He doesn't say it accusingly. He's only asking, even though I can see a spark of jealousy in him.

"Just talking, mostly," I tell him. "I felt like he was the only one who would listen about what I was going through. He was just outside of everything, and it was easier to tell him things because he didn't know."

Reid kicks off the car and walks away, his hands diving into his hair. "Is this who you were talking to this morning in the car?"

I blink. He must've seen right through me. "Yes," I tell him. Because he was who I was talking to, but it also feels like I should add an explanation to that sentence. I wasn't doing anything wrong. I was trying to get him not to talk to me.

"Briar," he growls, and a sliver of fear shoots through me.

"Let her talk," Lex says. "You don't know what's going on yet."

Reid throws him a gaze like fire. If it was actually fire, the center would've combusted right then and there, blown like a stick of dynamite.

To Reid's credit, he stops. He places his arms over his chest and glares at me like I'm already guilty. "I've actually told him not to contact me again," I say to Reid, making sure to hold his gaze. "I told him about you," I tell him, letting a smile slip out. Being with Reid makes me so happy. He fills a place inside me I didn't know I was missing, but now that he has filled it, I feel like I could starve to death if it wasn't there.

"Go on," Cade says. "We're listening."

"One night, he asked me for a picture." I clear my throat. "A tittie, pic, I guess."

Reid growls, making me so nervous to say my next words.

"I sent it to him," I say, looking at my lap now. "I

was so lost and sad, but none of that matters. It's just an excuse. I sent it to him even though I thought it was pretty tame."

"And what? He's threatening to show everyone now?" Lex asks. "What's his name? Where does he live?"

I wave him away. I don't think Ezra would do anything like that even though he's been acting strange lately.

"I'll kick his ass," Reid fumes.

At that, I turn my phone's screen back on and turn it around. Reid immediately grabs it as the other two look away. He studies it like it's tape from a previous game. "This is on my bed," he says.

I nod.

"That night at the party?"

I look away, and I'm sure my silence says everything my lips can't right now. It's even worse that I'm all over Reid's bed in this. Sasha might not have realized where the picture was taken, but I remembered. I knew it would hurt Reid all that much more to know that.

He plays around on my screen, and I'm sure he's looking back through my messages with Ezra. His gaze zeroes in on the screen when he reads something, then he looks up at me. "Who hacked you? What's going on?"

"What?" Lex asks, finally looking back over at his friend.

"She tells this guy she got hacked." This makes Cade snap to attention too.

"Sasha," I say, my voice like steel. "She came to see me while you guys were at practice. She hacked into my account. She got that picture, and now she's threatening to show you if I don't break up with you."

His head reels back, but he shrugs his shoulders. "Tough shit. You already showed me."

"She said if we stay together, she'll show the whole school."

"Fucking bitch," Lex roars. He turns toward Reid and shoves him. Reid's eyes blaze and they clash again. I inhale sharply on the car and jump down. I had no idea that would happen, but Cade is five steps ahead of me.

He throws himself into the middle of the two of them. "Calm down. Fuck! What the hell are you two doing?"

Lex lumbers there, his breaths coming quick before he looks up to meet my eyes and then spins on his heel and leaves. My heart reaches out to him. I don't have feelings for him like I do Reid, but I like Lex. I've always liked Lex and seeing him walk away right now, makes my insides twist.

Cade pushes Reid toward me. "Deal with your girl. I'll go to Lex."

Reid stumbles toward me. His arms move around me and suddenly my back is against the car, and I'm fully in his embrace. His taut muscles, swollen from practice, move around me. "I'm sorry," I tell him. "I didn't have any idea this would happen. I regretted sending it pretty much immediately afterward."

He caresses my back. "The picture is barely anything. You can't see your face, though I recognize the freckle." His throat works as his fingers brush against the freckle that's on the side of my breast. "I just want to throttle that guy because he probably jerked off to that picture."

I shake my head. "I don't think so. He barely wrote me after that."

"Don't sound so sad."

"I'm not," I say firmly.

He holds me again as if he's saying he's sorry for the comment. His hands are like steel bands around me, and I wish they would stay there forever.

"I don't want the whole school to see my picture. Sasha said she took screenshots of everything, so she could prove it was me even though you can't see my face in it."

He backs away, leaving a dark hole where he was. "I knew she was cold, but I didn't think she'd ever do this. It's on a whole other level of fucked up. That's not just pouring gravy on you or calling you names, this is your privacy we're talking about. Intimacy, even."

I bite my lip. "I'm so sorry, Reid."

He looks at me with his angular features that look that much more intimidating right now. "I'm not fucking happy about it, but it's not your fault."

"I mean about the picture."

His teeth grind together. "That's not your fault either." He sighs. "Though I'd love to be the only guy who's ever seen you, we know that's not the case, right? Lex," he says, like he's going to count the guys who have seen me, but that's it. There's just three people. Just him, Lex, and Ezra through a picture even though I'm pretty covered up.

My cheeks pink. "I don't want that picture to get out." My mind wanders to my parents, and I start to tremble. They really don't need this. Not after taking time away for themselves.

"I'm going to fucking talk to her," he says. "I'll make sure nothing happens." He takes his phone out of his pocket and brings it to his ear after hitting a button.

"Yeah, can you come back? I need someone to take Briar to my house while I pay Sasha a visit."

He hangs up after that, and it doesn't take long to see both Cade and Lex come striding back toward us. "Do you think that's a good idea?" Cade asks. "Maybe I should go talk to her. Or Lex."

"I can't fucking talk to her right now," Lex seethes. "I'll fucking—" He breaks off with a mottled curse. "It's just not a good fucking idea right now."

"She'll talk to me," Reid says, glancing at his friend. "She'll probably only talk to me."

I can't help that jealousy spikes the blood in my veins. I don't want Reid anywhere near Sasha. She's a conniving bitch.

In the same moment though, I know Reid. I trust him. Nothing is going to happen. He downright loathes her.

"You're probably right," Cade sighs. He comes over and drops his arm around me. "Come on, Shortie. Let's let Reid do his thing. Lex and I will drive you to his house and wait with you there."

I slide out from Cade's arm and throw myself at Reid, letting myself go to mush in his arms as he kisses the crap out of me. Cade drags me away again, warning Reid that he better take care of this soon. Sasha's off-the-wall crazy.

Lex picks my cell up from the ground, which must've fallen in the jostling between the two boys and hands it over to me. His fingertips brush mine. I look up at him and frown. It makes me sad to see him upset over me, but the heart wants what it wants, and right now, it wishes it could be next to Reid as he drives over to his ex-girlfriend's house and hopefully either unleashes his fury or talks some sense into her.

I'm not sure which I want more, but I do know, I want all this to end when Reid comes back to me.

27

*R*eid is moody when he returns. The door closes just as his family and I, along with Lex and Cade, are about to sit down to dinner at Mrs. Parker's insistence. He kisses me on the temple as he takes his seat next to me. My skin is crawling with unanswered questions, but little by little, I'm lulled by the fact that this seems so normal, eating over here with Reid's family surrounded by the boys. Mr. Parker talks football with the three of them while Mrs. Parker asks me about school. It doesn't make everything go away, but it puts it on hold for a moment.

As soon as we're finished and Mrs. Parker starts to clear the plates, Reid tilts his head, indicating for us to follow him. He takes us into the lived-in living room, sitting down on the couch and pulling me onto his lap.

Cade sits on the other end of the couch while Lex stands near the TV stand, his arms crossed, trying not to look at Reid while he talks. "She's placated for now, but we'll have to fucking watch her," Reid says. He shakes his head. "I can't believe I ever—" A shiver rolls through him that transfers to me. I hug myself, rubbing my hands up and down my arm.

"Maybe we could tell someone," I say. "The principal or her parents..."

Reid laughs harshly. "Her parents are worse than her. All they want is for her to be happy, so no, it won't help telling them. Things would just get worse."

"The police then?" Lex asks. "It's illegal to have pictures of a minor like that. Plus, she must've hacked into Briar's account to get them. That's an offense, right?"

I turn my head away. I really don't want anyone seeing those pictures. The police are just going to look at me like I'm this sad, pathetic girl.

"I think if we can just keep Sasha from showing the pictures, we should keep this between us. Maybe if she threatens to use them again, we'll tell someone."

"So," Cade says. "What did you have to do to get her to agree not to show them?"

My body locks up. I don't want to hear what he has to say. I don't know why I'm so worried about what's going to come out of his mouth. She wants him back. So, if she's decided she's not going to show the pictures off just yet, is that how he got her to do it? Did they kiss? Are they dating again?

Reid pulls me to him, holding me close to his chest. "I bluffed," he says. "I told her I had something that would ruin her if she did anything to hurt Briar."

"Okay…" Cade says, sounding skeptical.

"I didn't know what to fucking do," Reid spits. "I'm sure if I think about it, I probably do have dirt on her. I mean, shit, she's a terrible person. I'll have to think about it, or we can work to get something on her if I can't think of anything, but what matters right now is that it's over with. There's no imminent threat to Briar." He pulls me to him again like he can't get me close enough. His lips over my ear, making me shiver, he whispers. "I won't let anything happen to you. Promise."

I like that promise, and maybe that's my problem. No one can make promises like that. Not Reid. Not anyone. The truth is, we never know what's going to happen. That's why it was such a shock when Brady died. I put my world into him, if I think about it. My whole life revolved around him. He was my brother. His friends were my friends. When he was taken out of the equation, I had no one.

It scares the shit out of me to be that way again.

Cade slaps his thighs. "Alright. I'll see what I can't get out of um..." He snaps his fingers. "Um..."

"Jesus. Hayley," I say.

He smiles. "That's it."

"I have no idea why you had a hard time thinking of that. You're only fucking her," I say sarcastically.

Cade shrugs. "Don't judge, Shortie." He scratches his jaw. "I'll see if I can't get *Hayley* to spill her guts about Sasha. I'm sure those cheerleaders have dirt on her." He gets this twinkling look in his eye. "I'll just tell her if she wants the cock, she'll have—"

"We get it," Lex snaps. He walks forward, grabs Cade by the collar, and they both walk out of the room.

I snicker at Cade's reaction, but it's Lex I'm worried about. He didn't seem at all pleased with what's going on. Not about Sasha, not about Reid and me. I turn in Reid's lap. He looks so tired with having to deal with this shit today. "Hey, you talked to Lex, right? Everything's good?"

Reid blinks. "Everything's as good as it can be." He rubs down the side of his face. "I get how he feels. Seeing someone you like with someone else..." He shakes his head. "He'll be okay."

"I hope so," I say, worrying over my lip. "I like Lex."

"I know," Reid says, tightening his grip around me. "One day, he'll find someone else, someone that makes him feel how you did, how you make me feel, and then this will all be just a memory."

I sigh against his chest, perching my hand over his pec. I can feel his heart drum underneath it, a steady melody that's a great reminder that we're alive. We have a life to live unlike others who don't. "I hope he finds someone soon. I hate to see him so down."

"I think," Reid says, moving his hand over my chest and flicking my nipple through my shirt and bra. "We should stop worrying about Lex."

Just that one little touch is all it takes. A surge of need spreads through my limbs, settling in my core. When I turn to look up at him, both of us have matching looks of desire. "Your parents," I say, cautiously.

"They never come in here."

"Lie."

He lifts his hips into mine, and I feel the evidence of his arousal. "I don't care."

I close my eyes, trying to keep my head on straight. "Your parents are so good to me. I can't do this to them when they're just in the other room."

Reid slips his hands into his jeans and grabs his cock, moaning.

"Reid," his mom calls out.

He stills, and I swear my eyes bulge out of my head.

"Your dad and I are going out. Be back in a bit."

"Yeah, okay," he chokes out.

No sooner than we hear the front door close does Reid pull his hands out of his jeans to wrap around me, situating me on his lap so I'm straddling him. He rubs himself over me, sending sparks through my body that are bright enough to light up the night sky. We fumble around at first. There's a bundle of nerves inside of me, and probably in him too, from the shitstorm we had to deal with. This feels urgent and needy, like we need to make sure the other is still here.

I finally undo the button on his jeans and lower his zipper while he does the same to me. He tries to push my jeans down, but there's nowhere for them to go, not from this position.

He gets up, sets me on the coffee table and yanks at my jeans until they're around my ankles, then he pulls my panties down too before he moves back onto the couch. My bare knees slide against the couch cushions as he pulls his jeans and boxers down just low enough to free himself. My stomach tightens. I haven't been on top yet. I don't even know if I'll know exactly what to do or if I'll even be good at it, but I can tell Reid's mind isn't on any of that, so maybe mine shouldn't be either. I love Reid. I trust Reid.

He struggles with pulling his wallet out of his back pocket and frees a condom from inside. He smiles up at me. "I'm prepared now."

I bite my lip as he rolls it down his hard length, and then he takes my hips, poising me over him. I think he can see how nervous I am because he slows down then, capturing my gaze with his and not letting go the entire time he settles me on top of him.

I feel him at my entrance, then deeper, deeper, deeper until I'm sitting on him. I suck in a breath. It's not better or worse than the other positions, just different. I feel like *I* have the control.

"Holy fuck," he breathes. His hands skim up my front, under my bra, to close around my breast. "Mine," he says, his voice hard.

I'm still getting used to him inside me this way when he bucks his hips up. I make a strangled cry and twist my hands in his shirt. With that movement, he's unleashed a desire inside me to know what moving over him will feel like. I rock into him, feeling him slide inside me. I try every angle I can, searching for the one that drives he and I both crazy, but when I lean forward and grind my clit against him every time I move forward, I stay there, my mouth dropping at the delicious sensations that flutter through me.

"I can tell you like that," he breathes. He flips my bra out of the way and strokes my nipples.

My movements start out slow, but then I get faster and faster as the pleasure intensifies. I hold onto the back of his neck, forcing him to relinquish his hold on my breasts and move his hands to my ass. "Oh, Reid."

He groans. "Christ, Briar."

I feel myself building now, reaching for that waterfall of ecstasy. When I know it's going to come, I slow, grinding slow circles into him until I peak. "Reid!"

He holds me to him while I'm lost in the aftershocks, pumping inside me until he too comes apart, his fingers digging into my ass. I collapse against his chest. His hard breaths hit my hair, making it fan out against my face. It's a while before I lean back and look him in the eye. He's half-lidded, staring at me with bedroom eyes that make a smile come to my face. He reaches out to run a finger over my bottom lip. "We better get dressed in case my parents come back."

Gently, I remove myself from him, sitting right back onto the coffee table while I wiggle my panties and jeans back up. My tops are a mess. My bra is all tangled. I finally free the straps then get it hooked before pulling my shirt back down into place. Then, I just watch Reid. He walks away, pulling the condom off himself as he heads to the bathroom. I hear him unroll some toilet paper and then the crinkle of plastic as he drops them both in the trash, hopefully he's wrapped the toilet paper around the used condom to hide it. When he comes back out, he's all put together again, too.

He drops back onto the couch, and I climb right back onto his lap and hold him. There's about a hundred other things I could be doing. Calling my parents to ask how they are. Texting Jules to make sure she's okay and to tell her what happened with Sasha. Homework. But there's really nothing better than what I'm doing right now which scares the shit out of me. I feel like I've just transferred all that relying on only one person to make my life... from Brady to Reid.

But I guess that's what love is. Trusting that person to be around forever. Or maybe it's not just trust. Maybe it's just faith. Or maybe it's just despite the fact that something could go wrong, you want to be with that person no matter what. No matter if this ends in tragedy like Brady's life did.

I close my eyes while I think about this, weighing the two options. Never feeling this way or feeling it and having it taken away.

Honestly, both scare the shit out of me. I don't

think I can take another person close to me leaving me, but Reid's arms feel too damn good to deny me this one thing.

I don't know what all the answers are. Maybe no one does.

28

On Friday night, I hop in a car with Jules after school to travel to the away game. The boys are on a bus, heading that way too. My parents come home tomorrow. I'm actually looking forward to seeing them, hearing about their trip. But there's more than that too. I've been struggling with this idea of losing Reid now. I talked to the counselor about it at school today, asking her how people get over this feeling that people are going to leave them. Part of me just wants to see my parents back in our house so I know that they're okay. It'll be different than hearing their voices over the phone. Physical proof. That's what I need right now, and I don't know how these thoughts crept up on me. I was kind of happy when they said they were going away, but it's a completely different story now.

"You've been quiet," Jules says. "Is it the Sasha thing?"

I squirm in my seat as she takes a right. I've been to the school we're playing against many times. We're almost there, and I don't think I've spoken the whole time. "No, it's not that."

She side eyes me. "Well, what is it?" Her voice lowers like she wants to ask me if it's about Brady but doesn't want to bring it up if it's not. It's like putting hurt on top of hurt if that's not what this is about, but it actually is.

I hesitate to tell her. I don't know why. We've always been able to talk about Brady related things, commiserate with one another, but this feels a little different.

"Spit it out, Briar. You know I'm here for you."

I take a deep breath, letting her words sink in. I have what I thought I wanted. Other people in my life that care for me, but now it just scares me that these people will get taken away too. I clear my throat because it feels like I could really lose it about now. "I was wondering..." I say, feeling my voice tremble. "This is personal, so don't feel like you have to answer it."

"Okay..."

She's nervous now. She goes to turn the blinker on but misses it the first time and has to hit it again. "You

325

and Brady," I start. "Knowing what you know now, that he'd be taken away from us, would you still be with him?"

Her brows pull together.

"I mean if you knew in the beginning of your relationship that Brady would die, would you still have dated him?"

"Briar," she says. Her mouth opens to say one thing, and I think she's about to tell me that of course she would, but then her mouth snaps shut. She pulls into the opposing team's parking lot and finds a spot before shutting the car off and falling back into her seat with a look.

I think I know her answer. I think it's no.

"What brought this on?" she asks instead.

I shrug. "It's just everything that's happening now. I don't know. What if Reid dies? What if you die? My parents..." I choke up.

"What if? What if? What if?" she says. "You can't do that. You can't 'what if' your life to death."

"So, you would?" I ask. "You'd date him?"

She nibbles on her lower lip. Why can't she say yes? Why can't she just tell me yes, that that's what she would do? She'd date my brother. She'd fall in love. She'd feel the true ache when he's gone. She'd live the next few months practically falling apart in other people's arms missing him, looking toward her future and realizing that what she thought was going to happen just isn't going to happen now.

Like what the fuck? Why is the world so fucking cruel?

I sigh and move to throw the door open, but Jules grabs my arm. "Stop."

I turn toward her. I can tell my face is pleading with her. I feel like she holds all the answers right now. She'll know. She's gone through it. She's been there done that. Within her small frame lies all the answers.

"I don't know," she says simply. "It feels too easy to say yes and too easy to say no. I don't think we're meant to know."

"But what if we did?"

"But you can't possibly know, Briar, right? That's the point."

I shake my head. I'm not sure that is the point. Eventually something bad is going to happen. Sasha will release that picture. Someone else close to me will die. Hell, my parents will at some point. That's just the way of life. Accidents. Disease. Old age.

We're all fucked. Every single one of us.

"Should I call your parents?" she asks hesitantly. I can tell she thinks she let me down on this, but neither one of us can lie to the other.

I shake my head and force a smile. "No, I'm fine." I shrug. "You answered everything I need to know."

She looks at me warily. "Reid then? I can call him."

"Come on," I say, gently pushing her shoulder in jest even though that's the last thing I feel like doing right now. Is it dumb to think that all these relationships I have are meaningless? They're all going to end in death, so aren't they meaningless in the end? If all roads lead to your very life ceasing to exist, what's the point?

I feel a black cloud descend over me. This is some seriously deep shit I'm thinking about right now. It's way bigger than me, making me feel so, so small in an already fucked up world.

I kind of hate Brady right now. If he'd never died, I wouldn't be thinking any of this. I wouldn't have to have an existential crisis at seven-fucking-teen.

"Alright," she says. "I know what will make you feel better. Let's go see your hottie boyfriend obliterate this team. Okay?"

I nod, again smiling a smile I don't really feel. Maybe I'm good at hiding it though because Jules gets out of the car. While she's stepping out and closing her door, I take a deep breath. I know I'm not in the right head space to make any decisions right now. What decisions are there to make anyway? It's not that I don't like where my life is right now. I do have a hottie for a boyfriend. I have great friends. There's just... I don't know.

My phone buzzes in my pocket. I pull it out and see I have a message from Ezra. I went and changed every single one of my passwords to something ridiculously tricky. No one is getting into that shit anymore. **Hey,** it reads. **Sorry about getting hacked. I've missed talking to you. Things got weird there for a minute, but I didn't mean them to. I just wasn't feeling myself. I'm glad you have someone now. I'm here if you need me.**

Wow. Okay. That's more like the Ezra I remember. I shake my head and put my phone back in my pocket before meeting up with Jules at the front of the car and heading toward the stands in a back field. We pass the baseball field first before we get to the green of the football field. Then, Jules and I walk up the steps to find a good place to sit. Across the field, there's a smaller set of stands for the away team crowd. Technically, we should probably be sitting there, but there's a much better view from here.

The guys are all warming up on the field. Soon, they do the coin toss in the middle and the game starts shortly after.

Reid is killing it. Cade and Lex are doing amazing too, but we're pretty much kicking this team's ass. It makes me miss Brady. Then again, what doesn't?

During halftime, the SHH cheerleaders come over to "meet" these cheerleaders. Each team does a cheer for the other, probably one of their best to show off before talking for a bit. My eyes train on Sasha. She's like the evil queen dressed up with a huge bow in her hair and flawless skin. Before our squad leaves to make the trek back around the track to head over to the away team's side, a football player jogs over to her. They talk for a moment, and she puts her hand on his chest. I nudge Jules. "See that?"

"Oh yeah, I see that," she says. We both shake our heads. She acts like losing Reid was the worst thing for her, but if it was, why would she be going from one guy to the next? What happened to the lacrosse guy back at Spring Hill?

I pull out my phone and take a quick picture. It doesn't really prove anything, but hell, it might. The guys said we needed to get dirt on her and maybe if she thinks this proves she's cheating on the lacrosse player guy, she'll be more apt to keep the picture she has of me to herself. Maybe I should tell Ezra exactly what happened too. I've been grappling with that decision, but in the end, I keep saying it's not really any of his

330

business. It's not like we have a relationship, and I don't want to make it awkward for either one of us. This is Sasha's fault through and through.

The second half starts, and I'm watching the game with an intensity I haven't in a while. Maybe it's just because of how well Reid is playing. It makes me smile to think he's definitely getting out of Spring Hill. He's going to go to college on a scholarship for sure. That thought nags at me at the same time though. What about me? What about us?

Why do people my age have to make all these grand decisions that affect the rest of their lives? I'm finally realizing I'm not equipped to make these decisions. I feel like everything I do is going to be wrong.

This is what's running through my head when I hear the crack that ricochets through the stadium. I blink, trying to make the game come into focus. I hadn't been paying attention for a few moments. All I know is that SHH had the ball, but now there's a bunch of players standing together, necks bent at the field.

Jules stands. "Oh shit."

"What?" I say.

One guy wearing the opposing team's jersey pushes past the group that's standing there. He whips his helmet off, a smirk taking over his face. I watch as he runs and sits on the bench, taking a swig of water from one of the many plastic bottles around. It's the same guy who Sasha was cozying up to.

"What are you doing? Come on," Jules says, glaring at me. Finally, she takes my hand and pulls. We start moving down the stands as the players drop to one knee.

"What's going on?" I blurt out.

"It's Reid. He got sacked. Hard."

Breath escapes me. If it weren't for Jules pulling me along, I probably would've stopped right where I was. Instead, we run toward one of the gated entrances to the field as shouts rise up and radios go off. Jules claws at the lock that will get us onto the field.

"What are you doing?" the guy standing on the other side of the field asks. He's wearing a windbreaker and looks somewhat official. "You can't come in here."

"That's her boyfriend out there," Jules says, pointing to the field.

My boyfriend. Reid.

"Is he hurt?" I ask. I'm numb. I feel like my brain can't make connections. Reid got sacked. Okay, that happens. I heard a crack. The guy ran off the field smirking.

"Get out of the way!" the guy says, pushing at Jules's hands.

When we turn, the paramedics are right there, coming down the walkway toward this gate in the fence. There are three of them and they have a stretcher.

"Jules," I say, voice twisted in disbelief.

"We need to get in there," Jules says, grabbing ahold of one of the paramedics. "That's her boyfriend."

He looks from her to me. "Just stand back. There's nothing you can do right now. I'm sure he's fine."

Then, they all turn away, hurrying across the field. The crowd parts for them and I see a cleat. A fucking cleat and that's it.

Jules takes my hand and then we're running toward the other side of the field. "Cade!" she screams. "Lex!"

We're running and running, and it feels like the world is tilting. It feels like I've been here before in my head. It feels like if I'd been there when my brother passed out, this is exactly what it would've felt like. A great big fear of the unknown.

This is what I was so worried about.

The announcer overhead says, "Reid Parker, down on the field. Of course, we all hope he's okay."

We're on the other side of the field now. The team, everyone, is surrounding our quarterback. "Lex!" Jules screams again.

He turns back. Everyone heard Jules scream. Her

nails dig into me as he turns away from Reid and runs toward us. He whips his helmet off halfway and when he gets to the fence, he grips it like he might fall over. "I don't know what happened," he says. "I was there. I'm always there."

"Is he okay?" Jules asks, voice trembling.

I feel like I'm going to throw up. I feel like everything is bunching in my head together, like it's a beehive buzzing and buzzing, but I can't make sense out of any of it.

"I don't know," Lex says. He finally finds my face. "I heard—" He shakes his head. "It's not good."

I try to breathe, but I can't suck in air.

Reid's hurt.

Brady's dead.

"I'll find out," Lex says. "I'll come back." He jogs away backward. "I'll be back," he promises.

He can say that, but can he really promise that? No one can really make any promises about anything. We're all just spewing lies when we promise shit. I know that now. I finally get it.

29

I don't stay to watch the rest of the game. We know nothing as Jules and I get in the car to follow the ambulance to the hospital. Lex and Cade stayed behind to finish out the game, our back-up QB going in who has hardly ever played any minutes in his whole entire career at Spring Hill.

I don't know why the hell I'm thinking about that. I should be thinking about Reid, wondering how he's doing. It's almost like I'm too scared to know.

When we get to the hospital, the staff won't tell us anything because we're not family. Though, they have told us that Reid's family has been called. We wait in the waiting room, each of us holding onto the other, though it's almost as if I'm watching from outside of my body. This isn't really happening. I can feel Jules's pain. Hell, I can even hear it. She's sniffling beside me. But although our hands are clenched together tightly, I still feel numb. I realize that this isn't healthy. Something's not right with me right now. I should be breaking down like Jules, especially since Reid is my boyfriend.

Holy fucking shit. Reid is my boyfriend. I—I love him. And he's in the emergency room right now, and I have no idea what's going on.

… … … …

Nothing. Fucking nothing! I can think whatever I want in my head, but nothing comes out on the outside. I feel like I'm comforting Jules about her own boyfriend, not dealing with the fact that mine's been hurt. That my good friend of many, many years is currently inside a room buzzing with doctors. "I have to get in there to see him," I say.

Jules shakes her head. "We can't. You heard the lady at the front desk."

I blink at her. "I don't really care what the lady at the front desk said." I swallow. "What if he's as hurt as Brady was? I can't just sit out here."

Jules squeezes my hand, her fingernails biting into me. "Briar, they're probably working on him. They're doing what they need to do, so you can't just go in there." She looks me up and down. I think it's then that

336

she notices I'm not crying. I think she notices that my cheeks aren't red and puffy and that I'm somewhat lucid.

She gives me the strangest look that makes me feel even worse than what I feel for Reid being in a hospital bed right now. I've let her down.

I think I'm letting myself down too.

"You just stay with me," she says, patting my hand. She looks around the room, paying attention to the people walking around in scrubs. "You want something to eat?"

I shake my head. I feel okay. "I'm good," I tell her, and there's nothing inside me that says any different other than the fact that I just want to see Reid, make sure he's still breathing. I mean, he needs to still be breathing. What are the fucking odds that two guys from the Spring Hill High team would die within a year of one another?

I go to get up, but Jules pulls me back down. I stare back at her. "I need to see him."

She smiles at me, her lips quivering a little. "I know, Briar." Her face is tight when she looks away. She squeezes my hand again. "Maybe I can go see if they'll let us back. Okay?" Her voice has changed. It's comforting and condescending at the same time. Almost like I'm a child that has to be dealt with. "Will you be okay? I'm just going to go to the window for a second."

"I'm perfectly fine," I tell her, an edge coming out in my voice.

She ignores the hardness wrapped up in my curt words and looks me over from head to toe. Whatever she sees, she must decide it's okay to get up and go to the window because she does so. When she gets there, she looks back at me and then leans in toward the lady on the other side, speaking softly.

My whole body buzzes. I watch the Emergency Room doors like a hawk. Somewhere back there, Reid is in a bed. I wonder what's happening. Is he thinking about me? Is he thinking about the hit?

I run my hands through my hair. A nurse comes into view with pale yellow scrubs on. She hits the swinging doors with her backside and then walks in, not bothering to look behind her. I move without thinking. I slip just inside the doors before they swing in and out again.

Miraculously, there's no one in the hallway in the Emergency section of the hospital. I tiptoe down it, stealthily but also with an air like I'm supposed to be walking here. I peer into the open doorways. Ahead of me, the Emergency Room doors burst open and a stretcher gets reeled in. I press myself against the side of the hallway while a scream rips through the air. The hospital staff run the stretcher right past me. Bloody bandages are strewn all over it and the minute it wheels past me, nurses and doctors follow. Shouts rise up. Orders are given.

As soon as the guy in the stretcher is in a room, I walk down the hallway a little more slowly. Literally everyone is with that other patient right now, leaving me free to do what I came here to do. There were times I wished I was there when Brady got hurt. I wanted to be able to see him. Instead, by the time I was told, he was already gone. I didn't get to say goodbye. Everyone assured me I wouldn't have been able to anyway. As soon as he got knocked out, he was never cognizant again. It was like he just fell asleep. And then from being asleep, he was dead. Not even the other players got to talk to him. They all just thought he had a concussion, but no, it was much, much worse than that.

I grit my teeth and walk a little further in, still peeking in doors with my mind in the past. I peer inside one and almost move past it, but it's the dirty cleats sticking out of the bright white bedding that draws my attention. It's him. Brady.

I shake my head. Reid. I mean Reid.

Brady's gone. There's no way he's in a hospital bed because we buried him months and months ago even though sometimes it still feels like it could've been yesterday.

I look around, making sure there's no one in the room with him. When I find it empty, I step inside. There's a beeping going on in the corner. He's already hooked up to some machine. The only grateful thing I feel about that is the fact that the beeping means he's still breathing. I mean, people don't die from tackles, right? That would stand to reason. Maybe he has a broken bone or two. But that's probably exactly what they thought about Brady and look what happened.

It's like I'm watching a movie in front of me. They have his pads and jersey off. The sheets come up to hide his chest, his hands on either side of him. Reid doesn't sleep like that. He sleeps all haphazard like, as if he's struggled to get into a comfortable position all night and the one he ended up in just happened to be whatever position he was in when he couldn't ward off sleep any longer. Sometimes he's on his stomach with one hand up by the pillow, the other stretched out over the bed. Sometimes he's on his side with his legs spread wide. Sometimes on his back, one knee out with both his hands under his pillow. Never have I ever seen him laying like a mummy in bed, all straight lines. No, he was posed like this.

I sneak in a little further. Now, I can see his chest

rise, another piece of physical evidence that he's okay. He's still breathing at least. I wonder how long it took Brady to stop breathing... I don't think I was ever told.

I hear voices outside in the hall, so I traverse the last few steps to Reid's bedside in one giant step. I don't want to get kicked out now, not before I've touched him. Not before I've seen him with my very eyes. I grab his hand in both of mine, squeezing it. He's still warm. Still oh so warm, which makes my heart melt a little. For now, he's okay at least. I pick his hand up and kiss the back of it. "Reid, you're okay. You're okay."

His lips part slightly. His eyes are still closed, but his lips move like he's trying to say something even though a sound never comes out.

There are more voices down the hall. The screaming from the other guy has ceased, so I know I don't have a lot of time now. I'm sure Jules has also turned around and realized I'm no longer there.

I kiss the back of his hand again and again. "You're okay." I bite my lip. There are so many things popping up in my head, but only one actually seems all that important. "I didn't get a chance to tell you this yet, so in case I won't— In case I can't," I say. "I love you, Reid Parker. Part of me probably always has been in love with you because I slipped into it so easily. So fucking easily."

I kiss his hand again, knowing I'm on borrowed time. Someone's going to come in here any second now and I'm going to get into trouble.

Footsteps start for the room. They echo around the otherwise quiet hallway. It seems like the screaming guy put a hush on everything else, so other sounds echo loudly. "What happened?" someone asks.

Another softer, feminine voice says, "Don't know. Hurt on the football field, but the EMT's who brought him in said he kept saying someone meant to do it."

I still right there by Reid's bedside. In my head, I replay the things I saw tonight. Sasha talking to the guy on the other team. The guy on the other team running back to his sideline with an almost smile on his face. Is he the one who sacked Reid? Did he try to hurt him on purpose?

I stumble back from the bed, guilt slamming into me hard and fast.

My fingers fall from Reid's hand. His arm is outstretched beyond the sides of the stretcher now. His fingertips are just dangling there with no life. No life.

I turn around and head right back through the door. Instead of taking a right and going back toward the waiting room, I take a left. "Hey," a voice says.

I ignore them. My head's pounding. My heart's in my throat.

Did Reid get hurt because of me? Because I didn't want anyone seeing that stupid picture of me?

I trip over my two feet, but then right myself afterward.

"Hey!" the voice comes again. "You can't be in here."

The doors at the end of the hall swing open again and two paramedics walk through from outside. I slip to the side and make my way out. The sun is low in the sky, but it's still shining. I hold my hands over my eyes, blocking out the bright rays. All they do is ricochet off the darkness I feel in my heart right now.

I think I had it right before...when I ran away. I definitely had it right. No one to care about but myself, and I'm not sure I even care about myself at all right now. Look what happened to Reid because of me.

The hospital is on a hill, so I climb up it, putting as much distance between me and Reid and me and the rest of the world as possible. People walk by me in business suits. Cars honk their horns. I hear the beep, beep of the intersection crosswalk, telling people when to go. I mix in so easily with the people walking around the city. That was one reason why I liked it so much before. Everyone's so busy going to where they need to go that no one notices what's going on with you. I can hide. And if no one's asking me what's wrong, maybe I'll forget too.

Maybe I'll just forget everything.

I keep walking and walking and walking, leaving this life behind once more.

Maybe I had the Spring Hill blues worse than Brady my whole life. Subconsciously, I probably knew I'd always leave.

CHAPTER 30

A week later...

This room is so musty it makes my nose run. I've gone through all the scratchy tissues the motel provides and something tells me it's going to be difficult to get another container, especially considering it looks like these were purchased in the seventies with the puke green paisley pattern printed on the outside of the box.

I stretch back on the bed, fully clothed with my hands behind my head. The TV is on, but I can't really hear what it's saying. I've already seen this episode of *Supernatural* a bunch of times. I know I need to get out on the street, see if I can't drum up some more money to pay for another night in this place. People just like giving money to young kids my age. They all want to help, especially when I look as sad and confused as I feel all the time.

But at least I'm not home right now. At least I'm not at school worrying about what's happening with Re —. I shake my head. Nope. Won't think about it. I left that life. It's gone. What I need to do is find a permanent job instead of begging on the streets. I should probably hit up the local diners and see if I can't get a bussing job or even a waitress position even though I have zero experience.

A knock comes on the door. I bite my lip. It's probably the owner of the hotel. She's been pretty good to me. I owe her for last night and tonight. I'm sure she'll understand.

I swing my legs over to the carpeted floor. I briefly glance out the dirty window. Yeah, it's her.

I undo both locks and swing it open. It takes a second for my eyes to adjust from the shitty motel grungy light to the bright light of the sun from outside. I haven't kept the curtains open since I've been here, but when my eyes do adjust, I want to slam the door back in place.

"There you are," a sickeningly sweet voice says.

She bounces right in, throwing her arm around me tight. Too tight.

"Thanks," she calls out to the owner of the motel before kicking the door shut in her face. She yanks her arm off me as soon as the door's closed, tugging some of my hair out in the process that got wrapped around her bracelets. "You're so dumb," she sneers.

I glare at Sasha, wondering how the hell she found me, but maybe even most importantly, why the hell she found me.

She takes her phone out and wiggles it in front of my face. "Do you think you actually had an online boyfriend named Ezra? You think because you were smart enough to turn your old phone off that no one would find you, but what was one of the first things you did after buying a burner phone? Contact me."

I blink at her. I feel like my brain has already caught up to something my body doesn't want to admit yet. "What are you talking about?" I ask, but there's another question there that I want answered first. Another one that's burning me up from the inside even though I know it might hurt to know.

She walks close to me and laughs in my face. "*I'm* Ezra, Briar." She smirks. "That friend, the only one you think you had in the world? Yeah, that was me.

When you were touching yourself in that picture? It was me. When you were bleeding your heart out in messages? It was me. And I think you already know this, but I was laughing the entire fucking time. Your pain is funny to me."

I feel sick. My stomach wars against the idea. It revolts, sending bile up my throat. Ezra is Sasha? When I bought the burner phone, he was the only person I told I'd run away again. It was a moment of weakness. A moment of uncertainty. I just wanted one person to know, so I picked the safest one. The one I knew wouldn't come looking for me because he already proved he didn't care that much. He already proved he could talk to me or not. Either way was fine with him.

And it was Sasha the entire fucking time.

I have nothing in my stomach, so there's nothing to heave up, but my stomach tries to do it anyway. I cover my mouth and Sasha looks so disdainfully at me that if I had any feelings left, I might actually be hurt by that look.

I sent her a boob picture. She saw my nipple. She pretended to care. She pretended to be interested.

"Here's what's going to happen," Sasha says, her black eyes zeroing in on me like she's the devil himself.

I know I'm not going to like whatever comes out of

her mouth next. I know I'm going to hate it. I know that what I've just done is throw myself into the path of the enemy with no life vests. I'm on my own. Truly, this time, I have no one.

The End

If you enjoy a badass female main character,
UPPERCUT PRINCESS will be right up your alley!

About the Author

E. M. Moore is a USA Today Bestselling author of Contemporary and Paranormal Romance. She's drawn to write within the teen and college-aged years where her characters get knocked on their asses, torn inside out, and put back together again by their first loves. Whether it's in a fantastical setting where human guards protect the creatures of the night or a realistic high school backdrop where social cliques rule the halls, the emotions are the same. Dark. Twisty. Angsty. Raw.

When Erin's not writing, you can find her dreaming up vacations for her family, watching murder mystery shows, or dancing in her kitchen while she pretends to cook.

Made in the USA
Monee, IL
10 July 2022